bloody
waters

g . p .   p u t n a m ' s   s o n s
n e w   y o r k

bloody waters

a lupe solano mystery

carolina garcia-aguilera

G. P. Putnam's Sons
Publishers Since 1838
200 Madison Avenue
New York, NY 10016

Published simultaneously in Canada

ISBN 0-399-14157-X

Printed in the United States of America

Book design by Iris Weinstein

This book is dedicated to my three daughters,
Sarah, Antonia, and Gabriella,
the loves and passions of my life,
and to Cuba,
island of my dreams.
¡ Volveremos!

I would like to thank my agent, Elizabeth Ziemska, of Nicholas Ellison, Inc., for much, but most of all, for her faith in me and in my work. I would like to thank Celina Spiegel, my editor at G. P. Putnam's Sons, for her superb editing skills. I owe Quinton Skinner a debt, which I can never properly repay, for guiding me through the complicated business of writing.

My family certainly deserves special mention, especially my husband, Robert Hamshaw, for his endless patience; my mother, Lourdes Aguilera de Garcia, for her unfailing support of all the ventures and adventures of my life; my sister, Sara O'Connell, and my brother, Carlos Antonio Garcia, for the interest they have always shown in my work; and my nephew, Richard O'Connell, for his staunch belief that this would come to pass.

But mostly I am indebted to my daughters, Sarah, Antonia, and Gabby, for never, ever doubting me. I want to thank them for all the times when we would pass by a bookstore and they would point to the books displayed in the front of the store and say, "See, Mama, that's where your books are going to be someday." *Gracias, gracias, gracias.*

*bloody
waters*

miami, july 1991

Elio Betancourt hauled the straw basket toward his library, pausing at the French doors to make sure the baby was still sleeping. He didn't want the couple waiting inside to be confronted with a screaming infant—not that they would possibly change their minds.

Gently, he put the baby's hand close to her mouth, careful not to wake her. He opened her fist and edged her thumb between her lips—a particularly heartbreaking pose. Even at this final stage, presentation was everything.

Elio took a moment to admire his staging. The baby, the library beyond the glass door—all mahogany and leather, with rows of impressive books he had bought by the pound for their looks—it was perfect. He stepped in dramatically, holding the basket in both hands like a Christmas present. The clients got up anxiously, bumping into each other in their eagerness.

The husband, Jose Antonio Moreno, was a money man who had made a killing on some offshore Costa Rican banking accounts. The wife, Lucia, was younger than her husband. She was beautiful, but several fruitless attempts to bear a child had left lines of sadness around her eyes and mouth.

"Oh, honey. Look how beautiful she is!" Lucia said in her throaty voice, laughing and looking at Betancourt as though he were her best friend. "Elio, can I hold her?"

Jose Antonio coughed uncomfortably and ran a hand

through his thinning hair. "Of course you can, darling," he said, staring evenly at Betancourt. "She's ours now."

At that moment the deal was done. Now for the critical part: the money. Elio already had twenty-five; now he was due the balance. He cleared his throat. *All right, that's enough. Take the kid and go.*

Nothing. He cleared his throat again, twice as loud and doubly long. Still nothing. He shoved his hands in his pocket and sighed impatiently.

Jose Antonio reached into his pocket and produced an inch-thick manila envelope. "This is yours," he said, handing it over.

The money man had held on to his money until the last possible moment, as though it could gather interest in his pocket. Betancourt felt the heft of the package, cursing the day the Treasury stopped printing big notes, and decided not to count it there. He had more class than that.

"Well," Elio said. "Look at the time."

Lucia took no notice, entranced with the drooling baby, trying to get it to smile. At least Jose Antonio had the good sense to realize Elio wanted them gone. After interminable goodbyes and thanks, they climbed into their azure Jaguar, the wife gently tucking the baby into a waiting car seat. God, they certainly were prepared. Elio waited in the vestibule a full minute, listening to their engine recede, then walked outside. His feet crunched the gravel driveway.

After a hard morning, Elio was in no mood to play his daily hide-and-seek with the *Miami Herald.* He was convinced the paperboy was a Haitian Communist who took out his class resentment by tossing the paper in a different obscure place every morning. Elio's secretary called the *Herald* on a monthly basis to complain, but nothing helped. When the secretary told Elio that the woman who took complaints had a definite Haitian accent, Elio knew the paperboy had won. He took vengeance by giving the scoundrel only a five-dollar tip at Christmas.

Lately, Elio had taken to carrying a stopwatch and timing the search. He had it down to an art: he would walk the last few yards to the gate with his eyes closed to ensure that he wouldn't inadvertently find the paper before the timer was in position. His best time was five seconds. The worst was on a Sunday in a torrential downpour, almost a full four minutes, but that really didn't count because of the rain.

When he couldn't find the paper at all, it gave him perverse satisfaction to complain to the *Herald*'s circulation desk. Of course, he never mentioned that his Colombian neighbor's golden retriever might have stolen the paper—the fucking dog was three years old but acted like a monstrous, oversized puppy. Why the hell the Colombian didn't get a pit bull like the rest of the rich drug dealers was beyond Elio's reasoning, but to each his own.

Today was a good day. Twenty seconds, a good omen. With jaunty steps, he returned to the house. With any luck his wife wouldn't be awake yet. He was in a good mood and didn't want it spoiled.

Her Royal Highness slumbered on upstairs, resting for whatever social event loomed on that day's agenda. It was all the same to him what she did—Margarita abruptly moved him to the guest room one day when he was out, not long after he had one too many Cuba libres at a charity ball and declared that the only cause he believed in was a benefit for sexually transmitted diseases. Oh well. All those Cuban society ladies—even the mothers—liked to pretend they were still innocent virgins.

Elio thought about divorce, but he could just see one of those Miami divorce lawyers going over his financial statements. There was always murder, but he knew he couldn't do it. At least it gave him an excuse not to marry any of his girlfriends. They couldn't doubt that he was stuck in a marriage when his wife was in the fucking society pages every day with Elio at her side wearing a pained grin.

But his philosophy of life was as follows: Play the cards you're dealt. As with the *Herald,* turn adversity into challenge. If God saw fit to deny some couples the gift of children while giving others children they didn't want . . . well, it was in His infinite wisdom that He created Elio to be the emissary between the two. If this turned a profit, then who was Elio to doubt God's wisdom?

miami, may 1995

It doesn't take a genius to figure out that guns were invented by men—no woman would ever abuse her hands that way. If a woman had designed the first gun, she would have found a way to ensure that her nail polish wouldn't chip during reloading. And shooting at anything with wet, newly polished nails is simply out of the question. Even so-called "girl guns" are a pain in the ass.

Gun designers, at some point, apparently decided that women would be more likely to buy killing instruments marketed to feminine tastes. This inspiration at one point even led to pink guns, for God's sake. Really, what's the point of a cute gun? Weapons manufacturers must think women are mental pygmies. Guns are for killing—whatever their color, shape, or size, and whether or not they play "New York, New York" when they're fired.

These deep philosophical matters distracted me at the Tamiami practice range, where I was desperately trying not to embarrass myself. The Beretta felt strange in my hand, and my aim was really off. I had let it go too long. I thought I could even hear the gun groan from disuse as I fired off a few more rounds.

Thankfully the place was almost deserted. I had learned the hard way to practice off-hours. Once, years before, I came out on a crowded Sunday afternoon and ended up next to a cowboy shooting a .357 Magnum. Five minutes later I was nursing a burnt lip after a hot shell from another cannon ejected right onto my face. I still have a scar.

This wasn't going to work: I just wasn't in the mood. If I kept shooting like I was—badly and without inspiration—I would just end up pissed off and frustrated. I made sure the magazine was empty and put the gun in the zipper compartment of my oversized black leather Chanel bag. It was hard as hell to find a leather purse that could accommodate the Beretta without losing its shape.

I removed my plastic earplugs, wrapped them in cotton, and tossed them in the bag with the gun. Quitting for the day wasn't such a crime: in my seven years in the business, I've never had to actually use a gun. I don't even really believe in packing, but I know the day I leave the Beretta at home will be the day I need it.

Out in the parking lot I disarmed the Mercedes' alarm and opened the door, stepping back from the blast of hot air from inside. I love this town, but the weather is a complete bitch ten months out of the year. May means spring in most places, but here it's stifling, with the cruelties of summer just around the corner.

I blasted the air conditioner before I got in, hoping to cool off the interior enough to drive without sweating through my clothes. Well, that was optimistic. I knew I would sweat—everyone does in Miami—but I hoped to avoid becoming a dripping mess. I had to meet clients at the office in less than an hour, and I wanted to be reasonably presentable.

Stanley Zimmerman, our family attorney, had referred the clients to me. The Morenos were also his clients, which meant they had to be really well-off. Stanley Zimmerman didn't have poor clients. He thought pro bono was something Julius Caesar fed his troops.

Stanley didn't tell me much when he called to say the Morenos would contact me, only that they had adopted a baby girl and for some reason wanted to find the birth mother. This wasn't great news; I'm not particularly interested in adoption cases. My philosophy on that score is that the mother gave up the baby for her own reasons—and that should be respected. It never does anybody any good to dig up the past.

My drive down Flagler Street was interrupted by the harsh ring of the car phone. It was my sister Fatima.

"Lupe," she said, and I could tell she was anxious. As usual. "Papi is getting the boat ready again. You hear any news?"

Our father kept the Hatteras stocked with provisions, waiting to set off for Havana the minute he heard word of Fidel Castro's fall.

"No, but I haven't been listening to the radio. I'm sure nothing is happening. If it had, all the Cubans would be shooting off their guns."

Fatima sighed as though unconvinced. "Well, if you hear anything, anything at all, you call me. Papi is driving me crazy. He has the Cuban radio station blasting on the dock so he can listen to the news while he gets the boat ready."

Though my sisters and I were born in Miami and had never been to Cuba, never for a day could we forget the island's impact on our lives. From the minute one wakes up in the morning to day's end, somehow or somewhere there's always a reminder of the nation a scant ninety miles away. It's an unusual day when the *Miami Herald* fails to run a front-page story on Cuba. Anyone running for mayor here has to develop a foreign policy platform—unlike in other cities, where potholes and garbage collection are hot-button issues. It takes only a small spark to ignite the Cuban exiles' passion. Fidel Castro had been in power for thirty-six years, but it might as well have been yesterday that he took over. The exiles' resentment showed no sign of fading, and street-corner demonstrations against U.S. policy toward Fidel were as common as humid days in Miami.

If you asked my sisters or me where we were from, we would answer without hesitation that we were Cuban, from Havana. We spoke Spanish primarily, at home and among our friends, which wasn't at all unusual. Cuba coursed through our blood—and always would. Ever since I was a little girl, I dreamed of visiting the home of my ancestors. I wrote reports on Cuba in school and hungrily picked up every bit of knowledge that I could. I suppose you could say that I, like my father, was obsessed with my country—along with about a million other exiles.

I turned onto Douglas Avenue. Fatima was worried, but she should have known better. Readying for Fidel's imminent fall was Papi's favorite hobby. "Lupe, it's so hot outside, he shouldn't be out in this heat. I told him he could hear the news just as well inside the house, but he won't listen to me."

"Calm down," I said. Papi had spent his life in the heat; he could take it. "I'm almost at the office now. I'll make some calls and check it out. It's probably just those Alpha Sixty-six guys again, getting everyone stirred up. I'll call you, I promise."

Poor Fatima. Ever since Mami died five years ago, she had appointed herself Papi's caretaker. Her feeling of obligation went deeper than that, actually. She always felt she brought disgrace to our family because she was the first and only daughter to get divorced. Fatima was an old-fashioned girl.

Of the three Solano sisters—Fatima, Lourdes, and me, Guadalupe—Fatima was the eldest and the only to marry. My mother, for reasons known only to herself, named us after places where the Virgin had been sighted. It could have been worse; she could have named us after the Sacraments, the Immaculate Conception, the nativity, or worst of all, the stigmata. Believe me, when you're Catholic there are thousands of possibilities.

Fatima married Julio Juarez against our parents' wishes, but she was young, in love, and her hormones were in overdrive. Mami and Papi thought he was a gold-digger. I kind of liked him, but I was just fifteen years old—what did I know? I began to agree with my parents, though, just hours after the wedding, when I saw two pairs of legs—one male and one female—under one of the ladies' room stalls at the club where the reception was held. Full of adolescent curiosity, I hung around outside to see who it was. I already had a pretty good idea; after all, how many of the guests wore gray morning coats with tails? Sure enough, my new brother-in-law and one of the caterer's assistants emerged, sheepishly and one at a time, from the bathroom. Something had just been consummated, and it sure as hell wasn't my sister's marriage.

I should be grateful to Julio Juarez. Because of him, I became a private investigator. If Julio hadn't embezzled hundreds of thousands of dollars from Papi's construction company, we wouldn't have been forced to hire Stanley Zimmerman to look into the matter.

Julio was either unable or unwilling to hold down a job in the early days of his marriage to Fatima, perfectly content to live off her allowance. Papi went along grudgingly, but he cut off Julio's support when he learned Solano Construction was paying not only for keeping Fatima's household but also for a certain señorita's marginally more modest living quarters in Little Havana. There were limits even to Papi's generosity.

Julio was so drastically alarmed that one day he actually woke up, dressed, and reported for work at Solano Construction. Since he was categorically unqualified to do much of anything, he was given a ceremonial office job. It didn't take him long to figure out that since he was so useless, no one would bother to supervise him. He had the run of the place, as the boss's son-in-law, and no one questioned him. Within a week he had an inventive scam in place that allowed him to siphon money from accounts receivable by fixing duplicate client invoices. His great pot of gold was our government contracts.

Papi wouldn't be where he is in life if he were't a very smart man. But he kept his suspicions to himself. Mami had been diagnosed with ovarian cancer a few months before, and Papi didn't want a family scandal to upset her. My father was a proud and strong man, but the combination of his wife's illness and his son-in-law's betrayal wore him down in private. One night he took me out to the Hatteras and told me about Julio. Only I was to know.

The next day we met with the man Stanley hired as an investigator—Hadrian Wells, an overweight, chain-smoking ex-cop who kept staring at me in my sundress and heels. Wells suggested he start working undercover as a temp at Solano's, gathering proof against Julio.

Julio was out of Fatima's life in three days. She wasn't as distraught when he left as we had feared; maybe she knew all along she had made a mistake. Since the divorce was uncontested it was granted in thirty days. To this day she has no firm idea why Julio left. At least, that's what Papi and I hope.

As for me, I was fascinated by the case and how Wells had gone about his work. I met his boss, Esteban Morales. I asked a lot of questions and started hanging around, and, after I pestered him enough times, Esteban started taking me along to observe his investigations. Eventually I helped him work cases and met his contacts.

Even Esteban thought I was just playing around. I was a rich girl in my junior year at the University of Miami, majoring in advertising. I wasn't particularly ambitious—it's hard to agonize for long over your future when you live in a huge house in the exclusive Cocoplum section of Miami. If things ever got tight, I figured, I could always sell my Mercedes and live off the money for a while.

After getting involved with Esteban—professionally, that is—advertising looked pretty boring and tame. My parents saw that I would never turn into a respectable, conventional ad rep and, being practical people, decided not to fight it. They only asked that I finish college before doing what I wanted.

My degree behind me, I started working as an intern at White and Blanco, a fifteen-investigator firm in northwest Miami. Esteban set it up for me, explaining that I would need experience before going out on my own. The firm handled both civil and criminal cases and was old and well established—by Dade County standards, anyway. The state of Florida has a two-year internship requirement for investigators, which can be waived if the applicant has a background in law enforcement. My background was in partying, so I didn't qualify for the exemption.

In my two years there I saw everything. Esteban told me the internship would be difficult, but I think he meant the work, not the attitude I got from the other investigators. There was only one other woman at White and Blanco—Mary Matheson, a sixty-year-old grandmother and retired New York cop. Office legend held that she was once a first-class investigator, but the years had passed and she stayed on too long. When I started with the firm she mostly supervised office parties. I never saw so much fuss made over birthdays—no baby showers, but lots of birthdays, and we arguably gave the best Christmas parties in South Florida. Mary was great for office morale.

Still, I'm amazed I stuck it out. My desk was in an open pit of space shared with thirteen male investigators who smoked, drank, swore, farted, belched, and yelled instead of talking. It was more of an obstacle course than an office; the desks were set so close together that we had to climb over each other to reach them. More than once I stepped into an overflowing trash can trying to answer my phone. Of course, the clients never saw the pit. The partners, Sam White and Miguel Blanco, met with clients in their offices or the plush conference room.

After two years of this I had paid my dues. And Esteban had been right, as usual—I worked all kinds of cases at White and Blanco, from murders to missing persons, domestics, and frauds. I also worked undercover a lot, which I loved. I always secretly saw myself in TV or the movies, and undercover work is the next best thing.

I made contacts not only with future clients but with people in positions to help me when I was on my own: cops, reporters, state and federal clerks, fellow investigators. When my apprenticeship ended I started my own firm, which I grandly named Solano Investigations. I rented a three-room garden cottage in Coconut Grove for an office—a little paradise of orange poinciana shrubs, bougainvilleas, drooping palms, and squawking parrots, nestled back from the street. Papi gave me money to get started, so I bought good computers and office furniture to make the place look legitimate.

The only catch was that I had to hire my cousin Leonardo to work with me. He was Mami's sister's only son, and family consensus was that he was adrift. He had pretensions of becoming an actor—not a laudable ambition in a conservative Cuban family. Mami's sister Mercedes wanted Leonardo gainfully employed where the family could keep an eye on him until he came to his senses. After almost five years, everyone was still waiting. I had no problem with this—Leonardo and I got along famously, and since he was twenty-four now, four years my junior, he was just young enough for me to boss around.

Leonardo tried to be a good assistant, and he was great window dressing for the female clients. Working out was his primary purpose in life, now that he didn't have time for the theater, and he sculpted himself into a perfect physical specimen topped by thick, curly jet hair. Early on he convinced me to let him set up his exercise gear in the empty back room so he could work out during his lunch break. The room quickly started to look like a gym, with a Stairmaster in one corner quickly joined by a treadmill and an array of machines that looked like they were designed for obscure forms of medieval torture. Soon a team of workers showed up to install floor-to-ceiling mirrors. After all this it seemed only natural for Leonardo to come to work in sweats and track shoes, so he wouldn't have to change in the middle of the workday.

Also I'd lately noticed an array of pamphlets on health, nutrition, and spirituality planted around the office. Leonardo was thinking about broadening his horizons, I suspected, but he wasn't quite ready to approach me about it and was laying hints instead. But he knew I wasn't about to ease up on my investigations—especially for the touchy-feely New Age. I had worked too long and too hard to build the agency, and he knew that. We needed billable hours, and plenty of them, to make the rent every month.

Walking into Solano Investigations, it was obvious the place wasn't run like a high-powered corporate business. But we were efficient and honest, and I worked slowly and methodically to ensure that our client list was always growing. And through the years I had built up an investigator's most vital tool—my Rolodex file of top contract investigators and free-lancers. It was a list other investigators would have killed for.

Leonardo might have had a taste for the flaky, but don't get me wrong—he was my backup, and I could count on him. The office may have been informal, but we took our livelihood very seriously. We had to. In Miami, you could find yourself in deep waters very quickly. Staying sharp was a matter of life and death.

Leonardo greeted me from behind his desk, wearing a tank top and an exercise towel draped over his well-muscled shoulders. He handed me a stack of phone messages and folded back a page of the latest issue of *Muscle and Fitness*.

"Someone parked a sky-blue Jag in my spot," I said.

"New clients," Leonardo said, jerking a thumb toward my closed office door. "Lucia and Jose Antonio Moreno."

I left Leonardo to his magazine and quietly opened the door to my office. The clients Stanley sent, a middle-aged couple, were indeed waiting, sitting on the edge of my leather sofa. I watched their reaction.

They probably didn't expect an investigator who appeared as well-off as they. Maybe they expected a big, tough bitch with a bad haircut, smoking a cigar—who knows? On a good day I clear five feet. I've always thought I had too much figure for my height, but my boyfriends—and there have been plenty—never agree. I wear my long black hair in a very fifties French twist and keep my hands perfectly manicured with blood-red nails. My eyesight is lousy, so I like to experiment with colored contacts—the green ones are my favorites, even if they make me look like an alien who's lost her way.

"Guadalupe Solano," I said, shaking their hands. I motioned them back to the sofa and sat behind my desk. They both had avoided looking me in the eye. The woman stared at the floor, while the man looked everywhere but at me. It was obvious they were under a lot of strain—something almost all my clients have in common.

You have to be patient with distraught people. So I pretended to be fascinated with an illegible phone message left on my desk by Leonardo. Either Juan Garcia from First Miami had called about my stock portfolio, or else Johnny Carson had called about some slacks and perfumes. I couldn't be sure.

Giving up on that puzzle, I studied the Morenos. Jose Antonio Moreno was in his late fifties. He was tall, over six feet, with a dignified bearing. His dark brown hair was thin, but mercifully he hadn't resorted to stretching the remaining strands over his scalp to disguise the condition. His sharp black eyes seemed to have receded into his face, ringed by dark shadows.

Lucia Moreno held her husband's hand so tight that it had turned bloodless white. Lucia leaned back and stretched forward as I moved on to my stack of mail, as if she had a killer backache. Distressed as she was, she was meticulously groomed. Younger than her husband by at least five or six years, she was a beautiful woman with classic Northern Spanish features: blonde with fair skin, blue eyes, and fine facial bones. She was dressed expensively in an understated, elegantly cut sleeveless emerald dress.

I had the feeling she would talk first. I was right.

"Miss Solano, we're here on a matter of great delicacy." Lucia pulled her huge diamond ring up to her knuckle, exposing a plain platinum wedding ring underneath. "We need to be sure of your discretion and confidentiality."

"Of course. I will treat whatever we discuss here with the utmost confidentiality." All my clients make me say this. They don't understand that breaking client confidence would permanently wreck my reputation.

Lucia took a glossy picture out of her purse. It depicted a little girl about four years old. She didn't resemble either Lucia or Jose Antonio.

"This is our daughter, Michelle. We adopted her when she was only two weeks old," Lucia said. "We're here because of her."

She handed me the picture. Michelle was really an adorable little girl, with expressive dark eyes and curly black hair ringing her face. I examined the photo more closely and saw a star-shaped birthmark, about the width of my finger, across the girl's neck. Then I noticed that Jose Antonio was staring at me.

He cleared his throat, looked away, and put his arm tightly around his wife. She closed her eyes and rested her head on his shoulder. They stayed that way for a while.

"*Amor*," Jose Antonio finally said, helping his wife sit upright. "We have to tell her everything if she is going to help us."

Interesting. As if they had considered telling me only part of their story. Which, of course, most of my clients did.

I took out a yellow pad. "Before we begin I'll need to know a few things."

Solano Investigations' standard client form was simple: name, address, phone, employer if any, Social Security number, origin of referral. The latter was often the most important—it allowed me to check out the client's reputation. The Morenos were referred by Stanley, so I knew they were legitimate, not to mention rich.

My job would be easier if the Morenos trusted me, so I took my time filling out the questionnaire, making small talk along the way. They were more comfortable by the time I got their signatures, so I put away the form and gave them my most serious investigator's stare and asked them if they would like to explain why they had come to me.

"I'll tell her, *querido*," Lucia said, touching her husband's cheek. "Miss Solano, my husband and I have been married for twenty years. We are both Cubans—Jose Antonio is from Santiago and I am from Havana. Our families came separately to America in the early sixties, and we lived five blocks from each other in New York City. We were married when I was twenty and Jose Antonio was thirty-five.

That gave me pause. Lucia was younger than she looked. She gestured languidly as she spoke, placing Cuba here, New

York there. After thinking for an instant, I realized her sense of direction was perfect.

"God has blessed us in many ways. The only thing He did not give us is children."

Jose Antonio had been watching his wife, as though waiting for her to stray. "We always wanted a large family," he interrupted. "After five years of marriage we decided it was time. Lucia became pregnant right away, but she lost the baby six weeks later. We . . . Lucia had three more miscarriages, and the final pregnancy was ectopic. Lucia had to undergo surgery."

Lucia exhaled and shook her head, waving her hand. It seemed she was trying to brush the past away like dust floating in the air.

"The result of the surgery is that we cannot have children," Jose Antonio said, speaking quickly. "Five years ago we decided to come to Miami, to start fresh in a new place. We have family here."

Lucia patted her husband's hand, and he was silent. "We never gave up on having our own children," she said, her voice low and intent now. "We started to think about adoption. My cousin Elvira had privately adopted two children—a boy and a girl—a few years ago, from a lawyer. They said it was their best option. Elvira's husband is a German accountant, and when he said he looked into all the possibilities, we believed him."

I smiled tentatively, unsure how much she wanted me to enjoy the joke. Her expression didn't change.

"Elvira said children could be adopted through the Health and Rehabilitative Services of Florida, but there was a long waiting list and astonishing paperwork. And I, like Elvira, wanted a child of Cuban origin. HRS couldn't promise that, but the lawyer could. He provided Elvira with children within six months, at a great cost."

"What was the lawyer's name?" I asked.

"Elio Betancourt," she replied. I stayed silent.

"So we contacted Mr. Betancourt. It was just as Elvira told

us—it took less than six months, with almost no paperwork. After just two meetings and an exchange of funds, we were given our baby girl."

I glanced at Jose Antonio. He looked away guiltily.

"Betancourt was a charming man, very kind and understanding," Lucia said, leaning forward. "He said it pleased him to make others happy, and if he made money in the process, then so much the better. The only condition on the adoption was that we ask no questions. He said the babies he placed came from young Cuban mothers who didn't want their families to know they were with child. The girls lived together in a group home somewhere in the U.S. and received excellent prenatal care. You see, the main reason these private adoptions worked so well was because the young mothers knew their identities would always be kept secret."

Elio Betancourt was notorious in Miami for defending drug dealers, racketeers, anyone willing to pay top dollar for a lawyer who didn't mind immoral, dangerous clients. I doubted they hadn't heard of him before the adoption.

I started to write on my pad, but stopped. "Did Betancourt explain his reasons for all this secrecy?"

Jose Antonio frowned, as though I had been rude to mention it. "You have to understand, Miss Solano, we understood this secrecy in terms of who we are: Cubans. You know as well as I that even today, a Cuban girl's reputation is her life. These young mothers were being protected."

"We desperately wanted a baby," Lucia said. "We paid fifty thousand dollars and she was ours. A perfect, beautiful baby girl. It was ideal, until now."

The Morenos glanced at each other, and I tried to read what I saw. Fear, guilt, apprehension . . . but no regret.

"Tell me," I said.

"Last month I took Michelle to her pediatrician for a checkup. The next day the doctor called, saying he wanted to retest her blood. I knew something was wrong, even though he claimed it was routine."

Lucia put her hand over her heart as she spoke, touching some hidden core within herself. "The results of the initial tests were correct. Michelle has a rare inherited blood condition. The specialist at Jackson Memorial told us we have to locate her birth mother for a bone marrow transplant."

"Are you certain?" I asked. "There might be—"

"You must hear what I am saying," Lucia interrupted tersely. "The only patients to survive this disease have received transfusions of their mother's marrow. It's Michelle's only chance."

Without hearing more, I knew exactly what had happened next. They went to Betancourt for information about the birth mother, and he refused. This is where I came into the picture.

"What happened when you told Betancourt why you needed to find Michelle's mother?" I asked.

Jose Antonio stirred, smoothing his tie against his belly. "Betancourt couldn't care less," he said, his mouth tight with anger. "He said we knew the arrangement, that the child's mother would remain anonymous. At first he was sympathetic, but when we wouldn't leave he turned belligerent. He told us we entered into an illegal adoption, that we had bought a baby. If we went to the police we would lose Michelle and end up in as much trouble as him."

"We thought it was all legal," Lucia said. It sounded as though she was trying to convince herself as much as me.

"Betancourt said no one who adopted through him would help us either," Jose Antonio said. "Because they could lose their children."

They were honest enough to admit they had done something illegal, even if Lucia was hedging. It was a good start.

"I assume Betancourt gave you a birth certificate for Michelle?"

"Yes. Here." Jose Antonio reached into his briefcase and pro-

duced an envelope containing a duly certified birth certificate is-
sued by the state of Florida for a female newborn—Michelle
Maria Moreno, her date of birth listed as July 11, 1991. According to the document, the child was born at Jackson Memorial,
the obstetrician a Dr. Allen Samuels. There was no mention of
any group home for unwed Cuban-American mothers.

"Do you know this Dr. Samuels?" I asked.

"No. We tried to find him, of course, but we couldn't." Jose
Antonio pulled a cigarette from his pocket as he spoke, glancing
at me. I didn't offer him an ashtray, so he put it away. "There's no
listing for him in the Dade County telephone directory. We also
tried Broward County, Monroe, even Palm Beach County.
Nothing. I called the AMA and they had no current information
either. They said he probably retired, because their last record
for him was from five years ago. Now, how can he be listed as
the doctor who delivered Michelle if he was no longer practicing
medicine?"

I didn't answer. They should have known. "Did you call
Jackson Memorial?" I asked.

"They told us he wasn't on staff, and they wouldn't say anything more. We didn't ask any more questions because we didn't
want them to become suspicious."

Lucia stroked her cheek idly. The brass and strength
seemed to be gone from her now. "Miss Solano, we're very
frightened. Jose Antonio will not admit it, but I will." She
glanced at her husband.

Jose Antonio looked away. "We simply need to know if you
can help us."

"I can try, but I can't promise anything," I said. It was horri-
ble the way they looked at me, like children listening to their
parents. "At this point Betancourt has the upper hand, and he's
obviously knows it. You committed a criminal act, and he's
counting on that to keep you from forcing him to tell you where
he got your baby."

Jose Antonio pulled his checkbook from his suit jacket with

a flourish, a gesture he had apparently used often. "But you will help, right? We'll pay whatever you ask."

"Suppose I get lucky and find the mother," I said, ignoring him. "What if she doesn't want to help Michelle? She might want to be left alone; remember, she gave the baby up for adoption."

I felt terrible saying this. Lucia looked down at her lap, her eyes glistening. Jose Antonio spoke louder, as though the volume of his voice could banish all the problems he had created for himself.

"We've thought of all that, Miss Solano, but what else can we do? We have faith that the mother will accept payment for donating her bone marrow. We'll give her anything she wants."

"Well, it's her biological child," I said. "It stands to reason that she would be willing to help."

"Exactly," Jose Antonio said, taking his wife's hand.

"All right, I'll do my best. Before I draw up a contract, though, you both have to understand that it might all come to nothing. After a lot of expense, both emotional and financial, I might not ever find your child's birth mother."

Jose Antonio stood, practically pulling his wife to her feet. He tore off a check, signed and dated it, and put it on my desk.

"You fill in the amount you need to get started," he said. "Whatever you feel is fair."

I stared at the blank check. I hated this case already.

"Please, Miss Solano," Lucia said, her eyes dazed and her chin shaking. "The specialists say Michelle has four months at the most without the transplant. You have to succeed."

They closed the door gently behind them. I thought about needles in haystacks and my odds of winning the lottery.

three

It had been five years since my mother died, but to me it might have been just five months. I could still see the children in the sedate outer room at Jackson Memorial awaiting their turn for chemotherapy. Mami's dragged on for months, and her treatments were scheduled at regular intervals, so we became friendly with the other patients. The children there broke my heart.

Although no one would dream of being crass enough to ask about other patients' conditions, somehow everyone knew everything about each other's cancer. When someone missed a session, though, no one really wanted to know the details. It was never because they were improving: at that clinic, few were cured.

There was one little girl in particular, Elena Rojas. She must have been seven or eight years old at the time, but it was hard to be sure because of the toll chemotherapy had taken on her. She was a beautiful child, still, even with no hair and a bloated face, and the nurses all loved her. She was always upbeat and cheerful, and when I brought my mother to Jackson and didn't see Elena, it took all my self-control not to pry, just to make sure nothing had happened to her.

In time I noticed that she was seldom brought in by the same person twice; I figured she came from a large family. But I was nosy, and one day I found out that the people bringing Elena for treatment weren't relatives at all. They were workers from Florida Health and Rehabilitative Services. Elena was a foster child, her parents dead for several years. The nurse told me that from time to time, a relative would surface claiming to want to take Elena, but none of them carried through all the demands of the court and the little girl was always left in limbo. When Elena's leukemia gradually worsened, her relatives' perfunctory interest vanished.

My mother's condition turned critical, and we had to spend more time in the hospital. I talked to the nurses a lot, and they told me that Elena's situation wasn't all that unusual—there were quite a few children like her, in the care of strangers and at the mercy of workers from the court system.

In my mother's final weeks, she slipped in and out of consciousness so often that I took to wandering the hallways to distract myself. I visited the children, and I think they helped me through that time at least as much as I helped them. Soon my mother died, and almost out of habit, I continued coming to the floor and spending time with the kids. They made me a registered volunteer, in charge of twice-weekly story hours and paper doll duty.

After nearly three years, Elena died. I soon walked out and never returned. At the time I thought it was temporary burnout, but I was wrong. I simply couldn't face the place without her there to keep me strong.

In the air I could still catch a faint trace of Lucia's perfume. I studied Michelle's picture at my desk. If I could help it, she wouldn't end up like the kids in that waiting room. Here was my chance to make up for quitting on the others. I knew I was a little carried away with the notion—sue me, I'm Catholic. I believe in things like redemption. Common sense told me my chances of finding Michelle's birth mother were slim to none, but I never cared much for common sense.

Leonardo knocked softly at the door. "Lupe? You okay in there?"

"I'm fine, Leonardo." I put the picture in a manila envelope. "Just thinking about this new case, that's all."

Leonardo cracked the door enough to stick his head in. "Another referral from Stanley," he said, smiling with the bliss of the innocent. "I love it! All his clients are really rich, and they all pay on time."

"It certainly makes things easier," I said. Leonardo took care of our billing and books, to a degree. I had an accountant come in once a month to unravel our small financial messes before they grew into disasters. I wasn't hard on Leonardo, though. He gave it an honest effort.

I noticed Leonardo was still at the door, leaning in as though hesitant to come in all the way. "What's up?" I finally asked.

"Actually, I wanted to talk to you about something," he said, coming in and sitting in one of my clients' chairs. He had one of those metal springy things in his hand, which he flexed over and over to build up his forearms. "It's about my friend Serenity."

I really love Leonardo like a little brother, but some things about him irritate me. For instance, he has friends named after mental states. And he schemes. Recently he was caught up in selling high-energy, fat-burning fruit shakes out of our office kitchen. The place started to feel more like a health spa than an investigative agency.

Leonardo switched the springy thing to his other hand and started flexing. "She has an idea that I think you'll like," he said. "It's only twice a week, and after hours. You probably wouldn't even notice, but I wanted your approval."

"That's very considerate of you," I said. I tried to think what was coming, given what I knew about the hippie, spaced-out Serenity: Mud baths and chanting? Tea leaves and séances? Herbal colonics? Oh, God, anything but that.

"Serenity wants to start up yoga and meditation classes in the front area, with just a few students. You can take the classes too. She won't even charge you."

Maybe it was all the lush tropical vegetation around the cottage, or the wild parrots squawking out back with their brilliant plumage coloring the trees, Something about the little place seemed to lend itself to this sort of flaky, California-style stuff. Well, at least meditation wouldn't stain the carpets.

I rolled my eyes to the heavens at the idea of bringing in a client after hours to find a dozen Coconut Grove hippies with their legs wrapped around their shoulders. Leonardo took this for a resounding vote of approval.

"Great! I knew you'd say yes. I'm going to use our photocopier and paper to print up some fliers. Is that all right, too?"

The Bureau of Vital Statistics is in northwest Miami, sandwiched between the county jail and Cedars of Lebanon Hospital in a particularly dismal, squalid block. I hated going there, even though at midday the narrow streets teemed with people. I hadn't had any trouble there in the past, but it was just a matter of time. We live with the constant presence of crime and danger every day in Miami, and most people try to beat the odds by staying away from places like Vital Statistics. For me it was another day on the job.

As usual, parking there was impossible, especially since I was driving the Mercedes. I drove around the block several times without getting lucky, so I resigned myself to flirting shamelessly with the building parking-lot attendant so he would allow me to park in the restricted area reserved for public servants. For the usual five-dollar toll, he promised to keep an eye on my car.

Inside the squat mustard building, I paused outside the dank, windowless records room and squared my shoulders for courage. I always theorized that Dade County bureaucrats made the room so depressing—and the wait for information and documents so long—intentionally, to keep all but the hardiest citizens from even trying.

Instead of taking a number and settling in for the interminable wait before my name was called, I went straight to the window marked "Funeral Directors and Officers of the Court." I was neither, but my friend Mario Solis worked in that department. I knew he would take care of me.

Mario, a slightly potbellied man of about forty, had worked in county government since my days at White and Blanco. He was married with five children, but I could always tell he had a little crush on me.

His eyes lit up when he saw me, and he straightened his thick marine-blue tie. "Lupe! What a wonderful surprise!"

"Mario, you look great," I said. "How's Consuelo and the kids?" I asked innocently and enthusiastically as I discreetly air-kissed him. Consuelo was known as a world-class bitch.

"They're fine. Thanks for asking." I was relieved he made no move to pull out the album he kept in his desk, which chronicled his children's every birthday and lost baby tooth in scrupulous detail. Mario was a good man, but if I were married to him I would have been adding vodka to my orange juice at breakfast every morning.

We smiled at each other for a moment, running out of small talk. Then I took out my legal pad. "Mario, I need something for a case, a birth certificate for a little girl born in Dade County July 11, 1991."

That certainly broke the mood. "Lupe, you know I'm not supposed to give out that kind of information without an authorization," Mario said, looking at the other clerks to see if they had heard. "I know I've helped you in the past, but they've been cracking down lately. We get so many requests from adoptive children looking for their real parents, and we've had some legal problems."

I expected this, but I also knew how much Mario loved children. "Come on, Mario," I said. "I need the certificate for medical reasons, to save a sick child. If my clients have to go through normal channels it might be too late."

He didn't seem entirely convinced; the irony, of course, is

that I was telling the truth. But when I fixed him with a helpless pout, he leaned forward, the window between us filling with his oval head. "I'll do what I can," he whispered. "Meet me under the poinciana tree in the parking lot across from the jail. I have a break in a few minutes and I'll bring the document, if it's even on file here."

I gave the information to Mario—covering my bases by asking for birth certificates of all white females born in the county three days before and after the July 11 date given to the Morenos by Betancourt—and left without another word. Mario always indulged his dramatic flair with me, once delivering a death certificate to me in the building lobby by slipping it into my purse after I pretended to trip and fall. I guessed his home life wasn't exactly a thrill a minute.

So I waited for him under the poinciana tree. It wasn't all boring; I had the good luck to be around when the jail performed its daily prisoner release. A young guy in standard gang-wear noticed me and, after nudging his buddies, wolf-whistled at me and started walking my way. I flashed my investigator's ID, and he stopped, puzzled, and walked slowly away with a glance back at the jail.

An hour later I was just about to give up and try another tactic, when Mario appeared, clutching a manila envelope tightly to his chest. Looking warily at the traffic, he jogged across the street. He looked like he had put on a few pounds.

The exertion was apparently too much for him; he was winded and red when he reached me. "I could get fired for doing this, you know," he panted. "My supervisor was in the room the whole time, and she almost caught me copying the microfiche. She could've asked to see the request form if she thought of it. Never again! Not even for you."

Mario took out a handkerchief and wiped his face while I waited. This complaining was also part of our ritual. "If that woman caught me giving out confidential information about all those babies, she would have my ass! I must be crazy."

I figured a little expression of gratitude wouldn't hurt, so I leaned over and kissed his cheek. "Oh, Mario, thank you," I said. "I'm so sorry you had to go through all that for me, but remember: you're helping an innocent little baby."

He blushed with pleasure. "Now, Mario," I went on, "you have to tell me how the county records birth certificates."

The blush disappeared, and Mario looked around as though FBI agents might be watching us. "All live births have to be recorded within five days, by Florida statute 382.16," he recited. "Usually the hospital does it automatically."

"What about adoptions?"

Mario wiped his forehead again. The humidity was building to a typical midday sauna. "Adoptions are different. The baby's biological mother's name is listed along with the father's, if there is one. After the adoption is finalized, the courts send us an amended birth certificate listing the new parents. Both documents look the same, so it's impossible to tell the difference from just the documents. The original certificate goes into the sealed court records. After that it takes a court order to get to the information."

I glanced at the parking lot, but I couldn't see my car. Hopefully it wasn't on its way to a strip-and-cut operation. "What about home births, Mario?"

"In those cases there's usually a midwife or nurse practictioner. The law still requires all births to be recorded, and most people do it right away because everyone needs a birth certificate for government services. There are exceptions, though. Migrant workers sometimes don't bother if they plan to go back to their country. But the vast majority of them want their children to be American."

I jotted this down. I hadn't thought that a mother might not want her child's birth to be recorded.

Mario watched me write. "Hey, you're not planning to do anything illegal with those documents, are you, Lupe?"

I ignored him, because I didn't know the answer yet. "What about abandoned babies?"

"They're registered as baby Jane or Joe until adoption if the birth parents can't be found. There are cases of unregistered births, but not very often."

Betancourt had brokered the adoption, and it was almost certainly illegal. I tried to think: Where would he be likely to find a baby?

Mario reached out and touched my arm. "Lupe, be straight with me. I'll help if I can, but don't take me for a total fool. What's going on here?"

Mario, with his wife and houseful of kids, had the patience of five men, and I had finally worn him down. It made me feel sorry for him, for a second.

"You're right, Mario, I haven't told you everything." I took a deep breath, the air soupy and warm, and told him about the Morenos and the birth certificate they gave me. "I want to see if this document was filed with Vital Statistics. Frankly, I don't know if you have anything at all. My clients never checked with your department before coming to see me."

It made me nervous, telling him so much. I needed Mario to feel he could trust me; otherwise he might pull the plug on his help—on this case, and maybe on all the others to come.

"Well, what are you waiting for?" he said with an ironic smile. "Open the envelope and start looking."

I should have known Mario wouldn't cut out on me. What would he have left for excitement? I quickly ripped open the envelope and scanned the printout inside.

No Moreno was listed. I was astonished at the number of births in Dade County on a given date. No wonder Miami was overpopulated: in the summer of '91, Jackson Memorial alone produced more than thirty babies a day, and that was just the females. I reminded myself that this list represented only registered births.

Mario watched me closely, and I could see he recognized the disappointment on my face. I read the printout again, thinking maybe I had missed Michelle the first time around. No luck, and no Moreno.

There was nothing left for me there. I got up from the grass and helped Mario to his feet. He *had* gained weight.

"Well, I've already run over my break time," Mario said, wiping soil from his slacks.

I promised to stay in touch and gave him another kiss on the cheek. I never knew when I might need him again.

I was on my way home sweet home to Cocoplum when I remembered I'd forgotten my promise to Fatima to check into the
Castro rumors. Weaving through the traffic on Main Highway, I
switched on the radio. There wasn't anything to worry about—if
something had really happened in Cuba, all of Miami would be
going berserk. I fiddled around some more with the radio and,
finding nothing but music, turned it off. I could at least tell Fatima I had done something to look into Castro's demise, without
getting too specific about how hard I tried.

I stamped hard on the accelerator. My sister Lourdes was
coming home for the weekend, and I really wanted to see her.
She lived in a small, modest house in Little Havana with three
other sisters, all members of the Order of the Holy Rosary. She
usually lived a fairly simple life, but every so often she needed a
shot of home. I understood perfectly; I lived on my own for a
year after college, when I interned at White and Blanco, but
when the lease on my Brickell Avenue apartment came up for
renewal, Papi stepped in and tried to talk me into coming back
home to live. I considered it, and even returned for a month, but
as much as I loved my family I also needed independence. In
the year since I moved out I'd grown used to being alone, owing
explanations to no one and coming and going as I liked. Besides,
I liked my apartment.

I lived in a fairly nondescript building at the southern end of
Brickell, near the entrance to Key Biscayne. It had a reputation
as a "starter"—in other words, the tenants expected to move out
as their incomes grew. But I had two perfectly adequate bed-

rooms—one of which I used as a study—a living/dining room, a modern kitchen, a decent bathroom, and a balcony. My furniture was nothing to get excited over, sort of early undergrad decor. I was on the twenty-fifth floor, though, with a view of sunsets over the bay, so who cared about furniture?

What I really cared about, other than the privacy of living alone, was that Solano Investigations was finally beginning to make money. Leonardo and I had worked like maniacs, and it was finally starting to pay off. We started out taking lost-dog cases, collections, cases for bail bondsmen whose clients skipped town (desperate as we may have been, though, I drew the line at being a bounty hunter). At the end of our first year we were covering expenses and taking home halfway decent salaries. By year four I had paid Papi back the money he fronted me to start the agency. I had established myself as an independent and successful woman in a notoriously macho field of work.

Papi finally accepted that I was grown up—it took a while, since I was the baby—and that I had a life of my own. I think when Mami died he hoped I would move back in permanently, but he was satisfied that I ran home all the time for meals and laundry and often stayed overnight. All he demanded was that I accept a suitable car from him as a gift—which, in his opinion, could only mean a Mercedes. You can imagine how much arm-twisting it took to get a twenty-three-year-old girl to accept *that* gift.

Fatima and her two daughters, the twelve-year-old twins Magdalena and Teresa, also lived in the family house. It seemed natural, after Mami's death and the Julio Juarez scandal. All three of us, my sisters and I, would always return home one way or another. It was hard to explain, especially to Americans. Papi loved it; he always had company, and he got to complain about being the only man in a house full of chattering women.

Papi had been a contractor in Havana, building a sizable fortune in hotel construction during Batista's time, before he was forced into exile. He was educated in the United States, first at

Choate in Connecticut, then at Princeton. He formed friend-
ships with the kind of Americans who had traditionally invested
in Cuba.

When Cuba became too volatile and unsafe for business,
Papi started to shift the family's investments to the States, with
the help of his American friends. When Batista fell and Castro
took over, Papi had already transferred most of his wealth out of
the country. He and Mami had just married, and hated to leave
their homeland, but after a few years of Castro's dictatorship
they knew they had to leave while they could. Mami was three
months pregnant with Fatima at the time.

In Miami, Papi immediately got a contractor's license and
started work. Unlike most Cubans who came to the States in the
early sixties, he had no illusions about Cuba's future. He knew
the country wasn't going to return to the way it had been, and
this understanding put him miles ahead of the game. Papi and
Mami dug in for the future.

The family first lived in a modest three-bedroom house in
southern Coral Gables while Papi waited to build his perfect
home. His chance came about fifteen years ago, when the
Arvida Corporation started an exclusive development on a large
tract of land along Biscayne Bay, just south of Coconut Grove.
Papi bought three lots where the water was deepest, knowing he
would want to build a dock for a deep-sea fishing boat (his passion).

This development turned into Cocoplum. Some county
prosecutors call it *Coca*plum, because of all the drug money that
went into buying some of the houses there. But that's life in
South Florida. It may have had some elements of the tacky nou-
veau riche, it might have harbored some wealthy drug dealers
trying for legitimacy, but behind the guards and the gates was
my Cocoplum: the sprawling earth-tone homes and rich green
lawns, the canals and sea breezes. It was home.

And it was quite a home. Pulling into the driveway, I
thought for the millionth time that Papi went overboard on our

place. Lourdes called it "late refugee" style—the kind of house an immigrant who made piles of money in the land of golden opportunity would build. My parents were usually discreet, but they lost all restraint and proportion on the house. It was huge: ten bedrooms, all oversized, lots of living areas, terraces, patios. Your basic capitalist nightmare.

My sisters and I really don't know what got into Papi. He designed it when he was investigating our family's Galician ancestry, so he copied an obscure Spanish hacienda blueprint he found in an encyclopedia. Luckily we owned three lots to put distance between us and the others, but even at that remove we still overshadowed our neighbors' homes. I always suspected they hated us for it.

Old Osvaldo was watering the flowers when I pulled up, his bald head covered by a straw hat and his wiry, still-muscular frame hunched over a long hose. He and his wife, Aida, had been with our family for years, first as cook and butler for my grandparents in Havana. Upon arriving in Miami they called my parents, announcing they were ready to resume their service to the family. Mami, fully aware they were in their late fifties and that hiring them again also meant taking care of them for the rest of their lives, didn't hesitate a second. I can't remember a time when Osvaldo and Aida weren't around.

"Lupe, bring your car closer, this way," Osvaldo barked, mopping his forehead with a handkerchief. "How did it get so dirty? Did you park under that jacaranda tree again? I told you the sap from that tree kills the paint!"

I drove the car closer to Osvaldo. He watched with his hands on his hips, then opened the door so I could get out.

"It's the little things that are important, Lupe," he said, shutting the door and inspecting the paint as he scolded. "You must remember these things in life."

When I was younger I would have stuck my tongue out at him. "I'm sorry, Osvaldo," I said instead. "I won't do it again, I promise. Is Lourdes here yet?"

"She's on the dock with your Papi," he said, straightening. He was only a little taller than me. "Aida made some conch fritters, but you should hurry. Everyone keeps eating them all as soon as Aida makes them. You know how this family is. All they do is eat."

Once a week Osvaldo came to Solano Investigations and worked on the property around the cottage. He claimed to enjoy it; he said it brought out his creative side. Gardening and landscaping in disorderly Coconut Grove were a completely different matter than in Coral Gables. Foliage in the Grove was wild and lush, while the Gables preferred manicured lawns and immaculate hedges. There were practically no zoning restrictions in the Grove, while in the Gables homeowners could paint their houses in one of only sixteen approved colors.

Years ago when he first took over the grounds around the cottage, Osvaldo tried to consult with me about the trees and bushes. It didn't take him long to find that I was completely ignorant about nature. After that, the only time he approached me at work was when he discovered Leonardo's marijuana patch. To this day, my brilliant assistant is still amazed that old Osvaldo knew another kind of grass when he saw it.

I left Osvaldo in the driveway and stepped into the house, cooled for a moment by the air-conditioning. Then I was greeted anew by the Miami tropical blast when I stepped out to the dock. Lourdes was there, changed from her nun's habit into casual clothes from the Gap.

She seemed like a Cuppie—a Cuban yuppie—not like a demure sister of God. Actually, there are so few nuns left today that no one really knows what they're supposed to look like. Lourdes is the only nun I know. We compare our respective professions sometimes, and have to laugh and wonder where we went wrong.

I stepped out onto the dock and hugged my sister. Lourdes, as always, felt strong and solid in my embrace.

"Hello, sis," she said, her mouth full of conch fritter. She looked great, with her dark hair cut in a short, smart style that set off her gleaming brown eyes. Her skin was flawless.

She might not look it, but Lourdes is every bit the dedicated nun. One day I was at Tamiami for shooting practice on the range. Feeling around in my purse for the Beretta, I found Mami's white lacquer rosary beads wrapped around the barrel. I recognized Lourdes's handiwork and my eyes filled with tears—completely blowing the veneer of cool I try to keep at macho places like the shooting range. Lourdes worried about me, always giving me religious items to ward off danger. It can be downright embarrassing when I'm with a man in the throes of arousal and I have to call time out—so I can take off the religious medals she's made me promise to wear pinned to my bra.

I dug into the plate of conch fritters waiting on the glass table by the dock and poured myself a *mojito*—rum and lemon juice—to wash it down. Papi gracefully stepped off the deck of his boat, his lined features obscured by a big Panama hat and huge dark sunglasses.

"So there's no news?" he said to me. I could tell he had accepted the harsh truth—that he would still be in Miami tomorrow and that nothing had happened to Fidel. Papi never explained specifically what he intended to do when he landed the Hatteras in Havana harbor. I don't think he really knew.

We had dinner on the terrace. The sun set over Biscayne Bay with a brilliant splash of orange over a deep purplish blue, the clouds blowing lazily across the sky with the first stirrings of a cool night wind. Fatima argued with Teresa and Magdalena about riding lessons and whether they could have a horse. Papi ate in silence, his thoughts probably still filled with his dashed hopes. The older he became, the more he identified with our homeland and the more he wanted to go back.

Once or twice I noticed Lourdes staring at me strangely, but she didn't say anything. I teased the twins about how smelly horses were, then settled back and watched the pelicans perched on their pilings, waiting for some hapless fish to surface so they could gracefully swoop down to capture their prey.

Lourdes and I were alone at the table as Aida cleared the dishes. "Look," I said, pointing into the day's last light. "In the water. I think it's a manatee."

Lourdes didn't even bother looking. "Are you going to tell me what you're so worried about, or am I going to have to guess?"

She leaned back with her drink, her expression placid as she stared into my eyes. She was as close to me as anyone in the world, and I hate to think it, but since she became a nun she developed a real perceptiveness and intensity. It was spooky sometimes.

"It's nothing," I said. I knew she would be able to tell I was lying.

"All right, let's go through the list," she said. "Is it a man?"

"No, nothing like that."

"Then it's your work." Lourdes reached into her purse and produced a cigarette. She shielded the match from the wind and took a long drag. "Are you mixed up in something you shouldn't be?"

"I don't know," I said. "I just have a funny feeling."

Lourdes nodded and flicked her ash into a potted ficus tree. "You should listen to those feelings, little sister," she said, staring at the horizon. "They're trying to tell you something."

five

"Thirteen thousand, two hundred and thirty-two? You've got to be kidding!"

I was on the phone with Jennifer Harvey, who worked in the public relations department at Jackson Memorial. She sounded young and a little green, but she recited the number of births last year at Jackson the minute I asked the question. She knew her stuff.

"Let me see," I said, punching numbers on my calculator. "Divided by three hundred and sixty-five, that gives me thirty-six point twenty-five births a day."

"Approximately," Jennifer said perkily.

"Right," I mumbled, jotting down the numbers. I had the phone wedged between my shoulder and my ear, and it was becoming uncomfortable. Just then Leonardo grunted loudly from the next room, where he was lifting weights. He sounded like a cow giving birth. I wondered what Jennifer thought of that.

She didn't hear, or pretended not to. "I can't give you the breakdown on males and females," she said. "But you can just divide the number in half. That comes to six thousand, six hundred and sixteen females per year."

Jennifer was no help when I asked her about Jackson's procedures for registering births, but she transferred me to obstetrics, where a husky-voiced male nurse confirmed everything Mario told me. I also learned something interesting: Patients without their own private doctors ended up with "staff physician" on their birth certificates. Which confirmed that Allen

Samuels, whoever he was, had definitely delivered Michelle Moreno, and that the mother had been his patient.

I had already learned that there were twenty-nine community hospitals in Dade County alone, most offering maternity services. There was no way I could investigate the female births at all of them in the time I had. I was stuck with a certificate that listed Jackson Memorial, but in reality the Morenos weren't even sure Michelle was born in Dade County. All they had was Betancourt's word—and he had proven himself completely unreliable. All I knew for certain was that the birth certificate Betancourt produced had never been registered with the Bureau of Vital Statistics.

Speaking of births, Leonardo's delivery in the next room seemed to be progressing nicely. He screamed something incoherent in a high voice, then groaned again. A moment later I heard a loud thump as he dropped the weight to the floor.

I needed ideas. I got my magnifying glass out of my desk and inspected the documents the Morenos gave me. They looked just as genuine close up.

It bothered me that Betancourt hadn't registered Michelle's birth. Parents needed original, certified records for Social Security numbers, passports, government services. It didn't make sense for Betancourt to assume that his clients would never do any of these things. A snake like Betancourt would be too careful to screw up, unless he had been sloppy on just the Morenos' case. There was only one way to find out.

"Mr. Moreno? Guadalupe Solano speaking. I don't have anything to report to you at this time." I spoke quickly, not wanting to get his hopes up. "But I want to ask you a few questions."

"Anita, please leave me alone for a moment. Close the door behind you." I had called Jose Antonio at his office, and he dispatched his employee with cold imperiousness. But when he spoke to me, his voice became soft. "Anything, anything I can do to help."

"How many copies of Michelle's birth certificate did Elio Betancourt give you?"

"Ten—all certified. I remember the number, because I thought it was a lot of copies. Why do you ask?"

I heard grinding metal from the next room. Leonardo was about to start on his leg machine. "I'm working on something, Mr. Moreno, but I'd rather wait until I have more solid information before I go into it. I want to follow up on a couple of things before I get your hopes up."

Jose Antonio was silent, but I could hear him breathe harsh and jagged into the phone.

"One more thing. Your wife mentioned she heard of Betancourt through her cousin Elvira. Could your wife call Elvira and find out how many birth certificates Betancourt gave her for her children, and if she might give you copies? I want to take a look at them."

"Of course, of course," Jose Antonio said, pathetically happy to finally be of use. The poor man was probably about to break. I knew the Cuban male mentality enough to be sure he wasn't sharing his feelings with his wife. It isn't the macho thing to do.

Just as I hung up the phone, I heard a shriek from the next room. I called out and Leonardo answered he was okay. I lived in daily fear that he was going to hurt himself working out in the office. I imagined emergency rooms, a long convalescence, and an almost total work stoppage at the agency.

Next I called my cousin Luisa at home. She'd had a baby boy a few months before Michelle Moreno was born. I asked to borrow her baby's birth certificate for a few days, so I could compare a legitimate certificate with Michelle's. Luisa, bored to tears at home, was happy to help. Prior to having her son, she was a senior account executive at Barnett Bank in Miami. She was overjoyed being a mother, but I knew her brain was turning to jelly at home alone every day.

I hung up the phone and stuck my head into the next room

to see Leonardo contorted over his leg machine, looking like he was about to undergo a painful medical examination. Then my phone rang.

Jose Antonio didn't waste time with preliminaries. "Elvira also has ten birth certificates for each of her children. I sent a messenger to her home to pick them up. You should have them within the hour."

"Did Elvira ask Betancourt why he gave her so many?"

"Her husband did. Remember, he's an accountant. He probably worried he'd be charged extra." Jose Antonio laughed weakly. "Betancourt said he wanted them to have extra copies because it might take him a long time to file with the county."

I didn't say anything. Betancourt dealt with desperate people, the kind who didn't ask questions.

"Now, Ms. Solano, I need you to be honest with me. Obviously you've found something."

"The reason you and Elvira, and probably all the other adoptive parents, were given so many birth certificates is because Betancourt never intended to register your babies' births in Dade County. I went to the Bureau of Vital Statistics today, and Michelle was never registered there. As far as the county is concerned, she was never born."

Jose Antonio said nothing. I gave him a moment to take it all in. Then he shouted, "Anita, I told you to stay out of here! Leave, and close the door!"

I heard something in his voice I hadn't expected: embarrassment. "I'd imagine the same is true with Elvira's children," I said. "I'll be able to say more after I get the documents you sent me."

"Is this good or bad in terms of finding her birth mother?" Jose Antonio asked.

"I don't know what it means. I'll keep you posted on any developments as they arise, I promise." I knew my reassurance sounded weak, but it was the best I could do.

"There's one other thing," he added, a little sheepishly.

"Lucia . . . Lucia asked that you come to our home, to visit Michelle. My wife feels it would help somehow if you saw her."

"How about tomorrow, after lunchtime?" I said, without thinking. This wasn't the best idea in the world, I realized. The Morenos' emotions were so strong that I might become caught up in them. Jose Antonio said he looked forward to seeing me, and hung up.

In less than an hour I held Elvira's children's birth certificates in my hand. I put them next to Michelle's on my desk. The documents were identical except for the names of the children and parents and the dates of birth. The hospital was the same—Jackson Memorial. And the doctor was the same—Allen Samuels, his office address listed as the same as the hospital's. All the documents looked completely authentic, down to the notary stamp for the state of Florida.

Leonardo came into my office and dropped into a client's chair. He toweled sweat from his face for a while, then flexed his pecs through his tank top. He seemed pleased with his results for the day—so much so that I thought about offering him a mirror.

"Is there something you need, Leonardo?"

His eyes widened and he brushed a wet lock of hair from his forehead. "I just came in to say hello," he said sheepishly. "I heard you on the phone earlier."

"I'm surprised you heard me over your screaming. Did the birth go well? Should I send you a blue or a pink baby blanket?"

Leonardo shook his head and got up to leave. He was used to my sarcasm, but I was taking out too much of my frustration on him.

"Hey, Leonardo, I'm sorry," I said to his retreating back.

"Whatever. I'd keep the door closed, but I want to be able to answer the phone if it rings." His feathers ruffled for the moment, he waited in the doorway. "Anyway, I thought you'd want to hear my idea."

I bit my tongue—literally—before I said something nasty

about Charity, or Peacefulness, or whatever the hell her name was with the yoga lessons.

"You can't find out where those kids came from, right? And you're looking for a doctor at Jackson Memorial?" Leonardo shrugged. "I looked at the notes on your desk when you were out."

"Fine, fine. What are you getting at?"

"Gladys Rodriguez," Leonardo said. He waited for my memory to kick in and my eyes to light up, then happily left the room. I could hear him slapping out a beat on his tight stomach muscles as he made his way to his desk.

Gladys was the nurse who took care of my mother in the last painful months until her death. I remembered now, and apparently so did Leonardo, that Gladys worked for years in the neonatal unit at Jackson. She had retired a few years before, but she might have known Dr. Allen Samuels.

The moment she picked up the phone, the sound of Gladys's voice—creaky, a little loud—took me back in time. "Dr. Samuels? Dr. Samuels? Let me think."

Gladys was silent too long, and I was worried that her formerly sharp mind had dulled with age. "Lupe, *querida,* there were so many doctors there. Jackson is the teaching hospital for the University of Miami medical school. Sometimes residents, even medical students, delivered babies there. Also visiting doctors. There were so many . . . but Samuels, I remember him. I think he was there for a long time."

Gladys sighed with a musical little exhalation. She had to have been well into her seventies, but she still sounded exactly the same.

"You know, I'm sure I remember him now," she said. "A fine doctor. In fact, I think someone told me something about him not too long ago. Ay, my mind! Ever since I retired, I swear it retired too!"

I laughed with her. "You're fine, Gladys. It's good to hear you sounding so well."

"I know. I'll call my friend Regina. She was the assistant to the head of delivery at Jackson, so she'll remember your Dr. Samuels. What do you need to know?"

"I need to know where he's living now. I'm working on a case involving a baby he delivered."

Gladys's voice rose. "Oh, a *case.* I couldn't believe it when I heard you were a detective, Lupe. You were such a nice girl."

While I waited for Gladys to call back, I tried to think of a gift for Leonardo for helping me, and in case he stayed mad at me for making fun of him. I had settled on a jumbo tub of his favorite brand of disgusting bodybuilder's protein shake, when my phone rang.

It was Gladys. "I just spoke with Regina. She says Dr. Samuels retired about five years ago, and she thinks he moved to North Carolina. He used to have a house there, him and his wife. Regina remembers going to his retirement party, as a matter of fact. She said he was a good doctor, but she thinks he had some kind of problem and that's why he moved away. Is that enough, Lupe? Did I do all right?"

I could tell that for Gladys, this was more fun than watching *telenovelas* anytime.

"What kind of problem was she talking about?" I asked, getting the hot sensation in my ears I always felt when I was close to something important.

"No, I don't know anything about that." Gladys spoke abruptly; she liked to gossip, but I remembered she always felt protective of anyone in the medical profession.

"Gladys, do you think Regina would talk to me?" Now I really had the warm feeling.

"I'll call her and make sure it's okay, Lupe. I'll call you right back," Gladys said, and hung up.

It was Regina herself who phoned me. "Guadalupe Solano," she said in a deep, rich voice. "I remember Gladys telling me about your family. She said your mother was a wonderful woman."

"Thank you," I said quietly.

"Gladys told me what you want to know about. I will help you, but not on the telephone. I want to meet you face-to-face."

I quickly agreed. I was familiar with the mentality of the older-generation Cubans. Regina wanted to emphasize her importance by making me come to her. She was probably also bored and would simply enjoy a visit. Tomorrow I was in for a few hours on Regina's porch, drinking coffee and talking about Cuba. It was a small price to pay to find out what happened to Samuels.

When I came out, Leonardo was at his desk, gluing little mystical symbols to a piece of paper for a yoga flier. It didn't bother me one bit.

"Leonardo, you're a genius," I said.

He flashed a perfect smile. "So it worked?"

"It worked. Thank you."

"Great," he said. "You know, this might be a good time to ask you if I can—"

I held up my hand. "Whatever you want," I said. "Just don't tell me now. Things are going too well."

I locked my office and stood by the hall window for a minute, listening to the parrots cackling at each other. A late-afternoon breeze wafted through, carrying a sweet flower scent. Life was good.

six

"Emma, it's Lupe. Hi."

"Hey, girl, where have you been?"

"Busy, real busy. Listen, are you free for lunch today? I need to pick your brain on a case I'm working."

"Name it and claim it."

"Joe's at twelve-thirty."

"Great. I love a free lunch. Lucky me, I didn't even eat breakfast."

Emma Gillespie was one of my closest friends. We were classmates from kindergarten through high school, but we didn't really get close until later, when Mami was sick. Emma lost her own mother as a child, and looked me up when she heard about Mami. I found out she'd gone north to Harvard for college and law school, worked a stint as a federal prosecutor, then become one of the most respected criminal defense attorneys in Dade County.

I owed Emma a lot, and not just because she helped me get through a nightmarish time in my life. She was also a great contact for me because of her clout in the legal and law enforcement communities. After eating with Emma, I'd interview Regina. With any luck, I'd have enough leads to possibly nail down the Moreno case in a few days.

By the time I reached Miami Beach I was ravenous. I knew what Emma and I would have—two orders of the jumbo stone crabs, hash brown potatoes, creamed spinach, key lime pie for dessert, and a frigid cold white wine to wash it all down. The only variable was the wine—I liked it dry and Emma favored it sweet. Today was her turn to pick.

When I parked at Joe's I saw Emma's fire-engine-red Porsche pulling away, driven by a valet. It wasn't even twelve-thirty yet. Emma was the only person I knew who could make me feel late when I was early, but I ran on Cuban time; she ran on WASP time. I roared up to the valet drop-off area, nearly giving the attendant a coronary.

Emma was just giving the maître d' her name when I came into the dark waiting area. I was glad to see her dressed casually, in a pink cotton T-shirt, cotton pants, and espadrilles—it meant we could have a leisurely lunch without the hassle and stress of afternoon meetings or court appearances. She had on her favorite well-worn straw hat, with a fuchsia peony flower pinned to a black velvet ribbon around the crown. With her fresh good looks and perfect skin, Emma could pass for the Ivory soap girl. She radiated health and clean living and didn't seem to have a care in the world. Her opponents often learned the hard way that her innocent appearance masked a razor-sharp mind.

As soon as she spotted me she flew over and hugged me, almost knocking me down. We were only a few months apart in age, but she was a perpetual teenager.

"There's only a few people ahead of us," she said, straightening her hat. "It shouldn't be long until we get a seat."

I looked into the crowded dining room. At least it wasn't dinnertime; then, the wait ran from one to three hours. Joe's didn't take reservations, seating everyone in the order they arrived.

"You slipped the guy some money, didn't you?" I whispered.

"Of course." Emma smiled at the maître d' as he arrived with menus to take us to our table. Walking ahead of me, she turned and leaned down to talk into my ear. "Democracy in action," she said.

We were still giggling when we sat down. Joe's owners always vigorously insisted that theirs was a fair, first-come, first-served institution. Only two kinds of customers believed that: the truly gullible and tightwads who claimed to stand on principle.

We didn't talk for a minute because Emma was immersed in her menu. She truly seemed never to change. She was the only woman I knew who used Jean Naté cologne past the age of sixteen, and the few times she went hatless, mostly in court, she wore her hair parted in the center and flowing free down her back—just as in high school. One of the Miami social magazines did a piece on the ten most beautiful single career women a couple of years ago, and Emma was in it. When the editor asked how she kept her golden hair so lovely, Emma casually told her the truth—that she washed it with whatever shampoo was on sale at the time, and dried it by aiming her car air-conditioner vents at her head on the way to the office. Once, in her haste, she had even used her dog's flea and tick shampoo. The editor must have been completely humorless, because the episode never saw print.

Emma placed our order—everything I'd predicted, down to the sweet wine—and reached across the table and took my hand. "It's good to see you, it's been too long," she said, then took her hand back. "But it sounds like you mean business today. What's up?"

"Remember a few years ago, you told me you had a trial against Elio Betancourt?"

"That son of a bitch?"

"That son of a bitch."

Emma frowned like she had just bitten into a rotten lemon. She was trying to look disgusted, but she was simply too cute to pull it off.

The busboy arrived with a basket of bread and thick slabs of butter. The waiter came right behind him and started pouring the wine; as soon as Emma sipped it and pronounced it drinkable, we clinked glasses and drained them. The waiter, his eyes a

little wide, quickly refilled our glasses. I could see the hope
come to life in his eyes: we might be a two-bottle table.

"What do you want to know?" Emma asked.

"Well, I have a case he's closely involved in."

Emma slathered a quarter-inch-thick slab of butter on a roll.
"Good luck, and watch your back," she said.

I split an onion roll in half, stuffed it with butter, and took a
bite. Neither of us was cowed by the tyranny of the fat-free
brigade.

"Tell me what your case is about," Emma said, her mouth
full of bread. She reached over to the wine bucket and grabbed
the bottle in a smooth motion. Four men seated at the table
nearest us gave her an admiring look. Not many women today
display their appetites in public.

I gave her a brief account of what the Morenos told me and
the follow-up I had done. I knew I could trust Emma, both as a
friend and as an attorney.

"Wow," she finally said. "What a rat! I knew he was shady
and unscrupulous and all of that, but I never thought he was involved in anything downright criminal. I knew he was in bed
with some marginal clients, but this is unbelievable."

The waiter arrived with a huge tray that brimmed over with
our order. When Emma and I get together and eating is involved, there is no debate. We set Betancourt aside and concentrated on business. The waiter offered plastic bibs, but we
waved him away. Bibs are for tourists. We set into the cold stone
crabs, alternating between the mustard sauce and the drawn
butter. The hash brown potatoes were, as always, delicious and
greasy. It was only when we took a halftime breather that I ad-
dressed what Emma had last said.

"That's what I thought too," I said, wiping my hands. "I already knew he was no Mother Teresa, but what's a criminal defense attorney doing in adoptions—legal or illegal? Does the
guy need money? How's his practice going these days?"

"God, Lupe, calm down." Emma forked another load of

potatoes into her mouth. "What do you think I am, an Elio Betancourt expert?"

"Come on, all you criminal defense attorneys keep track of each other," I said. "After all, who knows when you might need representation of your own."

Emma crinkled her nose with amusement as she took another long drink of wine. "You should talk, Lupe. Have you broken any laws yet investigating this case?"

I dug into my food and didn't answer. "What about his personal life?" I asked. "Any skeletons you know about?"

"Well, I know he plays around like crazy on his wife. He considers anything in a skirt fair game."

"You sound like you're talking from experience," I said.

The guys at the next table had finished their lunch and all rose together. I could sense them trying not to stare as they walked by our table.

Emma seemed oblivious. "Well, it was certainly an easy proposition to turn down," she said. "Anyway, the wife—Margarita—is only interested in her social life. I heard he's had a series of mistresses through the years. Maybe that's why he needs the money. Those kinds of women aren't cheap."

"Come on, Emma, wake up. He's Cuban. Of course he has mistresses. It's probably built into his budget under fixed costs. What else do you know about him?"

"Hold on a second," she said. The waiter had just brought our key lime pie. "Can I have a cup of coffee with this?" The waiter nodded and made for the kitchen.

"I don't know what's worse," I said, "that Joe's refuses to serve Cuban coffee in the unofficial capital of Latin America, or that you're willing to drink that watered-down American junk."

Emma shrugged. "That Cuban stuff tastes like tar with sugar in it, if you ask me."

I bit into my pie. We could never agree about coffee or wine, but we were willing to tolerate each other's tastes.

"So anyway," Emma said, already half done with her pie

when the coffee came, "Betancourt's client list reads like a who's who of the drug crowd. I'm sure you know that. I've heard that he conducts himself in such a shady way to get back at his wife by playing head games with her. She's so preoccupied with social standing, and he's always trying to undermine her."

"Isn't that kind of extreme?"

"I don't know. Ask me when I get married," Emma said. "But the irony of all this is that he's considered a pretty good lawyer. He did some personal-injury cases a few years ago and got great results for his clients. He also took on the Dade County School Board for some teachers who got fired for some bullshit reason. I don't remember what—but he won."

"He sounds like a complex guy."

"That's for sure."

I motioned to the waiter to bring us the bill. The wine had made me sleepy, and I still had to meet the Morenos at their home, then drive to Sweetwater to meet Regina.

The bill paid, we stood outside in the bright afternoon glare, which blinded me and gave me an instant headache.

"If I hear anything else, sweetie, I'll let you know," Emma said when her car arrived first.

I took a pass by Ocean Drive. The sun played on the water, forming crescents of light that danced upon the blue surface. I always felt relaxed after seeing Emma. Her ease with the world rubbed off on me. Only the thought of a critically ill little girl, and that I was her last hope, kept me from having peace.

I didn't need to look in my rearview mirror to know that the cars were stacking up behind me. I was driving even slower than the little old ladies in their pink Cadillacs, but it was beyond my power to speed up. I hadn't thought much about going to Jackson at some point to visit Michelle Moreno since Jose Antonio's request the day before, but now the moment had arrived and I felt awful. It had been years since I was in the wards of Jackson Memorial, and I was in no hurry to return.

For the first time in my life I actually observed the speed limit on Old Cutler Road. Soon desperate drivers behind me started inching into the opposite lane, trying to pass. Self-preservation made me speed up—I didn't want to become road pizza if some cowboy tried to pass at the wrong moment. As soon as I accelerated, the drivers behind me settled down into routine tailgating. I could almost feel the soothed nerves back there when I finally shot twenty-five miles an hour over the speed limit.

Jose Antonio had confirmed with Leonardo when they would expect me, so I'd known he would be there in addition to Lucia. The wine from lunch was already wearing off, thankfully—it would be disrespectful to show up reeking of booze. I hoped it didn't wear off completely, though. I knew the visit might turn rough for me.

The evening before, after trying to sleep for hours, I'd had a nightmare. There was a child-sized coffin surrounded by white flowers on a stage in an empty Broadway theater, dramatically lit from behind. Dressed in black, I walked in slow motion to the coffin. Inside was a little girl, nestled in pink sheets, quietly asleep. Her skin was ivory white, save for the birthmark on her neck. Then the girl's eyes opened, full of tears that ran down to stain her satin pillow.

Needless to say, I awoke with my heart pounding, drenched in sweat. I got up around dawn and opened the balcony windows. I needed some Cuban coffee and an hour of watching the dark waters of Biscayne Bay before I could start the day.

I felt like a prisoner marching to her cell as I turned on my blinker to signal my left turn into Gables Estates. I slowed when I came to the gatehouse, stopping in front of the crash-proof barrier. I gave my name and said I was visiting the Morenos, then waited for the guard to take down my license number. He waved me through then, though when I looked back he was still staring at my car. This, of course, is what people pay for when they live in expensive gated communities: suspicious, paranoid guards who want to keep out everyone who doesn't live there— even, I suspect, expected guests.

Emma lived in Gables Estates with her family when we were in school, so I knew my way around. The Morenos lived only a block from Emma's parents' old house, and I smiled involuntarily when I passed the lake where we used to water-ski. The place hadn't changed much, though the houses seemed bigger than I remembered. Then I looked at the house numbers and realized I was close. It was time to take the exit ramp from memory lane.

Lucia and Jose Antonio's house was the last on its block, an imposing sand-colored, two-story Spanish colonial, hidden from the street by ficus trees planted tightly together. As soon as I pulled into the driveway and opened my car door, I heard a voice calling out to me.

"Señorita Lupe! Señorita Lupe!"

When my feet hit the driveway a tiny aged person dressed in traditional housekeeper's black and white had virtually tackled me. I had to wait for her to catch her breath to find out what was so urgent. I'm no giant myself, but this woman barely came up to my chest.

"Señorita Lupe," she gasped again.

This lilliputian had a puffy, tiny red doll's face. She pulled a handkerchief from her pocket and started wiping her eyes. I couldn't stand it anymore. "What's the matter?" I finally asked.

"Michelle is at the hospital. The Señora was waiting for you to arrive when Michelle started to feel ill."

My worst fears had been realized. I would have to go see the child at the hospital.

I almost reached out to console her. "Michelle looked very bad," she said. "Like the time before. The Señora, she called nine-one-one, and they came and took her away. The Señora went in the ambulance with her girl. She asked me to call you, but I didn't have your number."

"That's all right," I said quickly. "Are they at Jackson Memorial now?"

The housekeeper nodded and blew her nose loudly into her handkerchief. The situation was obviously serious, and I was also touched by her concern. Children are like that. You might not want to, but you can't help but care about them—usually a lot. I sort of patted the housekeeper's arm awkwardly and got back into the Mercedes.

There was nothing for me to do but go to Jackson. As I drove there now, I prayed the little girl was all right. Traffic was miraculously light, by Miami standards, and I reached the hospital in minutes. I parked in the "Doctors Only" lot behind the oncology wing, hoping that the Mercedes would blend in with the doctors' cars and keep me from getting towed.

I shuddered when I walked through the double doors, automatically looking for Mami's name on a bronze plaque on the north wall of the reception area. After she died, Papi made a half-million-dollar donation in her name. When I was a volunteer, I used to pray for my mother and rub my hand over the plaque before reporting to my position. I repeated the old ritual, looking around to see if anyone was watching.

I didn't need directions to the pediatric ward. I pressed the elevator button for the fourth floor and waited for those heavy doors to open in front of me again. It almost felt as though I'd never left.

When I stepped out of the elevator, I saw Jose Antonio leaning against a wall outside a room at the far end of the hall. I walked toward him, my heels clicking unnaturally loudly on the linoleum floor. Before I reached him I passed Elena's old room, almost expecting to see her there.

Jose Antonio shook my hand. "Thank you for coming. She is very ill," he said, looking away from me. "But the doctors think they have stabilized her. Until the next time, of course."

He spoke to me as though I were an old trusted friend. Lucia stepped from the room, an empty plastic water pitcher in her hand. She smiled wanly at me. "Thank you. Did Rosa tell you we were here?"

"Yes. She's very distraught," I added, I'm not sure why.

Lucia pondered for a moment and turned to her husband. "Go inside, Jose Antonio," she said. "Sit with the child for a while."

Jose Antonio obeyed like a robot, leaving us alone in the hall. "I want to speak to you without my husband present," Lucia said.

We walked together to the nurses' station, and I waited while she filled the pitcher with ice and water. The ward, as always, was quiet, with a thick feeling of gloom just beneath the surface calm.

"My husband is very upset," Lucia said as we made our way back. "He hardly eats or sleeps. The doctors tell us we are running out of time. How are you doing finding Michelle's . . . her mother?"

Lucia's voice was breathy and low. Soon there would be

three Morenos in the hospital unless I came up with something. Fear of failure sent bile up my throat, and I swallowed hard.

"I'm following several leads, and I'm working as hard as I can," I said, a little defensively. "Something will turn up soon, I'm sure of it. I promise."

I tasted bile again when Lucia turned to stare blankly at me. I don't know whether she really believed me, but she had no choice but to trust that I was trying. When we reached Michelle's room, she asked me to wait outside. I counted the speckles on the floor until the door opened again.

Lucia motioned for me to come in. I felt my heart in my ears as I approached the bed. When I saw her I had to hold on to the bed rail to keep from falling. Here was the girl in the picture, the girl in my nightmare. She slept, her closed eyelids ringed with purplish smudges. Apparently the storm had passed; there were no monitors, no respirators. Only a thin IV tube running from her arm indicated she was anything but fine.

I sensed Jose Antonio and Lucia retreat from behind me, and in a moment I heard the door close softly. Alone with the child, I reached out and caressed her cheek. Her eyelids seemed to flutter, just for an instant.

"I guess I should introduce myself." I felt ridiculous. "My name is Lupe Solano. I'm a private investigator."

She slept on. "I'll find her for you," I whispered softly. "I swear it."

Sweetwater was a town in western Dade County, founded by a troupe of acrobatic Russian midgets who had escaped from a circus touring South Florida. It was also called Little Managua because of its preponderance of refugees, primarily Nicaraguans. Scattered among them lived a few Cubans, reassured no doubt by the sight of ex–Somoza soldiers patrolling the orderly streets. It was here that Regina Larrea lived.

I was proud I'd made only three wrong turns before I pulled up to her small, tidy, freshly painted house. Lunch had done me in—I felt tired, fat, and a little hung over—and I arrived twenty minutes past our three o'clock meeting time. Lucky for me Cubans take tardiness for granted.

Waiting in the sweltering sun while she unlocked the chains securing the front door and gate, I had a good look at Regina. She was small, compact, probably in her early seventies, and exuded an air of total competence. I could see why she had held such an important job at Jackson for so long.

After watching all her elaborate precautions against crime, I took a brief paranoid look at my locked Mercedes parked in front of her house, as though it was the last time I would ever see it. Oh well, at least I was insured.

I followed Regina into her house. "Would you like a glass of lemonade?" she asked, already walking toward the kitchen.

I accepted, and had a look around until she came back. The place was immaculate, with crocheted doilies on the chair arms and embroidered curtains open to reveal windows sealed off with iron bars. A series of photos on a low wood shelf depicted a dark-haired family with Spanish features, first in the streets and backyards of old Havana, then on to color shots taken in Florida exile.

"Here, we'll sit in the rocking chairs," Regina said from behind me, startling me for a second with her husky voice. She pointed with her tray to a pair of matching white wood chairs. When we were seated with plastic glasses of lemonade, she asked how she could help me.

I told her most of the story of the Morenos and their daughter, withholding only specific details. I had pegged Regina as a no-nonsense character and thought it best to keep the bullshit to a minimum.

"Dr. Allen Samuels," she said, brushing a fleck of lint from her cotton housedress. She had been very distant when I told her the babies he delivered were later adopted illegally. "Ever since Gladys asked me about him, I've been trying to remember all I can. Here—I even found an old picture of him from his going-away party."

She gave me a slightly creased photograph of an older, distinguished-looking man surrounded by about a dozen women, all in nurse uniforms. The picture had been taken at the hospital; there were tons of medical equipment in the background. There were balloons and streamers, with a cake set on a steel examination table in the center of the room. I turned the photo over and read the date on the back: February 1991.

"Did you take this picture?" I asked her. "I don't see you in it."

"Yes. I developed it right away because the other nurses and I wanted to blow it up and put it in a frame for a nice going-away present to give Dr. Samuels. We were all fond of him, you know, and sorry to see him go. He was nice, not like some other doctors. Especially the young ones."

I showed her the date on the back of the picture. "I want to make sure I understand you correctly. According to what you're telling me, Dr. Samuels retired in February of 1991. You threw a party for him and he left right after."

Regina nodded sharply. In her high cheekbones and narrow, perfect nose I could see she had once been a beautiful woman—though maybe a little severe in manner. "In fact," she said, "he left so quickly we had to mail the picture to him in North Carolina."

"Do you have his address?" I gave her back the picture.

"I don't remember the town or the address; I would have to look. Sometimes I lose things now."

"Do you know why he left in such a hurry?"

"No. I heard stories, but I didn't give them any importance." Regina glanced at the photo and tucked it into her dress breast pocket. "Jackson is like a small town, you see. Almost ten thousand people work there."

"And people talk."

Regina met my eyes and frowned. "Exactly. I liked and respected Dr. Samuels. Besides, I'm not a gossip."

This was going nowhere fast. I couldn't afford to antagonize Regina, so I tried another approach. "Do you think you could find his address?" I asked again. "It's important I contact him to ask for his help."

"I have all my old papers in boxes in the garage," she said. "I had the picture in an album, but the address would be in a box with all the other papers since my time at Jackson. It's been years, you know."

That didn't sound encouraging, and she didn't exactly leap up with eagerness to dig through her old things in the garage. So, knowing it would make her happy, I asked, "I see you lived in Havana in the old days. What was it like?"

An hour later I left Regina with my business card and a promise to return after she went through her old papers. The trip hadn't been a total waste—I knew that Allen Samuels's name appeared on birth certificates years after he had left Jackson and ostensibly retired.

Back at the office, I was stunned to see Leonardo on the phone, trying to collect some of our past-due accounts. The last thing I wanted was for him to stop, so I walked past him on tiptoes and sealed myself in my office.

I opened my Rolodex and started making calls to some junior investigators I had used in the past. Within minutes I set up a round-the-clock surveillance on Elio Betancourt.

After a glass of water and a couple of aspirins, I jotted a note to Leonardo, assigning him the job of doing some phone work to find Samuels in North Carolina. Just in case Leonardo wasn't up to it, I also called a locating service I often used and ordered a nationwide search for Samuels. If the man was alive, they stood a decent chance of finding him.

Now it was just a matter of waiting, which I'm no good at. Still, I knew that information tends to come in torrents once it starts, so I started cleaning up old work on my desk. I spent the rest of the day doing what I hate most: writing reports. Leonardo had been on my case lately to catch up, and I certainly didn't want to discourage him from collecting old accounts.

Our work didn't come cheap, and Leonardo pointed out that most clients will pay our bills more cheerfully if they have a finished product in their hands. I had to agree, though I was fairly certain that he also had his eye on some new gym equipment. I think he figured that the more receivables we brought in, the less I'd object to his buying the stuff. He was probably right, but I would never dream of letting him know it. Early on, he would order the equipment and pay for it on a layaway plan, but when I pointed out to him the usurious rates of interest we paid, we just bought the equipment outright. Somehow Leonardo convinced me that we were actually saving money by buying all that stuff. He pointed out that he was much more productive if he could work out in the office at any time, and not have to go to a real gym.

As the afternoon turned into early evening, things started getting depressing. Leonardo had gone home, and the pile of reports on my desk grew taller and taller. I discovered some that were six months overdue. I hoped the clients would still remember me and the work I did for them.

"Well, cheer up, Leonardo," I said to the empty office. "I'll knock out a few more of these, and you're on your way to Soloflex city."

Two days later I had a pair of daily reports on Elio Betancourt done by junior investigators. I felt fresh and rested, having gone home early the past two nights like a good girl and slept like a newborn.

Elio, if the same two days were any indication, was an utter dynamo. His every waking minute was accounted for in either business or social functions. Any form of relaxation was apparently an alien concept to him. He worked all morning, drank like a fish at lunch, worked all afternoon in his office or at the courts, ate dinner with colleagues, then went to society functions—with visits to his mistress interspersed at odd hours. It made me tired just to read about it.

Accounts of Elio's life made for interesting reading, but they were worthless for uncovering his adoption scheme. I didn't care how many charity balls he attended with his wife, or how many girlfriends he had on the side. I was looking for something that stood out, something unusual. My one advantage was that I was familiar with the kind of upper-class social life Betancourt led, so I'd more easily spot anything out of the ordinary.

I was no closer to finding Samuels than when I started. Regina hadn't called, and Leonardo had struck out calling around in North Carolina. My locating service said they couldn't find him in a nationwide search, but they were moving on to other databases. The man couldn't have just disappeared from the face of the earth without a trace.

I picked up a phone message that Leonardo took for me before I got in that morning, and stared at it. Jose Antonio

Moreno. I had to call him and tell him how little I knew. I wasn't ready to panic yet—Esteban taught me never to rush a case, because that's exactly when you start to screw it up—but I knew Jose Antonio wouldn't take it well. It would be useless to explain to him that a case couldn't be forced, that it had to work its way to its own conclusion.

He answered on the first ring. I guess he was alone in his office, because his voice had the annoying tinny ring of a speakerphone. I told him I was trying to find Samuels, but hadn't yet.

There was a long moment of silence. "Mr. Moreno? Are you still there?"

"Yes. I'm sorry," he said, his voice distant through the speakerphone. "You have to excuse me. I didn't sleep at all last night."

I felt a surge of panic. "How . . . how bad is it?"

"Her blood count is low, and she's going in and out of consciousness. They have her stabilized, but the disease is progressing. My wife is at home trying to get some sleep before we return to the hospital this afternoon."

"I'm sorry, Mr. Moreno."

"There's time, Ms. Solano, but not as much as we thought." Jose Antonio's voice rose; it sounded as though he had his mouth right up to the speaker. "We need you."

A flood of emotion came over me: memories of my own fear and hopelessness when Mami's health failed over the course of weeks. The anger I felt then returned, and nearly turned against Jose Antonio. *Doesn't he know I'm doing what I can? I didn't make his little girl get sick.*

But then I closed my eyes and breathed deeply.

"Mr. Moreno, don't worry. I'll make something happen.

I hung up. *Now what?*

n i n e

The next morning, hours before dawn, my portable phone went off. It took me a minute to realize that it was the phone on my nightstand and not part of a dream I was having about chasing Elio Betancourt on horseback from South Beach to Sweetwater, with Emma in tow.

It was Nestor Gomez, the contract investigator I'd contacted to work the night shift surveillance on Betancourt.

"Lupe, sorry to call so late."

I switched on the light and looked out the window at the darkened sky. "What's up, Nestor?"

"I thought you'd want to know right away," he said. "At exactly two A.M. a couple in a dark Lexus pulled into Betancourt's driveway. They stayed for an hour, then left."

"Two in the morning is a strange time for a visit," I said, looking for my slippers. It was after three, but I knew I wouldn't be able to go back to sleep.

"That's why I didn't wait to call. I took some pictures with the telephoto lens, but I don't think they're going to be any good. I was too far away, and it was too dark."

I knew what he was talking about. To decide where the investigators should park for the surveillance on Betancourt's home, I drove by the place several times. It was hopeless: surveillance in Coral Gables is always a bitch. There's not much cover, the cops are overzealous, and the residents are always ready to freak out over a car parked on the street with someone in it. It was too easy to get burned.

"Anyway, Lupe," Nestor continued, "I'm going to get the

photographs developed. I'll stop by later today to drop them off."

"Nestor," I said quickly, afraid he was about to hang up, "you got the tags on the Lexus, right?"

Nestor chuckled. He had been playing games with me. "Of course I did, Lupe."

"Good boy, Nestor." I opened the closet and started trying to select an outfit. "You get the happy face *and* the gold star on today's homework."

By daybreak I had already run the Lexus's tags. They came back to an address owned by a Carillo family in Bay Point, an exclusive development just north of downtown Miami. I had a friend from high school who lived there, so I knew the area. I remembered Bay Point had a guardhouse to keep out undesirables, and without a call to the guards from a resident it was impossible for a visitor to get in.

Sonia, my old friend, was a scream in high school but somewhere since took a turn for the bland and bitchy. She did the usual thing: husband, two kids, nanny, charity work. I had a terrible habit of agreeing to meet her for lunch and canceling at the last minute.

"Sonia? Hi, it's Lupe. How are you? How's your mom?"

Sonia's kids screamed in the background. A TV blared.

"Listen, could you do me a favor and get me into Bay Point for a case I'm working? Just leave my name with the guards. Ay, thanks. Lunch? You bet. Just set the day and call me. Hey, *querida*, thanks."

Sometimes I'm ruthless.

I had to conduct the surveillance myself, and I really hoped I wouldn't have to spend the entire day locked up in a hot car. I wore a sedate khaki pantsuit, hoping it would make me look inconspicuous, but I didn't know how I would hold out in the outfit when the morning turned into blazing afternoon.

Sonia had done her part well: getting in was a breeze. I quickly found the house, but to call it a house would be an understatement—the place was a mansion. Right on the bay on Palm Road, it was a pink-columned Miami palace.

A house was up for sale right across the street. The gods were definitely with me. It was also vacant, so I happily parked in the driveway, hidden from view but with a perfect vantage point across the street. There, parked in a cul-de-sac in front of a smaller house, was the Lexus that Nestor spotted at Betancourt's house.

I didn't wait long to see action. No sooner was I safely hidden than a steady procession of expensive cars poured into the driveway. All the drivers were women, all carrying presents. Three florist trucks showed up, delivering huge baskets of flowers.

After the last truck drove away, I knew there was a new baby boy in the household. After all, why else send blue carnations? I took a few pictures, mostly to stay in practice, then pulled away, hoping I looked enough like a real estate agent who had been stood up on an appointment to show a house.

Nestor Gomez was waiting for me at the office with black, concave circles under his eyes, nestled in one of the client's chairs in my office, sipping one of Leonardo's mango power-vitamin shakes.

He flipped through the packet of photographs in his lap, trying to pick out the best shots. "These aren't great," he said wearily. "But they're not as bad as I thought they might be."

I sat at my desk and had a look. It was possible to distinguish through a grainy fuzz the middle-aged couple entering and leaving Betancourt's house with what appeared to be a baby seat. The time and date automatically stamped on the bottom of each picture indicated they had been inside for precisely one hour. I knew some details would emerge more clearly when I took the pictures to be blown up.

It didn't exactly break the case, but it was a start. "Good job, Nestor," I said. "I know it's a tough surveillance."

Nestor rubbed his eyes with the back of his hand. He wasn't even thirty years old, but he could have passed for fifty. In addition to taking night classes, he held down two jobs. He was Dominican, and he was slowly saving to bring his entire family to Miami. He told me he was one of twelve brothers and sisters, so it was going to take him a while. I called him all the time with jobs. He was steady and dependable, qualities hard to find in this business—plus, he always needed the work, so he never turned me down.

"Thanks, Lupe," he said. "But no more Coral Gables jobs, please. They're a real bitch."

"You've got it. Betancourt will be your last." I pulled out a notepad. "Now, tell me everything you saw."

Nestor took a deep breath. With what little sleep he got, I don't know how he remembered anything.

"At two o'clock the Lexus drove in," he said. "No one else came or left. I'm positive of that. And that's all."

If Nestor said that's all that happened, I knew the story was over. He was precise, almost to a fault. On a job once he stared, motionless, at a doorway for hours. There was no way anyone else entered Betancourt's house from the street without Nestor spotting them.

"So where did the baby come from?" I asked. "After we talked I called Missy and Kenny." Nestor frowned at the mention of the investigators working the two shifts before his. He didn't trust anyone else's work, except maybe mine. "According to them, no baby arrived at the house during their watches. But that baby was in the house when the Bay Point couple arrived, right?"

Nestor scrunched his tanned face into a mask of concentration. "Maybe the baby was there before we started the surveillance. I know for sure that no baby arrived at the house in the three days I've been on the job. I don't think it was born there, do you?"

I shook my head. "No, I don't think so. None of you reported seeing a pregnant woman entering the house, and I doubt Betancourt has a birthing room installed in there. Besides, none of the visitor's tags we've run has come back to any doctors or nurses."

"Lupe, I was making a joke."

"Oh, sorry." You could have fooled me. I could have taken his picture and sold it to the dictionary publishers to be printed next to the entry for "poker face."

But it made me think. The babies weren't born in Betancourt's house, but they also couldn't have been there for very long. Elio took on notorious criminals for clients and acted up in public, at least in part so he could piss off his socialite wife. So he was peevish and perverse, but that didn't make him stupid. He wouldn't want Margarita to know he was doing anything grossly illegal, what with her preoccupation with public image, and it would be hard to hide a screaming baby from her for any length of time.

"Keep talking, Nestor," I said. "What does all this tell you?"

I needed Nestor's literal mind at just that moment. "The only thing I know is that the baby didn't arrive by car," he said cautiously.

"Wait a second. There are two ways of getting onto Betancourt's property," I said. "From the street, or from the bay via the canal behind the house. If we rule out the street, that leaves the canal. That baby had to come by boat!"

Nestor wasn't at all excited: imagination wasn't a quality he cultivated. "From where I was stationed, I couldn't see the canal. It very well could have arrived by boat. Maybe that's the only explanation."

He stood up to leave. I quickly wrote him a check for his payment. "Thanks," I said. "You did great. This job might go on for a few more weeks. Do you think you can handle that?"

"Sure. I figure I can bring over one of my sisters with what you're paying me," he said proudly as he made to leave. "I only have seven left to go, you know."

"Get some sleep!" I screamed as he closed the door behind him.

When I picked up the phone and started dialing, I could hear Leonardo trying to sell Nestor some of his vitamins. He had just warmed up his sales pitch—I liked the part about "getting by on six hours' sleep and feeling great," since Nestor was probably lucky to get three hours a night—when Lucia Moreno answered.

"Señora Moreno? This is Lupe. I need to ask you a few more questions. Do you think you and your husband could come by my office today?"

I should have known they would speed right over. They arrived in the time it took me to find out that Leonardo still hadn't unearthed anything about Samuels in North Carolina—but he had succeeded in selling Nestor thirty bucks' worth of vitamins and dietary supplements.

"What that guy needs is a private room at a rest home for about six months," I was saying when the Morenos walked through the door.

Lucia looked as though she had aged years in the week or so since I last saw her. She had clearly lost weight, and seemed frailer than ever. I was genuinely worried about her. This case had to be resolved one way or the other, and soon.

To my amazement she stepped across the room and, without a word, embraced me tightly. I could feel the heat of her body, and her shoulders begin to tremble with tears. Jose Antonio looked mortified. I was embarrassed, and felt guilty for feeling that way.

"Here, Señora," Leonardo said, handing her a handkerchief

and taking her hand. She looked shocked for an instant to be confronted by a handsome young man wearing a "Muscle Club" tank top and jogging shorts, but he was obviously so genuine and concerned that she let him lead her to the office refrigerator. There he mixed her a mango shake and spoke calm words to her in a low voice.

"I'm sorry," Jose Antonio said. "Lucia is very emotional."

Of course, Jose Antonio, a typical Cuban man, felt compelled to act as if he were made of granite. "How is Michelle?" I asked.

"The same," he said, staring at the floor. "She's stable for now."

Leonardo and I led them into my office, where I sat behind my desk and tried to project an all-business attitude. I was on the verge of getting caught up in Lucia's despair, and needed to stay calm.

I had written up all the reports on the case, so I read them a complete update. They both listened intently to what I had to say, Lucia sipping slowly at her mango drink.

"What happens now?" José Antonio asked. "Are we really any closer to finding Michelle's birth mother?"

"That's why I asked you to come here. I need you to remember that night four years ago when you went to Betancourt's house to pick up Michelle. Think hard. I want you to tell me exactly what happened, beginning from when you got there. Take your time."

The Morenos looked at each other warily. Jose Antonio spoke in a low, dispassionate voice. "Betancourt called to tell us the baby had been born, and that we would receive a call sometime in the next week telling us exactly when we could pick her up. He said it could be anytime, night or day."

Lucia cleared her throat. Trying to remember had obviously helped her calm down. "He called us at midnight three days later," she said. "He told us to be at his house in Coral Gables at exactly two in the morning, and to bring a baby carrier. We had all the equipment, of course. Michelle's room had been ready for months."

"Did you ask him why it had to be so late at night? I mean, two in the morning seems pretty late for a newborn to be out."

Lucia seemed to ponder this. "He told us the mothers simply wanted to drop off the babies and not be seen by anyone, because they were so ashamed of what they had done. He kept saying these were good Cuban girls, that they would be ostracized from their families if anyone found out what they had done."

"You have to understand, Ms. Solano," Jose Antonio said. "We were desperate for a baby. We didn't ask many questions. Maybe we didn't want to know too much, and that's our fault. But Michelle shouldn't have to pay for our mistake."

I interrupted him. "Think back to when you arrived at the house. I need all the details. Where was the baby? Was she waiting for you?"

"No, she wasn't there when we arrived," Jose Antonio said. "At least, not in the library, where Betancourt took us. We were there for a half hour or so, finishing the paperwork, while Betancourt left to fetch the baby. We stayed in the library from the time we went into the house to the time we left with Michelle, I'm sure of that."

"So you don't know how the baby got into the house, or if she was there the whole time you were there?"

I could see in their eyes they were trying to figure out where I was going. "No, we don't know," Lucia said softly.

"Did you hear anything unusual while you were there?"

They both shook their heads.

"Did the library have windows? Could you see anything outside?"

Lucia and Jose Antonio were silent. I could almost see the wheels turning as they searched their memories. It was lousy to torment them like this, but I couldn't stop now.

"There were French doors, weren't there, Jose Antonio?"

Lucia asked in a distant voice. "French doors leading to a patio or garden, or . . . I'm sorry. It was dark, and I was so excited. I know I'm not helping you much."

Jose Antonio put his arm around his wife and kissed the crown of her head. He looked at me. "Ms. Solano, why are you asking all these questions? What are you thinking about?"

I could see they were done, and a trace of indignation had entered Jose Antonio's voice. I told them my theory, that the baby arrived at the house by boat. They quietly accepted what I had to say, listening as though gleaning my words for some slight hope.

And my options had narrowed to one: to wait until the next baby was delivered to Elio Betancourt.

I was bone tired after ushering the Morenos out to their car, but I had one more call to make before I could go home. The reception area was empty; Leonardo had slipped out, probably for a self-defense-through-nutrition class or something.

There was an already opened bottle of white wine in the office fridge somewhere, I just knew it, but first I had to dig through a small mountain of chilled recyclable bottles full of multicolored health drinks. I finally found the wine, behind a big plastic bag full of some weird tuber that looked like it was growing eyes.

I downed half a glass before dialing the phone. I would need some fortification.

"Sonia? Hi, this is Lupe. I wanted to say thanks for your help today. I really appreciate it."

For the second time that day I was on the phone with the old friend who got me into Bay Point. I put my hand over the mouthpiece and took a long drink of wine; it was usually hard to get through a conversation with Sonia.

"Lupe!" she nearly shouted. "Did you get in all right? Sometimes those guards can be really rude. I keep telling Ricardo I like to feel safe, but I don't need to feel like I live in Fort Knox!"

I made the appropriate noises in response. The hair on the

back of my neck had begun to stand on end, just as it had during high school when I had to listen to Sonia's aimless ramblings. I poured another glass of wine; Sonia was worth half a bottle, at least.

"Sonia, *querida*," I said in an all-business voice, "while I was in Bay Point today I noticed a lot of florists delivering to the Carillos' house. Are they having a party? The flowers were absolutely beautiful."

"The Carillos? No, no, Lupe. They're not having a party. Didn't you hear about them?" I grunted to keep her going. "They adopted a baby boy! Finally, after all those years of waiting!"

"I didn't know they were trying to adopt for so long," I said. I didn't know the Carillos from Adam, but I knew Sonia would use any excuse to spill everything she knew. She hadn't been voted Miss Chatterbox three years running in high school for nothing.

"Oh, yes, Lupe, for years. I heard they kept getting turned down because Maria was too old—over fifty, I heard, even though she says she's only forty-three. Maria said it was because she couldn't get a Cuban baby, but it's because she's too old. They've got rules about that kind of stuff."

"So if that's true, how did they get a baby?" I asked innocently, holding my breath.

"I heard it was a private adoption, from some girl who got into trouble. Some girl they knew," Sonia said brightly.

"Can you do that?" I asked. "Is that legal? If the government says you can't adopt, isn't it against the law to go ahead?" I sounded as naive as possible, if only for practice. I knew it didn't matter much what I said to Sonia.

"I wondered the same thing," she said. "I asked Ricardo about it. He said it depends. A lot of adoptions are done privately, but the real question is where the babies come from."

That was the most intelligent thing I'd heard Sonia say in a long time. I wanted to hang up, but I also felt strangely lonely.

"Come to think of it, I don't even know that many people who adopted babies, or gave one up for adoption," I said, just to make conversation.

"Oh, come on, Lupe. Of course you do," Sonia said suggestively. "Remember Caridad Gutierrez, our junior year? Remember how she dropped out of school?"

"Vaguely," I said. "Oh, right, Caridad. She went to live with her aunt in New Jersey."

Sonia giggled. "You really don't know why she left? She was knocked up by that sleazy boyfriend of hers, the one from public school. She went to New Jersey to live with her aunt, and to have the baby. You really didn't know that? God, Lupe, you're so naive!"

I put her on the speakerphone and poured another glass of wine while she cackled into the phone. That pretty well took care of my loneliness and my need to talk to someone.

"Sonia? I just got a call on another line. I'll call real soon, I promise. We'll have lunch, all right?" I hung up.

I sat at my desk writing notes based on the Morenos' visit and what Sonia told me—leaving out Sonia's venomous gossip about a girl I hadn't seen in years—until it was too dark to see without the lights on. I had a theory, and a concrete trail of evidence to support it. But still, there was nothing I could do but wait.

After I locked up and turned on the alarm, I drove home to my apartment on Brickell. The car phone rang once, but I didn't pick up. I really wasn't in the mood for any more talk, or any company that night.

"Esteban, since Betancourt just delivered the last baby to the couple from Bay Point two days ago, we have some lead time. Do you agree?"

"*Sí*, probably. At least a week, maybe a little more. We should have enough time to set up surveillance at the dock."

I'd realized it was time to bring Esteban into the case, and he had arrived an hour after I called him, looking fit and ready. He was slender and well built, with features that grew more handsome with the lines of age. I spent two hours telling him what I had found so far, showing him the surveillance photos so he could familiarize himself with Betancourt's property.

Esteban had no equal in setting up surveillances. If anyone could cover Betancourt's house from the water, it was he.

"Which canal is this house on?" Esteban asked, turning a picture upside down and looking at it as though this perspective gave him a fresh new insight.

"The Granada canal," I said. "Walking distance from Coco-plum, but we'll have to motor all the way out to the bay and cir-cle back toward Coral Gables."

He looked up from the pictures, fixing his dark eyes on mine. "You've arranged with your father for the Hatteras?"

"Of course," I said, a little peevishly. "We have it all after-noon."

Esteban had been my guru, and I owed him a lot. I was a full investigator now, though, with my own firm, and though I had contracted him a couple of times in the past, it still felt that some part of Esteban had a hard time accepting me as an equal.

It wasn't that he was sexist; on the contrary, he was a true gentleman, and he always treated me with complete respect. I think his feelings were like those of the father who can't see his only daughter as a full adult, even after she's left the house and gone into the world on her own. I hoped it wouldn't be a problem this time out. The job was too important, and there was too little time. If Esteban wasn't fully with the program, I was prepared to knock some sense into him.

Coral Gables was founded by George Merrick, one of Dade County's true pioneers, in the 1920s. He envisioned a development based on a Spanish model of Moorish architecture, and laid out canals and waterways intersecting the streets. He was staggeringly strict in enforcing his vision, and even now Coral Gables has the most rigid building codes and zoning restrictions in the country. Some houses on the canals are lavish, growing even more expansive closer to the bay. And the closer to Biscayne Bay the homes are, the larger the boats the owners can dock behind them. Not only is the water deeper, but more important, the boats have to pass under fewer low bridges to reach the bay.

Coral Gables, and Cocoplum within it, lie together in Miami's dense geography and make up much of the upper-class social world of the city. I've always had a slight prejudice about Coral Gables, passed on to me by Papi—who had a lot of problems building our cozy monstrosity of a home under the town's restrictive building environment.

We slowly motored our way up the canal in Papi's boat, heading toward Betancourt's house. Even though, technically speaking, I was working, I still enjoyed myself. Papi taught my sisters and me to drive all the boats we ever owned. He knew that to live by the water, you have to be capable of dealing with it. My sisters and I swam before we could walk.

When we turned into the Granada canal, I cut the engines

so we wouldn't leave a big wake. Sure enough, only one bridge lay between Betancourt's house and the bay. He had quick, easy access to the open water.

We approached the place cautiously, even though we were certain he wouldn't be home in the late afternoon. Unlike at his neighbors', who had boats docked behind their homes, the space behind Betancourt's house was empty. The dock was made of long, dark-stained wood planks, with floodlights above and an American flag snapping in the wind on a tall aluminum pole.

The dock was well kept, the metal rails polished, and the wood floor spotless. About a half-dozen neatly coiled ropes lay stacked by wooden posts. Other ropes were tied to cleats on the deck, ready to welcome any boat that might tie up there. Betancourt had also built up the area around the dock, so it was almost impossible to see the house from the canal. Instead we saw a long expanse of very green, perfectly manicured lawn.

So it was possible to arrive at the dock by boat without being spotted from the house. And vice versa.

Esteban and I passed the property without stopping and idled in the canal for a few minutes before turning around. Esteban scowled in concentration and was silent. I could tell this wasn't going to be easy.

"You said money was not a consideration in this case, right?" he finally asked as I slowly drove the boat forward.

"Right."

He nodded with satisfaction. "Look closely at the bridge," he ordered. "Remember where it is in relation to the canal entrance."

Esteban made me turn the Hatteras around and cruise past the house one more time. Dusk had begun to shift to night, and visibility grew more limited.

"Slow down," he hissed. "Slow down as much as you can. Now look at the pink house across the canal from Betancourt's, and the boathouse next to it. If we place someone on top of the boathouse, they will have a perfectly clear view of Betancourt's dock."

I stared at the relatively modest pink house and boathouse. Esteban was right: it had the best view in the area, and couldn't be seen from Betancourt's. But there was a problem.

"Esteban," I said gently, "how can you get someone up there ten hours every night for God knows how long without being spotted?"

"That person won't be up there the whole time," he said in a distracted voice, like a professor explaining an idea to a pesky student. "We're going to use two people, one stationed on the bridge with a cellular phone. The other will have arrived earlier by dinghy."

My attention wandered for a moment when I saw a large parrot watching us from a tree limb hanging over the canal. I had the paranoid sensation that he was eavesdropping on us.

"Remember, these homes can be accessed only by road and from the canal," Esteban continued, oblivious. "We don't want our second guy stopped for prowling across people's yards to get a clear view of the boathouse. He has to come in by boat."

The parrot above us let out a cackling wail. Esteban stopped speaking and searched above him for the bird. When he saw it, he smiled and whistled at it. Esteban had always loved animals.

"You see what I'm saying," he continued, turning back to the water. "People fish the canals at night by dinghy, so our man won't attract much attention. He can hide in the boat, anchored to one of the banks we passed on our way in. The eucalyptus trees will hide the boat, and when the investigator on the bridge sees a boat approaching Betancourt's house, he can call on the cell phone. The man on the boat will have to hustle like hell to get up the canal and tie off the dinghy to one of the posts under the neighbor's dock quickly, without being spotted.

"It's almost dark now," he said, pointing at the pink house's dock. "You can't really see anything under the docks. And that tree with branches hanging over the boathouse? He has to climb that tree. We can keep our chances of getting spotted to a minimum—he only has to climb on the boathouse the night of the delivery."

By now we had passed the surveillance site almost completely. Esteban pointed to structures and locales that I nearly had to reconstruct from memory.

"It sounds like it could work, but who the hell am I going to get to do all that?" Whoever worked the boat had to be strong and agile and willing to sit in a dinghy night after night in the dark, eaten by mosquitoes. Then when the signal came that a boat was finally coming, they had to row like hell, tie the dinghy up, and climb a tall boathouse while weighed down with bulky camera equipment. Quite a nice job.

"It sounds fine. I can think of at least a thousand ways it can go wrong," I said sweetly. "Is there a plan B, or is this my only choice?"

Esteban glared at me. He was normally one of the most relaxed and accommodating people I knew, except when it came to his work—especially when his judgment was challenged. I had insulted him with my tone; after all, he had trained me, so it turned things on their heads for me to question him.

"I hate it when you turn macho on me, Esteban," I said. "It really doesn't suit you."

"Lupe, I'm doing you a favor here. You can call in anyone else you want. My feelings won't be hurt, believe me."

I also hate it when men lie to me. It's not becoming, and they're rarely very good at it. The degree to which they lie varies, but they all do it. I used to think men lied unintentionally just to spare women's feelings. But my years at White and Blanco taught me it's their egos, mostly, that make them so loose with the truth. There's nothing like working in an open pit with thirteen men to cure a girl of her naivete. I can guarantee it.

"Esteban, calm down," I said. "I didn't say it couldn't work, now did I? I was just thinking out loud."

That seemed to placate him a little. "If you tell me who

you're thinking of using, I'll do a couple of training runs with them so they'll be ready when it all comes down," he said.

Esteban leaned on the boat's railing and looked into the distance. A few words were enough to restore his macho sense of dignity. "Does your father have a dinghy we can use, or a Zodiac?" he continued. "I'd prefer an old one, so it doesn't look like it's stolen. Actually, two boats would be better—we could switch off and look less suspicious. You only need them in place from around eleven at night until first light. There aren't too many people out in Coral Gables then. If this was South Beach then it's a different story. That's when people start their days there."

Esteban always talked too much when he was excited. I just nodded and smiled, though I knew his idea was good. It was risky, but insightful. I probably couldn't have thought of it on my own.

Soon I could see my house in the distance. It really wasn't hard to spot: to my embarrassment, it was lit up like a colossal Christmas tree. Osvaldo and Aida didn't believe in conservation of any kind. Where they came from, you flaunted it if you had it.

The water on the bay was a little rough, but it was nothing I couldn't handle. I docked the Hatteras on the first cut, without any problems. I could do it in my sleep during a hurricane.

Esteban had grown quiet, probably still nursing his hurt feelings. I was still busy trying to figure out who I would call in on this one.

I guess he couldn't stand it any longer. "Well, Lupe, what's it going to be? You want my help or not?" He glanced up at the house. "I'm willing to do this for you, but I won't beg for your permission."

This was exactly why I never married. I couldn't deal with the male ego on a daily basis. If I wanted to deal with fragility, I could just as easily go out and have some children. I really have no patience for mothering someone taller than me.

"Esteban, I'm sorry. That would be great for me, thank you."

I put my hand on his shoulder. "I also expect you to keep track of your hours and submit a bill. It's my one requirement for accepting your help."

Esteban had insisted on working for me as a favor in the past, but I knew that he was building an addition behind his house. He wouldn't turn down a shot at extra cash.

"That's fair," he said, softening. "But who are you going to use for the second man?"

"Who said it has to be a man?"

e l e v e n

"Get ready. I think this is it. Hustle!"

It was my fifth night posted on the first bridge overlooking the Granada canal. The Mercedes was parked under a tree just beyond the nearby traffic circle, and I was at a spot more or less out of the streetlights. I was meditating on how much tonight's slew of mosquito bites would swell, when I saw the wooden sailboat and phoned Miranda.

I had night-vision binoculars with fresh batteries inside, and through them I saw Miranda frantically push the dinghy into the canal. The binoculars were good on long watches, even though the padding on the lenses dug into my face, and through a green shadowy gloom I saw Miranda quickly close the distance between her post on the banks of the waterway and the pink house. Miranda was on the crew team at Penn and was built like an Olympic athlete. I imagined the only similarity between the Coral Gables water and the Schuylkill River was the stench of the rapidly approaching low tide.

I prayed this wasn't another false alarm, which would make number five. But we were in luck if another baby was being delivered to Betancourt so soon. I added a prayer for Miranda.

The motor's soft sound purred below me as the boat passed under the bridge. Through the binoculars I saw Miranda fumble with the ropes as she tied up the dinghy deep under the dock. This was going to be close.

"Please, let this be it," I begged the Virgin. "You have to know we're running out of time."

I knew I was in shadows and wouldn't be seen by anyone in

the boat who happened to look back. But Miranda had just managed to tie the boat up and hoist herself onto the lowest tree branch over the canal when the boat grew close. In an instant, though, she climbed the tree and leapt from it to the top of the boathouse. I couldn't believe she did it. I would have been in the water, spluttering before the approaching boat, in a second.

Miranda paused on the boathouse and hunched for a second, grabbing her leg. She had hurt herself climbing, and I hoped it wasn't too severe. The Skin-So-Soft I gave her was all right for keeping the mosquitoes away, but the little beasts would come in droves after her open wound.

Miranda was on her own now, so I pointed the binoculars at the canal and focused on Betancourt's dock. "Damn," I whispered. The boat was passing Betancourt's property.

But then I heard the motor being cut, and looked into the water to see the craft slowly turning around. The pilot intended to dock facing the bay, no doubt to make his getaway quicker.

I focused on Miranda and saw that she had her own set of binoculars fixed on the canal. I was too far away to see details, but she was in the perfect spot. There was a slim crescent moon—both a blessing and a curse, because it would mean Miranda was less likely to be seen, but the reduced visibility also made her job harder.

"Wait a minute," I said, a little too loudly, when I saw a man and woman emerge on the sailboat's deck. There was something about this boat—made entirely of wood, even the mast— that reminded me of sailing in the summers in the Northeast when we visited Papi's college friends. It wasn't a common kind of sailboat in South Florida—in fact, I can't remember ever seeing one down here at all.

As for the couple, I couldn't see much. I saw a mustache on the man, and recognized the other figure as a woman because of the enormous breasts clearly outlined against her man's shirt. They weren't all that was big about her: she had a big belly, and waddled with fat as she walked.

Docking easily, the man and woman waited on the boat's deck. Soon a tall man showed up—Betancourt. He had probably come from his huge house, past the long lawn.

Miranda had her camera out and was taking pictures. I hadn't told her the facts of the case, by her request and my preference. In this business, the less an investigator knows about a surveillance, the better. If the case turned sour, she could truthfully claim ignorance and maybe stay out of trouble.

The couple on the boat handed what looked like a basket to Betancourt. At least, I thought it was Betancourt. The moon had passed under a thick cloud, and my binoculars were near useless for determining details at that distance.

But I had told Miranda to take tons of pictures if anything went down: of the boat, anyone involved, anything that might change hands. When it was all over I would tell her she had helped save a little girl's life. I hoped.

Betancourt turned toward the house and carried the basket inside. As soon as he started his stroll across the lawn, the boat's engines came to life. The woman fended off and took care of the ropes. She was surprisingly agile for her weight, even nimbly leaping from the dock to the boat after the last rope was untied.

The sailboat made its way up the canal and out to the bay, as quietly as it had arrived. I turned back to the boathouse and saw Miranda's lean figure. She was shaking her sandy blond hair from under her bandanna.

Before leaving the boathouse roof, she looked around carefully as though checking to see if she had left any trace of her presence.

"Good girl," I said. Gingerly, she shimmied down the tree and boarded the dinghy. I saw her examining her leg, and wondered when she had her last tetanus shot.

The registration for the sailboat—the *Mamita*—came back to Alberto M. Cruz, at an address in the northwest section of town near the Miami River. I knew that area well, with its dozens of seedy apartment buildings and waterfront warehouses. The residents, mostly transients, included a lot of people who made their living through any illegal means they could find. I can take care of myself, but I wouldn't want to go there alone, especially at night.

When I got there I saw no reason to linger and take in the sights. I drove Leonardo's Jeep because I knew if I took the Mercedes I'd never see it again. After I parked and left it, it would probably end up on a freighter bound for Port au Prince before I could even report it missing to the police. And the cops wouldn't exactly sympathize with my plight—they'd tell me I knew better than to go there with a car like that, and put my report in the circular file.

Cruz had to be our man. The boat's arrival the night before coincided with the arrival of yet another well-heeled Cuban couple at the Betancourt house. In my purse, alongside the Beretta, were the dozen photographs Miranda took of the boat docked at the lawyer's house. I could have kissed her when I picked them up at the one-hour developing shop. We had registry numbers, faces, and a shadowy figure with a lean build and broad shoulders that had to be Betancourt.

I walked quickly from the Jeep to Cruz's house, a three-story pastel green apartment building replete with peeling paint and a set of steel mailboxes that had long ago been jimmied open. The place was almost unnaturally calm and quiet, except for the blare of a TV out a second-floor window, as I made my way down the walkway outside the building to Cruz's door.

I knocked on his door with my fist and called out his name. Every time I struck the door, huge green chips of paint fell to the stained hall carpeting. There was no answer. While I stood there debating my next move and feeling the hair rise up on the back of my neck, the door opened a crack.

"Who are you? What do you want?" I didn't know much, but it was obvious Alberto found the concept of an unannounced visitor in the midafternoon cause for alarm. I had an advantage.

"Are you Señor Cruz?" I asked politely. He opened the door a little more, and I knew it was he: the mop of short hair, the mustache, the lined, dark face were those of the man on the boat.

"Why do you want to know?" he asked in a voice that would have been perfect for an antismoking advertisement. He opened the door more, and I saw a dimly lit kitchen inside.

"My name is Lupe Solano. May I come in?"

He slammed the door so hard I feared for a second it might fall off its hinges. Dumbstruck, I stood there staring at it like an idiot until a hand parted one of the curtains behind the small dirty window next to it. Cruz was checking me out, trying to decide whether to open the door again. He would. The temptation would be too much for him.

Sure enough, I heard a series of rapid clicks: I counted six in all. He had a lot of hardware securing his place.

With surprising courtliness, Cruz opened the door, stepped aside, and waved me into his scrupulously clean, airy studio apartment. Overwhelmingly furnished in early aluminum, with a mauve couch doing double duty as his bed and purple shiny vases filled with cream-colored fluffy feathers in all four corners, the place oozed tackiness. It took me a few moments to adjust.

"You have a nice place here," I said as he motioned to one of four aluminum chairs grouped around a gleaming stainless-steel dining room table.

Cruz, dressed in shiny gray slacks and a worn polo shirt bearing a naval insignia, shrugged like a baron complimented on his manse. "In this neighborhood you don't let people know what you have. That's why I let the window get so dirty and the door stay so messed up."

I sat down carefully, not wanting to muss the rose velvet upholstery on the chair. "Good idea," I said.

Looking around, I saw only one out-of-place element that contradicted my overall impression of Alberto as a seriously obsessive neatness freak: ashtrays, lots of them, in various shapes and sizes, some of them soiled with unfiltered butts and ashes.

It didn't matter that he didn't light up in front of me, because I knew his brand by the smell in the air—thick and tarry. Alberto was a Gauloise man, a smoker's smoker. I'd know the smell anywhere since I'd been to France two years before. I quickly looked around for the familiar light blue paper packet, but saw none. Strange. There were at least half a dozen ashtrays in easy reach, so I didn't imagine he was used to going too long without lighting up.

I entertained the idea that someone else was the smoker in the house, but when Alberto walked past me he disabused me of that notion. The man smelled like a lit Gauloise, and I caught a glimpse of his yellowed teeth and stained fingers.

He took the chair opposite me and stared for a second, as though trying to figure out if I was putting him on. "Well, Lupe Solano," he said, looking away, "what can I do for you?"

"I'm helping a friend find someone. I was told you could help me do that."

He put his hands flat on the table. "I'm sorry. I forgot to ask you if you want something to drink."

"Don't bother, thanks."

Cruz looked slightly offended. "Well, I'm afraid I don't

know what you're talking about. Why don't you explain what you mean."

"Maybe these will help you." I handed him the envelope containing the photographs Miranda took. I watched him slowly examine each one, and I savored the play of emotions as his face registered shock, fascination, confusion, and finally suppressed anger. After he looked them over he raised his eyes to me.

"This friend of yours, exactly what kind of help is it that he needs?"

"My friend wants information about the whereabouts of her adopted child's natural mother. And my friend is willing to pay to find out."

"I would need to know more about your friend's problem," Cruz said, flashing a yellow smile. "There have been so many babies, you know."

I smiled back. This wasn't what I expected. I figured Cruz would deny everything, even with the pictures in front of him. That's what *I* would have done. I couldn't have imagined it would be this easy, though I knew what came next—he would try to determine how badly I needed his help, so he could name his price.

"What would it take to refresh your memory about a boat trip you took about four years ago, in July of 1991?"

Cruz shook his head regretfully. "Well, you know, I'm not such a young man anymore, and my memory sometimes fails me. I would have to think a lot to remember that. I could do it, you know, but it would be hard."

We smiled at each other some more. "How much trouble are we talking about?" I asked. "I have to tell my friend, so it could be arranged for you."

Only the knowledge that Alberto Cruz was my only link between Michelle and her mother kept me from leaping up and strangling him. I knew he had the details I needed. Anyone who kept an apartment this obsessively clean would remember every aspect of the baby scheme.

"I think twenty thousand dollars would help me remember."

So Alberto wasn't so smart after all. I had warned the Morenos that I thought he would ask for twenty-five thousand, so I at least had the pleasure of seeing him underbid himself. It was still a huge sum of money, but when there's a life involved, people will pay. I know. My father would have given away his fortune to save my mother's life.

I also knew I couldn't trust Alberto, but this was at least a chance. "I can come back tomorrow with half," I said. There was no point being coy now. "I'll give you the rest when we locate the mother. Here's a photograph of the baby taken just after she was delivered to the parents. She has a distinctive birthmark on the side of her neck—that might help you remember."

Cruz examined the picture thoughtfully, running his tongue along his back teeth. "Okay, I'll think about it," he said. "Ten thousand cash tomorrow, ten thousand when I tell you about the mother. I have to make sure she's where I think she is, but it shouldn't take long."

I had to try. "Where are the mothers, Alberto? Does all this have something to do with Jackson Memorial Hospital?"

He looked at me with something like admiration. "This has been a pleasant visit," he said, rising and walking to the door. "A bright spot in my day."

I stood in the doorway. There was no reason to smile now. "Tomorrow afternoon, then," I said.

Alberto was stalling me. I could see that he remembered the mother but insisted I play it his way. It didn't surprise me: his immaculate place was the lair of a control freak. You learn everything about someone by dropping in at their house.

Back at the office, Leonardo sat at his desk, all aglow with post-workout fatigue. I rushed by him to my office and shut the door.

In minutes I had Jose Antonio Moreno on the phone. He gasped when I told him about Alberto Cruz.

"It's important you have the entire ten thousand in cash ready for me to take to Cruz tomorrow," I said. "Don't take it all from the same account, because the banks are required to report either withdrawals or deposits of that amount to the government." That law was enacted to control the drug money coming into South Florida—a smashing success, as I'm sure you've heard.

"I know about the law," Jose Antonio said dryly. "The money will be ready."

"With luck you'll never have to pay the other ten," I continued. "I contracted an investigator to follow Cruz as soon as I left his apartment. Cruz will have a constant shadow, and if he goes to see the mother, all this will be over."

I heard the confidence in my voice. Nestor Gomez would follow Cruz into a blast furnace if he had to.

Jose Antonio said nothing. I thought for an instant he had hung up the phone and I hadn't heard the dial tone yet. I said his name.

"I'm sorry, Ms. Solano," he said. "My mind drifted. I hope something happens soon. But if we have to pay the full amount, I'm certainly prepared."

"Has something happened to Michelle?" I said quickly.

"She's . . . she's sick again. She had a relapse this morning. She was starting to improve, but it didn't last."

"I'm sorry, Mr. Moreno, but we're close. I can feel it."

Jose Antonio sighed, and I realized I shouldn't give him false hope. Everything could fall apart in an instant. "I trust you, Ms. Solano," he said. "But my wife is very frightened. I don't want to tell her anything that might make her disappointed later."

A Cuban man to the last, he talked about his wife's feelings when I could hear in his voice that he was barely hanging on.

After we hung up I called Regina again. She still had nothing on Dr. Samuels, and only wanted to talk about old Havana. I wasn't convinced she was doing everything she could to locate the doctor, and I had started to suspect that she was trying to protect him for some reason. She wasn't under any obligation to help me, so there wasn't much I could do. I listened to her reminisce for fifteen minutes before I told her a client had arrived and I had to go.

I cracked my office door and caught a glimpse of Leonardo reading an actual book at his desk. I walked over to him with Miranda's pictures, curious about what he was reading.

He had taken the act pretty far, even sporting a pair of dark-rimmed reading glasses that I had never seen before.

"What's the book about?"

He sat up a little in his chair, a shy smile on his face. "Finding your cosmic center," he said. I knew instantly it had to be for a girl.

"This is for Clarity, right?"

"Her name is Serenity," Leonardo said, putting the book facedown on his desk. "And we're just friends, but I went out with a really terrific girl last night. She's into fitness and nutrition and she teaches night aerobics classes at the community center."

When Leonardo found a girl he liked, he regressed into a bug-eyed teenager. It was actually pretty cute. "So what's her name? Tranquillity? Moon Child?"

"Actually, her name is Alice."

"You really like her, don't you?" I spoke with as much insinuation as I could muster, knowing how easily I could get him embarrassed.

"Stop it," he said, blushing and looking around the room. His eyes lit on the pictures I held in my hand.

I put them on his desk and gave him a brief summary of what they were, figuring it was time to stop tormenting him about his latest fling. He took the glasses off—he probably couldn't see through them, anyway—and pointed at the obese woman on the deck of the *Mamita*.

"Who's that supposed to be?" he asked. "And how in the

world is she able to do all that physical stuff with the condition she's in?"

I had completely forgotten to ask Cruz about the woman, and he certainly hadn't brought it up. I stared at the big woman in the grainy picture, wondering for the first time what her role was in all this.

thirteen

In the morning I dropped off Alberto's money at his apartment. He said he'd call me "within the next few days," and quietly closed the door in my face. I reminded him I knew where to find him.

I spent the rest of the day and most of the next making calls, reading surveillance reports on the Moreno case, and generally waiting for inspiration to arrive. It didn't, and I was pondering calling it a day, when my phone rang. It was Tommy McDonald, asking for a dinner date. Since I wasn't planning to apply for sainthood anytime soon, and since the Moreno case had filled my waking thoughts since the first day, I figured I deserved a nice time. And Tommy would certainly provide it.

Tommy was an American, or, as they are called here in Dade County, a "non-Hispanic white." I met him by chance working on a case a few years before. I was set for deposition by his law partner in a civil case, but at the last minute his partner couldn't make it. Rather than cancel, he asked Tommy to sit in for him.

It was a total bullshit case—a slip and fall—so Tommy and I decided to make it interesting by flirting shamelessly with each other. The court reporter had barely put away her equipment when Tommy and I were out the conference room door on our way to have drinks. I awoke at dawn, tired and hung over but admiring the view from his penthouse apartment on Brickell Avenue.

I quickly learned that Tommy was a cowboy, a criminal defense lawyer—which made him, almost by definition, irritatingly condescending about civil cases. Nothing got his testosterone rushing better than a trial, especially when his client didn't stand a chance of acquittal. Uncharitable prosecutors called him "the criminal's best buddy" because of the kind of clients he represented. But he was a quixotic believer in the Constitution in his own way, particularly the part about universal entitlement to legal representation . . . especially for rich clients. Dating him was fun, but sometimes it was too interesting even for me. I still remember a time when he was involved in a controversial homicide involving a runner for the drug cartels, and we had to check under his Rolls for bombs before going out.

At one point in our relationship, we almost considered marriage, but then we turned sane again and decided we liked each other too much. We went out to dinner maybe once a month and somehow stayed friends. Tommy liked to shock his friends by declaring that he was dating a Cuban Catholic whose sister was a nun! What the hell. I enjoyed his company better than most men's, and the sex wasn't bad, either.

We ended up at the Strand, one of the older restaurants on Washington Avenue in South Beach, for an early dinner. They have a sophisticated menu, but as usual I ordered the meat loaf. It was my favorite, and I loved the decadence of washing it down with Dom Perignon.

"What's up, Lupe?" Tommy asked, his handsome Irish face set in dramatic shadow by the candle on our table. "You haven't even touched your mashed potatoes."

I nudged the plate closer to him, and he eagerly dug in. Tommy could outeat almost anyone. "There's a case I'm working, and it's driving me nuts. I think I might be spinning my wheels."

The crowd that night was the usual South Beach assortment of movie stars, starlet wanna-bes, models, gay couples of both sexes, even a couple of cross-dressers. Tommy and I made quite a pair—even in my high heels, he was easily a foot taller than me, and he was as fair as I was dark.

"Anything you want to talk about?" he asked.

A bottle of champagne arrived at our table. Tommy looked perplexed until the waiter pointed toward a table in the corner. I glanced over and saw a small crowd of Colombians. The eldest among them raised his glass and smiled. Tommy waved.

"That guy would have got thirty-five years if it wasn't for me," he whispered.

For a moment I thought about asking him about Elio Betancourt. They ran in some of the same circles, they knew a lot of the same people. But no, I was trying to forget. I would drive myself crazy thinking about Michelle and her parents, about Betancourt and Cruz.

"Hey, something's really bothering you." Tommy reached across the table and took my hand. "Why don't you tell me?"

I paused. No, I wanted to enjoy myself a little. It might be my last chance for a while. "Hey, remember the time you sent me to the county stockade to interview that guy on the home invasion case? Remember, it was a total junk case, and the guy fell in love with me?"

Tommy stared into my eyes. He knew something was bothering me, and he also knew better than to pry. "Yeah, he started writing poetry to you," he said, smiling gently.

" 'As I sit here looking through the bars of my cell,' " I recited, " 'I dream of the day I am free, and can come demonstrate the depth of my love to you.' "

"That stuff got pretty graphic, didn't it?" Tommy said, wincing but mischievously delighted. "Damn, that guy was scary."

"Well," I said, "he had a flair for words."

After dinner we passed on more drinks and drove to his place. Tommy was surprised when I said I didn't want to stay the night, but for some reason I wanted to sleep in my own bed. He didn't act hurt or try to make me stay. I drove home as the last light of day vanished over the city, thinking that Tommy was a good man. Thank God I hadn't ruined everything by marrying him.

On nights like this, when I came home relatively late or not at all—depending on the success of the evening—I would always return to my apartment on Brickell. There was no point hammering home to Papi that I was no longer his sweet, virginal little girl, the one in the pure white First Communion dress framed over the mantel at home in Cocoplum.

Lourdes was the only one in the family who ever asked about my love life. Everyone else seemed perfectly content to live in a complete state of denial, which was fine by me. It was easier on all of us that way.

This made us like the rest of the Cuban-American families in Miami. Girls were considered forever chaste and virginal, even after they grew into women, married, and had babies. Still, it's not as though I slept around randomly; in fact, for the past three or four years I hadn't been with a new man.

But I did sleep with former lovers. I found that the older I became, the less energy I wanted to put out in seeking new relationships with men. So I came to prefer the men I already knew and trusted. My select group of men friends were happy to entertain me when I called, and they all were content (at least they seemed to be) with my stringent "don't ask, don't tell" policy.

I knew that other men were interested, and in my line of work I met plenty of available guys in varying walks of life, but somehow I never bothered. Health risks apart, I didn't want to go through the work of opening myself up to someone new, someone who didn't understand me or my MO. And after spending my days confronted with human deceit, treachery, contentiousness, and violence, it was hard to take a stranger at face value.

My building was quiet that night, and as soon as I got off the elevator on my floor, I sensed something was wrong. I stood in the vestibule outside my apartment and stared at my locked door. For a second I considered turning around and walking away, but I felt ridiculous and paranoid. This case was getting to me.

I put the key in the lock and tried to settle down. After all, my building had good security: guards at the entrances, and locks that only Medeco keys could open. The entire time I lived there, I never heard a report of a break-in. This was all very reassuring. Until I opened the door and knew someone had been in there. I just knew.

There was a lingering smell of something musty, something out of place. And things didn't seem to be where I left them. I took my gun out of my purse and walked farther in, trying to hold my hand steady. My second bedroom, the one I used as an office, had definitely been searched. Whoever had been in there was gone, though, and I couldn't see that anything was missing.

I picked up the house phone and called security. I groaned when I learned who was on duty that night.

"Bernard?" I sighed. "This is Lupe. Can you come up here, please?"

A minute later he huffed and puffed into my apartment. I wanted to find out if anyone had asked for me that night or if anything strange had happened, but I knew it was pointless. Bernard couldn't find his way out of a shopping bag with a high-beam spotlight.

Bernard was a full-time student at beauty school, studying to be a hairdresser and making ends meet by substituting when one of our regular guards took the night off. All the tenants genuinely liked him, but the general consensus was that we had more to fear from him than from burglars. He was more likely to shoot himself or one of us by mistake than he was to shoot any criminal.

"Hi, Lupe, what's up?" Bernard gave me his goofy grin and

looked around, completely at ease. It was impossible not to like him; his incompetence was part of his charm. I noticed he had his gun on backwards, the holster pointing the wrong way.

"Bernard, fix that." I said, pointing at the holster. He grabbed it like a toy. "And be careful."

"Thanks," he said, fiddling with the strap. "I always do that wrong."

"Don't worry about it." I kept an eye on him, ready to dive behind a sofa if he had any undue trouble. "But Bernard, I think someone has been in my apartment tonight."

"Really?" he asked, moving closer. "Is that a problem?"

I thought I should start again. "Bernard. Someone broke into my apartment tonight."

"Anyone you know? One of your friends?"

I sure as hell hoped Bernard was a better hairdresser than security guard. Otherwise he had some lean years ahead of him.

"No, Bernard, no one I know." I spoke very slowly, enunciating each word. "That's why I wanted to talk to you: to find out if anyone came by for me tonight, or if anyone was asking for me."

Bernard took out his logbook and checked it. "Nope. I'm sorry. Is anything missing?"

Maybe there was hope after all. "No, nothing's missing. I just know someone was here, that's all. Are you sure no one came by?"

"I can't help you," he said apologetically. "If anyone was here, they didn't stop at the gate or the security desk."

That's what I was worried about. Whoever came into my apartment was good enough to get past my building's security. I was certain about one thing: it had to do with the Moreno case.

Bernard and I said good night, and he gallantly made me promise to call him if I had any trouble. I kept a straight face and sent him back downstairs.

After I closed the door behind me, I stood for a moment in the middle of my living room, listening to the quiet. Then I looked in my office again; nothing was missing, but someone had been very interested in my desk and files. They had done a pretty good cleanup job, but one thing bothered me—the place was too neat. My papers were stacked too nicely. I wondered what Alberto Cruz was up to that evening, and what the contract investigator's report would tell me at the end of his shift. I fervently hoped the wily old Cuban had not been able to shake my investigator off during the night. Alberto Cruz looked like a man who could blend into the woodwork with no problems.

I looked at my unmade bed, checked the fridge for leftovers, and sat down to glance at my mail. It was then that I felt my gun tucked into the back of my skirt. This was ridiculous. The place was too quiet, and I was walking around like a paranoid survivalist. I could sacrifice my privacy for one night. I needed to go home.

fourteen

Cruising through the night to Cocoplum, I started to wonder if I was imagining things. I tried to think: If I were in court, could I definitely testify that someone had broken into my place that night? I had suspicion, intuition, and a feeling of dread. I'd probably cave under cross-examination.

I was surprised to see Emma's Porsche parked in the driveway when I pulled up to the house, especially since it was after ten. I didn't remember her telling me she was coming over, but I couldn't put it past me to have completely forgotten. I thought quickly about whether to tell anyone about my "break-in" and thought better of it. Papi would just insist I move home again. I focused on the temporary bliss I'd shared with Tommy earlier, and hurried inside—if Emma arrived expecting me, she might be ready to leave.

There was no need to worry. I found Emma happily perched on a wooden kitchen stool, gossiping away in perfect Spanish with Aida while attacking a white fluffy meringue. They'd been at it for a while, because the counter in front of Emma was covered in white sugar powder.

Emma saw me come in and patted the stool next to her. "Hey, *chica!* Have a meringue."

I reached into the crystal jar where Aida kept the homemade treats and helped myself to a couple. After the wine and food with Tommy, I was already planning on spending an extra twenty minutes on Leonardo's treadmill.

"You look like you've had quite a night," Emma said, smiling like a devil. She was still in her suit from work, and she winked at Aida.

After hearing about Aida's day—she was affectionately annoyed with Osvaldo, as usual, this time because he'd climbed a high ladder to clean the gutters that day—I led Emma out to the dock.

"Aida's so much fun," Emma said as she sat on a cushioned bench. "I need to come around more often."

"You should," I said. "It's been a long time since we sat out like this."

"Is something bothering you? You seem tense." Emma cocked her head, as though truly looking at me for the first time that night.

Before I could answer, Osvaldo emerged from the house bearing a silver tray. He beamed at Emma. "No one told me you were here!" he said. "I was upstairs watching the television. I could have missed you."

Emma rose and hugged the old man, who kissed her on each cheek. I think everyone in my family—including Aida and Osvaldo—felt a lasting gratitude to Emma for helping us stay strong and sane after Mami died. I'm sure if Emma asked to move in, no one would object. Osvaldo held on to Emma's hand for a moment, his lined face seemingly full of memory and affection, before he went back into the house.

The sky above had turned violet, a deepening shade of clear night that made the world below seem brilliant and distinct. Even the pelicans took time out from their manic foraging to look at it.

"This calls for a celebration," I said. Osvaldo had brought us a pitcher of *mojitos,* along with some freshly fried conch fritters. "You know, Aida and Osvaldo never would have done this for me alone."

We poured drinks and dug into the food. Emma seemed starved. Knowing her, I guessed she'd worked late and come straight over without eating dinner. She grunted with pleasure and extended her glass for another drink, obviously forgetting whatever she saw in my face moments before.

"I hope you don't mind that I dropped by unannounced," she said, still chewing. "But I wanted to tell you some gossip I heard about Elio Betancourt—that is, if you're still interested in him."

"Of course I don't mind you stopping by," I said. So I *hadn't* forgotten. "And I'm still up to my neck in the case that involves Betancourt. As a matter of fact, I think it's driving me nuts. What do you have?"

Emma stood up quietly. "Lupe, look at that shape over there. There, look! Is that a manatee?"

She raced to the edge of the dock, her long hair flowing around her shoulders, and leaned over as far as she could. She looked just like she did when we were younger. "Look, Lupe, it *is* a manatee! Look, she's got a baby!"

I had to see this. It wasn't unusual to see manatees lumbering by our dock, but I'd never seen one with her calf. Emma leaned even farther out over the rail.

"Be careful, you're going to fall in!" I screamed.

"What's all the noise about?" a voice said behind me, and I almost jumped into the water myself. It was only Lourdes, but she'd sneaked up on me in complete silence. She looked stern and dour, barefoot in her habit. "Hi, Emma, long time no see. I heard you guys from all the way upstairs."

Emma climbed down off the rail, and I exhaled loudly with relief. "Emma saw a manatee and her calf," I said. "Look, it's there."

In the moonlight I saw, swimming in the clear water, the mother and baby. I felt a chill when their searching, soulful eyes locked into mine.

"Beautiful!" Lourdes exclaimed, leaning over the rail that Emma had just vacated.

In a split second she was out of her habit, stripped down to her bra and underpants. "I have to do this. I just have to."

Emma and I stood with our mouths agape as Lourdes stepped up on the rail, almost naked, and executed a perfect swan dive into the canal. She landed just to the left of the manatees, barely disturbing the water.

I looked at Emma, and she looked at me. With a shrug, I stripped off my skirt and blouse and joined my sister the liberated nun in the cool water. It took Emma longer to get out of her suit, but she joined us too, and we swam around the dock's wooden pillars.

The mother was incredibly gentle and trusting. We swam next to the manatees, over and under them, even hanging on to Mom's flippers and letting her pull us in lazy circles. Her flesh felt cool and slippery, and her dark eyes followed us with friendly interest as we moved closer and farther away.

We must have been out there for fifteen minutes before Fatima appeared above us, leaning over the dock rail. "What are you doing down there?" she yelled, panicked. "Does anyone need help?"

Fatima must have seen the clothes strewn on the deck and thought we'd all stripped down before tumbling into the canal and drowning. Well, Fatima was never known for her gray matter. Emma, Lourdes, and I looked up at her as her eyes adjusted to the darkness and she saw what we were up to. The manatee glanced up at Fatima and, seeing the games were over, escorted her calf away toward the bay.

By the time we climbed back up, Aida had brought towels and bathrobes for us three wayward girls. Fatima glared at us, alternating between fury and concern.

"I can't believe you," she said to Lourdes. "You can die poisoned from drinking that filthy canal water. These two crazies I can understand, but you! A nun! A bride of Christ!"

Lourdes couldn't contain herself. She burst out into deep laughter, and pretty soon we were all cracked up—including, finally, Fatima. We all trooped inside like obedient little girls to dry off and dress. The impromptu swim had sobered me up quickly—either that or I drank too much canal water, because the *mojitos* and the champagne I'd shared with Tommy had completely worn off when Emma and I showered and put on our clothes.

We stretched out on my bed together, just like when we were schoolgirls. "Now, what were you going to tell me about Betancourt?" I asked.

Emma was on her back, staring up at the ceiling, her wet hair pulled up in a bun. "Do you remember me telling you about Marisol Velez, a Uruguayan woman who used to work with me as an investigator?"

"I think so," I said. "She's great with video, right?"

"That's her." Emma yawned. It was getting late. "Well, I called her yesterday to work a custody case for me—a really dirty one. My client is the mom. It's an old story—the dad doesn't want to pay child support, so he's suing her for custody."

"Of course," I said. "He doesn't want the kids, he just wants to screw her over."

"Exactly. The mother says the father had sex with his girl-friends in front of the kids. Dad says Mom holds Santeria animal sacrifices in front of them. The truth is definitely not somewhere in between. Anyway, I called Marisol because I want to get videos of the father's house during his visitations with the kids. She told me she couldn't do it because she was starting on an-other case, and she mentioned it was for Elio Betancourt."

Emma rolled over and grabbed a couple of pillows, fixing me with a "Now I'll bet you're interested" look. She took her time adjusting the pillows, getting comfortable. She always loved a captive audience.

"So today at around five I get a call from Marisol," Emma said, "asking if I still want her, because the job with Elio is off. Needless to say, I asked her about it. She didn't want to talk, but I got it out of her."

I knew the routine well. Emma could weasel anything out of someone—even things they didn't realize they knew. Marisol didn't have a prayer against Emma with her curiosity on full power.

A loud bump came from upstairs. "Don't worry about it," I said when Emma started. "It's just Lourdes doing her calisthenics."

"Oh," Emma said, looking at the ceiling. "She's amazing, you know. Did you see that dive?"

I hit her with a pillow. "Come on, don't get sidetracked."

"Oh." Emma moved closer. "So Marisol said that Betancourt wanted her to commit an illegal act. This was more than just investigator's-license problems—we're talking criminal charges."

"What did he want?"

"She didn't come right out and say it," Emma said. "Elio's hired her before, and she didn't want to burn any bridges, but she basically said he wanted her to get into someone's apartment to take a book."

My breath caught in my chest. "What? He wanted her to break and enter?"

Emma had the same look she'd get years ago, when we were gossiping about boys we liked. "He told Marisol that it was just a person's notebook, without any monetary value, so it wasn't technically stealing."

"Did he think she'd go for that?"

"I don't know. Marisol hasn't been in the country that long." Emma shrugged. "Maybe he thought she'd believe him, since he's a lawyer."

"What an asshole," I said. I got up and started pacing, trying to think this through.

"You said it," Emma said. She stood up and stretched. "Well, you asked me to find out what I could about him, so there you have it. He's into some serious stuff, from what you told me, but trying to talk an investigator into doing a B and E—the guy's pretty much lost it."

"Did he tell Marisol anything else?"

Emma brightened. "Yeah—get this. He told her this job was for him personally, not for another client."

"I don't get it."

"Well, when Marisol said she wouldn't break into this guy's place, Elio blew up. He said he needed the book because this guy was blackmailing him."

"Blackmailing him? How?"

Emma undid the clips that held her hair in place and shook her head, sending her hair flying out in a halo before it settled on her shoulders. "He didn't say. I guess he recovered and realized he shouldn't be talking to her at all if she wouldn't take the job."

"Of course," I muttered.

I looked up to see Emma staring at me. "Is there something you want to tell me?" she asked.

I shook my head. "No, no, I'm just paranoid. It's nothing." I was lying, of course, but this wasn't the time to draw Emma into whatever I was up against. It's a rule with me: Don't spill your guts just to make yourself feel better, especially when you might put a friend in danger.

I sent Emma home with a brown bag of meringues, and as I watched the Porsche's taillights recede into the humid night, I stood outside the house, thinking about what she told me. Betancourt's recent problems, I knew, would soon become mine as well. It was just a matter of time.

Two days after I delivered the Morenos' cash to Alberto Cruz, I got a call from Nestor while I was relaxing in my bedroom in Cocoplum after taking a slow evening off. There was so much noise where he was, I could barely hear him.

"Lupe, I can't talk much. I'm calling from a pay phone outside the men's room in Dirty Dave's." I heard someone shout in the background. "Your boy Alberto just returned from Betancourt's office."

"What?"

"That's right. He got there at three oh-five and left at three twenty-five," Nestor said without hesitation. I knew he had memorized the times and didn't even need to consult his notes. "As a matter of fact, I'm looking at him right now. I don't want to get too close to him, because I don't want him to burn me. But I thought you'd be interested."

Nestor could give a college course on understatement. "You're right. I'm very interested," I said. "You got pictures?"

"Hey, Lupe, how long have you known me?" Nestor said. "Of course I have pictures. Don't insult me. I have him going into and coming out of Betancourt's office building. Listen, I don't want to stay here much longer, so I'm going outside. I'll stop by in the morning when I get off my shift."

Nestor hung up, and my room felt eerily silent after listening to the din inside Dirty Dave's, a sleazy waterfront bar not far from Cruz's apartment.

I had guessed this might happen. Alberto Cruz had no reason to go to Betancourt's office during the day except to tell him about my visit. The lawyer would never allow Cruz to have such public contact with him unless Cruz insisted it was urgent. It hadn't occurred to me before, but the break-in Betancourt wanted Marisol Velez to perform might have been at Alberto's apartment.

Cruz probably sat around after I left and thought about how to turn the situation to his advantage. Once he received the first payment from me and saw that my offer was for real, he made his move. A calculating guy like Cruz would understand that his activities had been found out and that it was only a question of time before his job with Betancourt as well as his profits were gone. I just hoped Cruz didn't get too greedy.

The air-conditioning in the house was turned on too low, so I opened my window, breathing in the rich night heat and the breeze from the bay. Papi was already in bed, and Fatima and the twins were on Key Biscayne visiting one of her friends, so I had the house to myself except for Osvaldo and Aida, who were done for the day and were in their quarters watching TV. At times like these, it was hard to imagine places like Dirty Dave's and people like Cruz and Betancourt, but I knew I had to concentrate. Things could start to get dangerous for me.

As far as I knew, Cruz hadn't personally contacted Michelle's mother. He might have called her on the phone, but I was certain he hadn't met with her, because so far my constant surveillance on him was tight. According to the investigators' reports, Cruz mostly stayed to himself in the apartment, daily venturing out to Dirty Dave's to get drunk and then staggering back home.

As far as I was concerned, however, I couldn't take anything for granted as far as Alberto Cruz was concerned. The old sailor's deviousness had been proven in the way he had shaken off his tail and broken into my apartment, for although my investigator had sworn that Alberto had not left his apartment that night at all, I was convinced he had, somehow. I had not imagined the stink of those cigarettes.

To call Dirty Dave's a bar was probably giving it too much dignity. It was a wooden shack on the river that teetered dangerously toward the water when it was full of people. Its patrons were all locals, men mostly, and almost every one of them was probably wanted or involved in something that would lead him to the county jail.

As usual, I had run a routine background check on Alberto Cruz. I did an employment history and found that he held no steady, regular job. I ran a Social Security check on him for his prior employment, but nothing came up on the printout. This meant he was always paid cash for whatever jobs he might have worked, maybe even that his only income came from Betancourt. He was listed at the same home address for the last four years, which somewhat surprised me. Alberto was fastidious, but I didn't see him as stable enough to live for long in any one place. Maybe I just couldn't see someone staying in that magenta palace for so long, but you never can tell about taste— good or bad.

If his money came from Betancourt's adoption business, then no wonder Cruz seemed worried for a second when I showed him the photographs, before he could catch himself and start scheming. No more babies, no more money, no more aluminum furniture.

My only question now was what he said to Betancourt. Did he warn him I was snooping around, or did he ask for money to keep quiet? As long as he delivered Michelle's mother he could play all the dangerous games he wanted, as far as I was concerned—as long as he didn't screw up before he helped me solve the case.

I wasn't really worried that Betancourt would openly come after the Morenos or me. He was far too smart for that. He knew the Morenos wouldn't try to act publicly, because that would expose their involvement in the illegal adoption and might jeopardize Michelle. Alberto, on the other hand, probably didn't know the nature of Betancourt's arrangements with the various adoptive parents. He knew his knowledge was worth a lot to someone, but he didn't know why.

There was another possibility, of course. Betancourt might know all about me now, and might have already phoned one of his former clients—a contract killer for the drug cartels, maybe—to have a talk with me. I shut off my bedside lamp and got under the covers—after I checked to make sure my spare gun was in the nightstand drawer.

It was hard to sleep that night.

The next morning Nestor's report was waiting for me when I got to the office. Nestor was gone.

I'd overslept when I finally dropped off, and Leonardo beat me to work. He was overdressed by his standards, in an authentic Venice Beach Gold's Gym T-shirt and a pair of khakis.

"Looking good, young man," I said as I picked up the reports from his desk. "We'll have you in wing tips and a double-breasted suit before you know it."

"Alice isn't into that yuppie thing," he said, staring at a legal pad filled with figures and totaling them up on the office adding machine. "You know, I sold Nestor two bottles of vitamins this morning. One more and I'm over my quota for the month. Then I get a bonus."

He smiled at me sweetly. "No way," I said. "I get all the vitamins I need without taking one of your horse pills."

Leonardo was about to begin one of his dissertations on health, exercise, and why I was headed for a life of ruin and varicose veins, when I waved him off and made for my office. The last thing I needed that morning was to be told my digestive enzymes were probably out of kilter. Whatever he meant by that.

At my desk I wondered if I should tell Leonardo about Cruz's visit to Betancourt and my suspicions about my apartment, but I stopped myself just as I was about to rise from my chair. What was I going to do, tell him to look out for armed gunmen in ski masks crashing through the front door? The case was moving forward, and it was no time to turn totally paranoid.

But it had been three days since I gave Alberto Cruz ten thousand dollars of someone else's money, and I still had nothing from him. It was time to start sweating. If Alberto knew where the birth mother was and planned to deliver her, he probably would have done so by then. He wanted the balance of the money too much to wait for no reason.

I looked over Nestor's meticulous report and referenced it against those made by the other contract investigators. Cruz had followed a routine that week: he got up late, worked on the *Mamita* for a little while, went back home, and inevitably ended up at Dirty Dave's. No visitors came to his apartment, and he didn't meet anyone in particular at the bar. He usually ate a brown-bag lunch on the boat, then had his dinner at the bar. It seemed he was just marking time.

Regina didn't answer when I called, and I had a phone message from Jose Antonio Moreno that Michelle's condition was stable again. It seemed I had to do something that ran completely against my nature: wait and see what happened.

I found Osvaldo on the couch in the reception area when I returned from a quick lunch. That was strange: Osvaldo usually did his work at the cottage outside and left without speaking to either Leonardo or me.

Maybe Leonardo was growing pot again. That was the last thing I needed. Ever since the first incident, Osvaldo had almost completely avoided Leonardo. The only reason Osvaldo was civil to him at all was because the young man was Mami's nephew, so there had to be something good about him. I suspected Osvaldo felt he just hadn't found it yet.

The old man sat quietly, in his gardening clothes with a straw hat in his hands. He looked worried. Leonardo was silent at his desk, staring at a poster of the Mr. Miami Beach contest that he'd recently tacked up on the wall.

Osvaldo leapt up when he saw me. "Lupe," he said, "I have to talk with you. Now."

It was completely out of character for the old man to order me around like this. In a joking way, sure. But this was serious, and something had to be truly wrong. With a glance at Leonardo—who gave me a frightened "I'm innocent" look—I escorted Osvaldo into my office.

Osvaldo gingerly took a seat. "You know the birds-of-paradise I'm trying to grow outside your window?" he asked. "The ones giving me all that trouble?"

I nodded, even though I had no idea what he was talking about. I knew, though, that this had to do with more than flowers.

"Look, Lupe." He dug into his pocket, pulled out five cigarette butts, and shoved them under my nose. I pulled back quickly. They were Gauloises. I knew the smell.

"Where did you find these?"

Osvaldo took my arm and led me out of the office. We didn't stop until we had circled the cottage and ended up in the back, facing my office window. He pointed to some scraggly plants underfoot. "There!" he said. "I found them there this afternoon. Someone has been watching you, Lupe!"

He yelled so loud that he scared the family of parrots living in the upper branches of an avocado tree on the edge of the property. The big royal-blue-and-green birds squawked and complained for a moment, until the mother bird saw nothing was wrong, took charge, and settled everyone on their perches again.

"Calm down, Osvaldo," I said. "It's not good for you to get so agitated. This is no big deal. Remember your blood pressure."

I patted his arm affectionately, trying to control his sudden trembling. The thing was, he was right to be shook-up. I was now dead certain it was Gauloises I had smelled in my apartment earlier in the week.

I took the butts from Osvaldo and inspected them. They were in varying stages of decomposition—two were almost identical and seemed to have been smoked fairly recently, while the other three were all different from each other. It hadn't rained the last few days, so they were all in pretty good condition.

Alberto Cruz had visited Solano Investigations on more than one occasion, that was obvious. For what? He hadn't been inside, because the alarm would have gone off. I knew the cigarettes were smoked at different times, but that was it.

Had he started watching me before I went to his apartment to see him? I had to stop myself from getting too paranoid. I couldn't let myself think people were after me the whole time or I would go crazy. I had to think clearly. Nestor was too honest to lie about losing Cruz, and I had Nestor's reports inside. This raised more serious questions. When did Cruz start watching me, if it was indeed Cruz and not someone else trying to make me think it was, and how much did Betancourt know about my investigation? The circle was narrowing, and too quickly.

To steady myself I decided to catch up on other cases I had going—nothing nearly as pressing as the Morenos'. I had a hidden-assets case in which Hugh Bresnan, a rich stockbroker from New York, moved to Florida to escape his creditors up north. He declared bankruptcy, but meanwhile bought a fifteen-million-dollar oceanfront home in Miami and called it his homestead. There was nothing his creditors could do, since state law protected his primary residence.

No wonder Florida is called "bankruptcy heaven." But I found a couple of other properties this guy owned—a condo for his mistress and a townhouse for his college-age son. The client was going to be very happy, and Solano Investigations would earn a fee. I guess the only unhappy part was Hugh Bresnan, but he would never even know my name.

My very first client had been a domestic, a referral from Osvaldo, of all people. A seventy-eight-year-old neighbor of his from Havana was convinced his seventy-five-year-old wife was cheating on him. A job was a job, especially the first one, so I started following the old lady around. For the first three days I found nothing. She visited her two daughters daily, stopped off at her church to help set up flowers on the altar, then played canasta with her friends. I thought the old man was definitely nuts, and started feeling guilty about taking his money.

On the fourth day, while I searched my mind for a way to tell my client I was quitting, the wife drove to a seedy hot-sheets motel off Eighth Street in Little Havana. I was fascinated and shocked when I saw her sneak into one of the back rooms.

Soon an elderly gentleman arrived, parked his car, and walked slowly to the old lady's room. At this point I had to pinch myself in the side to make sure I wasn't hallucinating.

They stayed in the room for almost two hours. She emerged first, followed by the disheveled older gentleman a few minutes later. I got pictures and sat alone in my car for a while to compose myself, then dropped off the film at a one-hour developing place. I had a shot of Cuban coffee while I waited. The photographs turned out perfectly. Both their faces were so clearly defined they could have been professionally taken portraits.

I called my client at home and told him I needed to see him. He said his wife would be away for a few more hours, and he wasn't feeling well. I wanted to get it over with as soon as possible, so I agreed to stop by his house instead of making him come to my office.

The client lived in a neat, modest apartment on Coral Way, near the entrance to the Key Biscayne bridge. I hesitated in his tiny living room, dreading telling him what I'd found. To stall for time, I accepted his offer of a glass of ice water.

When he went to the kitchen to get it, I looked around the

living room and saw rows of photographs displayed on the side tables. I could easily recognize the wife. And in one ornate silver frame I noticed a picture of three people: my client, his wife, and to my horror, the man I saw coming out of the motel room.

I almost jumped through the low roof when my client appeared behind me. He caught me staring at the photo and told me that the third man was his brother, Modesto, who had never married and lived only two blocks away. The picture was taken at my client's fiftieth wedding anniversary.

There was no way I could break the old man's heart. I said his wife was completely faithful to him and that he was imagining things. I told him I wouldn't charge for the case, since there really was nothing to report. That day I found Modesto's home address and anonymously mailed him the photographs with a note attached: Unless he stopped the affair, copies would be mailed to his brother. It was a bluff, but I was certain it worked.

I lost money on that first case, but I learned an invaluable lesson: Nothing is ever as it seems. And when someone suspects something is wrong and comes to me for help, ninety-nine percent of the time they're right.

The Morenos knew what was wrong when they came to my office. And now I knew something wasn't right with Alberto Cruz. The question I asked myself was: Would I find out the answers before problems I couldn't even imagine found me?

If I kept thinking this way—about break-ins and cigarette butts—I was going to drive myself crazy. I had to find something to divert myself, if only for the rest of the day, so I fished around in the pile of phone messages on my desk, trying to find an interesting one. In that mess there were three in the last two days from Ethan Chapman, a lawyer I'd worked for in the past. Leonardo's message said Ethan needed me for a quick domestic case. It sounded perfect.

Waiting for his receptionist to get Ethan on the line, I pictured his office. It, like Ethan himself, was a sort of old-guard bastion of East Coast WASPiness and propriety stuck in the swirling chaos of Miami. I always liked Ethan, with his Boston accent and prep school background. He met and married a pretty Honduran woman at Yale Law School, and she insisted they move to Miami to be close to her family. After fifteen years he still wore wool slacks on hundred-degree days.

"Lupe, I was starting to think you weren't going to call," he said.

"Hello to you too, Ethan," I said. "How's Ruth and the kids?"

"Fine, fine," he said distractedly. Ethan always had about five pots boiling at the same time. "Look, I have a domestic for you. The case is going to trial in two days, so I only need you for one day's work plus maybe court time. I'll pay your usual outrageous fee."

That was Ethan's idea of humor. "That's fine, Ethan," I said, "because I'm really only free today. I'm on an important case, but I'm in a wait-and-see mode today."

"Fine, fine," he said. He covered his phone's mouthpiece and mumbled something, probably to his secretary. "Lupe, still there? All right, well, this is definitely a low-budget case. My client is a waitress whose ex-husband owes her thirteen grand in child support for her three kids. The divorce happened a few years ago, and he paid at first, but it's reached the point where the money's stopped coming in altogether."

Ethan paused to catch his breath. "Sounds like the usual story," I said.

"Right. She's been after him for a while, and I've represented her in the last couple court appearances. The ex-husband always shows up, but he looks like crap." Ethan almost never swore, and I smiled at his delicacy. "His clothes are torn up and dirty, he has bandages from purported injuries. Sometimes he carries a cane. He's a photographer by profession, and he claims he can't work because of physical disability. He cries in court, begs with the judge—and he's lucked out so far, because he got a real bleeding-heart judge hearing the case. At this point the guy's on his sixth extension."

"What a scumbag," I said. That was another reason I never got married—ex-husbands.

"The worst," Ethan said. "But we're in luck. The father-friendly judge got transferred to another division, and I had a talk with the new judge. He said that if I can prove the ex-husband is working, he'll send him to jail for nonpayment."

"If he's in jail, he can't pay," I said. "County jail wages take a long time to add up to thirteen thousand bucks."

"That's what I told my client." Ethan paused. "Her need for money won out over her vengeful streak. If we can come up with proof that this guy is working, I can nail him and attach his wages."

"Give me his name and number," I said. "I'll have something for you by the end of the day."

I hung up and gave the case some thought. This would be an easy one, and I would enjoy it—there's nothing worse than a lying bastard who won't support his kids. I got into character and dialed the phone.

"Can I speak to Cesar Menendez, please?" I said in my best Cuban-housewife voice.

"Speaking." His voice was rich and sharp, the voice of a man with no worries. Music played softly in the background.

"My name is Carlotta Suarez. I would like to have an appointment to have my picture taken. It's for my husband."

"Certainly. How did you hear about me?"

"My friend Maria from Hialeah," I said adoringly. "You took her picture last Christmas. It was so beautiful."

I figured that was safe enough. Everyone knew a Maria from Hialeah.

"Sure," he said. "I can fit you in next week."

"Oh, I'm so sorry," I said, my voice breaking. "But I have to do it today. I have to go to Orlando tomorrow to visit my brother. He's very sick, and I don't know when I'll get back."

Cesar turned down the music. "All right," he said, a little annoyed. "I guess I can do that. Do you want to come to my studio?"

That wasn't a good idea, in case anything went wrong. "No," I cooed, "I want my picture taken outdoors. My husband likes a natural look."

"Meet me at Kennedy Park in Coconut Grove at three this afternoon," he said. "Do you know where that is?"

"I think so," I said uncertainly. It was just down the street from my office. "I'm sure I can find it. But there's one more thing. I need you to have the picture ready tomorrow."

"I thought you said you had to go to Orlando?"

"Oh, I do, but I'll pick up the picture in the morning and leave it for my husband. He doesn't like me going out of town, you know, so I'm getting this picture to make him happy."

"If you say so," he said. "But there's a surcharge for overnight service."

Before setting out for Kennedy Park, I stopped off at home to change into a matronly blouse and sufficiently dowdy long skirt, pulling my hair back into a bun and applying some blush and eyeliner. I also exchanged the Mercedes for Aida and Osvaldo's station wagon, which I'd used in the past for a cover.

Cesar was waiting for me in the park, impeccably dressed in white linen trousers and a spotless white cotton shirt, with a Hasselblad camera in hand. He introduced his assistant, a dapper young man going through a leather bag full of film and lenses. Cesar was handsome, with a nice nose and a tousled hairstyle—but more important, he had no bruises, no bandages, and certainly didn't need a cane.

This was going to be good. "Thank you for meeting me, Mr. Menendez," I said shyly. "I have never had my picture taken by a professional like yourself before."

Cesar and his assistant exchanged glances. "May I say," he said, taking my arm and leading me under a tree on a lush patch of grass, "that I'm lucky to have such a beautiful subject."

The man knew his business. He posed me in a number of different ways. It was the assistant's job to help with the staging, moving some branches around me and putting a flower in my hair. Cesar wasn't above helping out too, and each time he moved me into position he would touch my arm or my waist. The man was a dog.

When they were done, I smiled with delight and opened my purse. "Here, let me pay you now," I said.

"No, Señora, you pay when you get the prints," Cesar said, wiping his forehead with a silk handkerchief.

"I insist, really." I didn't give him a chance to reject the wad of bills I pressed into his hands. "Is this enough?"

Cesar stared at the money. "It will be a hundred and twenty dollars. But really, Señora, it is not necessary to pay in advance." He glanced at his assistant, as though he felt something was wrong that he couldn't quite identify.

"Please," I said, giggling. "It would make me feel better. How about if I give you half now and the other half tomorrow?"

"Well, if you absolutely insist." He took the money. I knew he couldn't hold out.

"Could I have one of your business cards?" I asked innocently. "I lost the one Maria gave me."

He fished around in his shirt pocket for a card. "Could you also put down that I gave you sixty dollars, please? I have a terrible memory, and I don't want to forget." I gave him my most hopeless, pathetic look, ensuring that he would think I had a double-digit IQ.

It was almost too easy. Cesar, deadbeat dad, wrote, "$60 received," and the date on the back of the card. We said our good-byes and he left, presumably for his darkroom. Or maybe to buy a new pair of slacks. I snapped a couple of pictures of him stowing his equipment in his truck, even catching him hoisting a spare tire to make room for his bag.

I called Ethan when I got back to my office. Leonardo, immersed in *Modern Nutrition* magazine, glanced at my dowdy outfit and went back to his reading.

Ethan chuckled at how I'd handled Cesar. "Terrific," he said, as pleased as if he'd just made a hole in one. "Have the receipt and the pictures sent over today or tomorrow, with your report. I'll give you a call if I need you to testify."

"Can do, Ethan," I said. "And thanks, Ethan. Thanks a lot."

"For what?"

"I'd almost forgotten why I like this business so much."

seventeen

The early edition of the *Miami Herald* confirmed what I'd known for hours: Alberto Cruz had been stabbed and killed in the alley behind Dirty Dave's late the night before. It was a small item in the local section. There were no witnesses and, apparently, no one with any knowledge of the assault. The police asked anyone who knew anything about the murder to contact them, listing a number to call.

Kenny Alston, one of my contract investigators, was at Dirty Dave's when it happened, and he'd called at three A.M. to tell me that Alberto had been jumped in the alley on his way home. Kenny had spent the evening in the bar, watching Alberto drink his usual quota of beers. After Alberto left the bar, swaying as usual, Kenny waited a few minutes before following him outside.

Kenny reported that there was nothing unusual in Alberto's behavior that night. He assumed Alberto was going home from the bar, as always, so he gave Alberto time to walk away from the bar toward the apartment and piss in the alley, which was also part of his routine. It couldn't have been more than three or four minutes after Alberto left the bar that Kenny followed. Alberto was nowhere to be seen. Kenny checked around and found Alberto slumped on the ground, hidden from view among the aluminum trash barrels behind the bar's back door. Someone had obviously been waiting for him.

Kenny went back inside Dirty Dave's and told the bartender to call an ambulance. Then he called the police and reported finding the body. Kenny didn't volunteer any more information, and the police asked him hardly any questions at all. In that neighborhood, a stabbing was about as rare as a pinecone in the forest.

Now I was in my office, listening to the parrots laughing among themselves outside, and I was wrestling with my conscience. Alberto had the money for three days, and was killed two days after going to see Betancourt. It was too much of a coincidence, and I had to think through my responsibility as far as telling the police what I knew about the crime. Right now the police classified it as an attempted robbery, and as far as I knew, that might have been true.

I had lost my only link to Michelle's mother, as well as the ten thousand dollars the Morenos had staked for Alberto. Since Alberto was a sailor, I guessed he hid it on the *Mamita*. And if he was dumb enough to blackmail Betancourt, the money probably was stashed with the photographs I left with him—and, maybe, the notebook Betancourt sought. If so, I wouldn't be alone looking for them.

I knew the Miami police were inefficient investigators, especially for a low-priority victim such as Alberto Cruz, so I had some lead time. I doubted they had found the *Mamita* yet.

Alberto's death left me with one, unattractive option: I had to find the big woman from the photos taken at Betancourt's dock. Unfortunately, I had no idea whom she was. I meticulously laid out pictures of her in different poses from a set of enlargements I ordered, just trying to make something happen. The woman was obviously familiar with boats, so maybe I would find her around the Miami River, where Alberto kept the *Mamita*. If I couldn't find her, I could pass the photos around the neighborhood. Maybe someone would identify her.

I again borrowed Leonardo's Jeep for the expedition. I parked across the street from Alberto's berth, under a banyan tree, and just watched the wooden sailboat for a while. It was suffocatingly hot, even with the windows down. I was glad I had dressed in shorts and a T-shirt, even though I got a few stares from the few lowlifes passing by on the street.

I must have said my prayers right the night before. Within a half hour a large, heavyset woman in baggy cotton pants and a print short-sleeved shirt slowly bicycled by my car. She passed the *Mamita* once, pedaled laboriously to the end of the block, waited a couple of minutes, then circled back.

She crossed the street right in front of me and tied her bicycle to a stunted, half-dead palm tree. She was wearing a big straw hat and sunglasses, but I was able to get a glimpse of her face. It was the woman in the photographs. With surprising agility for her girth, she jogged along the dock planks and jumped on board the sailboat. Now that I finally saw her a little better, I realized she wasn't just overweight. I had seen women move their bodies like that before: she was pregnant.

I gave her ten minutes in the boat alone before I surprised her. Creeping onto the deck, I knelt and saw her through the porthole, frantically searching the main cabin, then moved closer. She had emptied an oversized drawer full of Alberto's sea charts and turned it upside down, all the while puffing on a cigar.

She obviously knew where to look. She was about to pull back a slat from the shelf when I loudly cleared my throat. She instantly jumped three feet in the air, grabbed a machete leaning against the wall next to her, and pulled the thick cigar out of her mouth.

"Who are you? What are you doing here?" she spat, brandishing the machete threateningly above her head.

I ignored her questions. "Are you looking for these?"

I held up a couple of Miranda's photographs featuring her, Alberto, and Betancourt. The woman sprang at me and tried to grab them from my hand. I let her—after all, she had the machete. There were plenty more copies back at the office.

She glared at me with intense confusion, hatred, and fear. She was a mulatto with beautiful light brown skin and almond, almost Asian black eyes. Her hair was loosely braided down her back, falling nearly down to her waist. Even when she wasn't pregnant, I guessed, she must have been huge.

"I know who you are," she said, her eyes locking on mine. She gripped the machete tighter. "You're the one who came to see Alberto about the mother of that baby. He told me you gave him some money."

"I did give him some money, but he never told me where to find the mother. He was going to, but he passed away." She put the machete on the table and closed her eyes. "But I could always do the deal with you instead," I went on. "I know you were there. You always went with Alberto to get the babies."

The woman's eyes narrowed, and I could see she knew I was bluffing. "Alberto didn't pass away, he was killed," she said. "He got stabbed because he was going to tell you about the babies. He said you threatened him, that you made him tell you about the trips."

"And did he tell you he went to Betancourt and tried to blackmail him?"

The woman moved for the machete but apparently thought better of it. Instead she took a particularly furious drag on her cigar. I tried not to think about what she was doing to the baby inside her.

She sat there studying me, as though I would take back what I had just said or burst loose with answers. I wasn't moving either, but I was doing some mental arithmetic, trying to figure which of us could get to the machete quicker if things turned sour. I had the Beretta in my purse, but I couldn't count on getting it out before she cut in. Pregnant or not, she was agile.

"Why the hell should I believe you?" she said, still staring. "Alberto would never go to the lawyer like that. He hated the *hijo de puta,* but he was scared of him too. You're a liar."

She adjusted herself, trying to get her belly comfortable. "I'm not lying," I said. "I had Alberto followed from the day I went to his apartment. I suspected he might try something."

She exhaled an enormous cloud of smoke directly into my face. If I hadn't been Cuban, growing up with Papi and my uncles smoking around me all my life, I might have vomited on the spot. I swallowed hard. This wasn't someone you wanted to throw up in front of. I couldn't see her kindly giving me a Wash'n Dri afterward to clean my face.

"Why should I believe you?" she asked, apparently disappointed she couldn't turn my stomach. "I've known Alberto for years. You're just some skinny bitch who wants something out of me."

I reached into the envelope containing Nestor's photographs and pulled three from the bottom of the stack. I slid them over to her and waited for her reaction.

"You see, I'm telling the truth," I said gently. "Alberto went to Betancourt's office to blackmail him. It didn't work. Now he's dead, and you're in big trouble. Betancourt will come after you next."

She shook her head as though talking to a confused child. "Why would he come after me? Alberto went there alone, and I'm not going to blackmail the lawyer. Betancourt has nothing to fear from me."

I was making progress. Maybe she'd always suspected she couldn't completely trust Alberto. Thank God for Nestor and his camerawork.

"You're in deep shit," I insisted. "I can tell you're a smart woman, so don't play dumb. Betancourt might think you'll step in where Alberto left off, and you're the only link left between him and the babies. You yourself told me Alberto was afraid of him."

The boat began to sway in the wake of a speedboat passing by in the marina outside. I reached out for the bulkhead until the waves subsided.

"Betancourt is a bad man," she said, ignoring the boat's rocking. "But he wouldn't come after me unless he was sure I was up to something." For the first time I thought I detected a slight doubt in her voice. She puffed some more on the cigar.

I took a deep breath. It was time to get personal. "What's your name, anyway?" I asked.

This woman gave away nothing easily. Her lips tight, she said. "Barbara. Barbara Perez."

"Look, Barbara, you know the kind of trouble you're in. You've known Betancourt for years." A guess, but she didn't deny it. "Do you think this man cares about right and wrong? The man traffics in babies."

Barbara's face turned red. "You're the one that got Alberto killed!" she yelled. "If you hadn't gone to see him, he'd be alive today and I wouldn't be in all this trouble!"

"Let's get one thing straight. Alberto got Alberto killed." I slapped the table. "He tried to blackmail Betancourt. I'm not going to take the blame because he was stupid." Barbara shrugged as though what I said was true. "You lie down with dogs, you get fleas. Right?"

She chuckled softly. "You know so much, girl detective. Tell me, then. What happens next?"

That took me by surprise. Barbara was tough, but she had started to accept me. We weren't going to be best friends, but at least she wasn't eyeing the machete every few seconds. Finally, she was listening.

"First of all, I need to know about the mother of that baby you picked up four years ago. I'll make the same deal with you that I made with Alberto. He told you the details, right?"

Barbara rubbed her belly, almost reflexively. She was in trouble, as far as I could guess, but I was partially bluffing and she seemed to know it. "What good is money to me when I'm dead?" she asked. "Look at Alberto. He doesn't care about money now."

"But Alberto tried to blackmail Betancourt. Alberto got greedy," I reminded her. "You could leave Miami."

Her eyes widened; like me, she was Cuban. I could see leaving Miami wasn't something she had ever considered. "You're going to have a baby in a few months, right? Give me the information I want, and you can start fresh someplace new."

Barbara sat quietly, brooding over her limited options. At first she had frightened me, with her sudden violence and the menace in her eyes, but I could see now that she was more scared of me than I was of her. I let her take her time. She was Michelle Moreno's only hope, and I seemed to have done nothing but screw up all the others.

Seeing that Barbara was going to take a while, I looked around the sailboat for the first time. She made no move to stop me.

The place was the polar opposite of Alberto's purple apartment. This was a man's domain, all dark colors and wood paneling. It was a boat designed for serious sailors, with no frills, just the bare necessities for life at sea. The only sign of Alberto was the beautiful, meticulously polished wood—and a lingering smell of Gauloises.

"I'll help you," Barbara said from behind me, and I realized I had forgotten myself and turned my back on her. "But you have to guarantee that Betancourt won't hurt me. I don't want to leave Miami. I have six children—seven with this one." She patted her belly. "Guarantee me that lawyer will leave me alone, and I'll tell you about the little girl's mother."

"How do you expect me to guarantee that? I don't know what the man is going to do!" I started to get angry, then remembered Barbara could beat me senseless in under a minute if she wanted to. "Look, I'll more than double the money. I'll pay you twenty-five thousand dollars."

She stared into my eyes. "You have to guarantee my safety as well. I don't care how you do it, but those are my terms."

Well, this was a kink I didn't expect. I sympathized with her, but how could I guarantee how Betancourt might act, especially now that it seemed obvious he was willing to play hardball? He probably hadn't killed Alberto himself—men like him seldom did their own dirty work—but I was growing certain that he was responsible. With his client list, he could have opened an employment agency for killers and thugs.

I left Barbara sitting in the captain's chair, her arms resolutely crossed over her ample chest. I really didn't blame her for dictating outrageous terms. Unfortunately, now each of us bore the fate of another in our hands.

eighteen

After leaving Barbara to the steaming afternoon, I called ahead to Assistant State Attorney Charles Miliken. He was an old friend, and he could help me get some perspective on this situation. Charlie and I also once had a pretty intense relationship. It lasted two years, but really went nowhere. He wanted a stable, constant relationship with a woman who wouldn't tell him when he was wrong. You can imagine how well I fit in with that ideal.

The receptionist remembered me when I walked up to the bulletproof cubicle outside the prosecutors' offices at the Metro Dade Justice Building, and she waved me past the double doors to Charlie's office. I trudged down the long, drab corridors, making four turns before reaching his tinted-glass door. The place was a maze, and I'm sure the prosecutors liked it that way, just in case anyone got past the guards downstairs.

Charlie's office was no different from the others I passed along the way—cramped, institutional, and absolutely packed with file cabinets. A battered desk sat askew in the middle of each room, opposite two old-fashioned wooden chairs, the kind with slats up the back. The industrial carpet in most offices showed so many coffee stains that they resembled relief maps of the world.

I knocked on his door, first softly, then louder. He was probably on the phone, as usual. Tired of waiting to be asked in, I pushed the door open. Charlie never was very hospitable.

I guessed it. He was on the phone, his chair tilted back as far as it would go, almost horizontal to the floor and facing away from the door. He was so engrossed in his conversation that he hadn't heard me come in, so I sat down in his lap and started kissing him.

He hung up in a hurry, cutting off his rambling in midsentence. For a moment I was tempted to let history repeat itself and have a go at it right then and there, but I'd made enough hassles for myself lately without adding another.

"Charlie," I said, pulling away.

"Oh, God." He pulled me closer and started in on my ear. He knew it was my weakest point.

"Charlie, I have a problem."

"Later," he said, getting up when I rose from his lap. "Let me lock the door."

He obviously remembered past afternoon delights, and I realized I'd given him the wrong idea. "Charlie, please. This is serious."

He sat down at his desk, trying to catch his breath, and ran his fingers through his straight, longish hair. "Okay, I can tell you're not going to be any fun until you tell me what's on your mind."

Charles Miliken was the man I came closest to marrying. Five years ago he proposed—on one knee, all of that. I spent a week agonizing over whether I would let him make an honest woman out of me, but I finally turned him down. I didn't reject him completely; instead, I said I wanted to keep seeing him, this time without mentioning marriage again.

Charlie agreed, probably thinking he'd wear me down eventually. We still saw each other, but eventually he couldn't take the strain of uncertainty. We didn't fight, but the marriage question started to overshadow everything else. Things are never the same after a man proposes.

We still had a physical relationship from time to time. That would have been hard to give up—for a WASP, Charlie was unusually passionate. In fact, as far as I could see, we got along better in our post-breakup state than when we had a formal relationship. Once, late at night, Charlie confessed I'd ruined other women for him. I tried not to take pride in that, but it was hard.

I sat primly on one of his wooden visitor's chairs and tried to pull myself together. Charlie looked a mess, and I was more into it than I'd realized when we stopped. I should have known not to play around with old chemistry.

"Before I tell you anything, Charlie, I need a promise from you," I said. "You have to keep evrything I say in confidence unless I give you permission later to go public with it."

Charlie's light blue eyes fixed on me, suddenly clear and focused. He ran his oversized ink-stained hands over his prominent chin.

"You got it," he said. Ignoring the no-smoking law restricting all Dade County public buildings, he opened the window behind his desk and pulled a Marlboro out of his shirt pocket, lighting it with a plastic Dolphins lighter. Charlie never cared much for rules, which probably explained why he was still only an assistant state attorney instead of division chief.

"Lupe, darling," he said, "you know I'd do anything for you, but I have to ask: Could I go to jail for this?"

"Probably not."

He shrugged and took a puff on his cigarette. "Good enough for government work."

I told him the whole story, beginning with my initial meeting with the Morenos and ending with Barbara Perez at the *Mamita*. I showed him Miranda's pictures. He listened without interrupting and seemed uninterested in the photos, his brow wrinkled in concentration, lighting another cigarette off the butt of the last.

"That's a hell of a story, Lupe. Thanks for involving me," he said sarcastically and with a bitterness that was new to me. "Let's start with the charges you could face for withholding information in a murder case—not to mention the fact that you may have set this Alberto Cruz up for a murder hit."

"I've thought of that already," I said.

Charlie flicked some ash into a can of diet Coke and shook his head in wonderment. "All right," he said. "Why quibble over the little things? What do you want from me?"

"Can you protect Barbara Perez?"

Charlie blinked, just once. I'd succeeded in surprising him.

"Let's see what we have," he said, sitting up straight in his chair. "You clients took part in an illegal adoption, and almost surely knew it wasn't kosher. The baby isn't present in Dade County records, and you can't find the doctor who delivered her—unless some dotty old widow comes through at the eleventh hour. You bribed a lowlife for information, and because of that he's dead. You may also have signed his pregnant partner's death warrant, and you're nowhere near solving your case. Interrupt me when you disagree."

I nodded miserably. "You're right, Charlie. So are you happy now?" I thought for an instant that this was what my married life would have been like if I had accepted his proposal. Thank God I didn't.

Charlie leaned forward in his chair, which sent a shuddering creak straight to my brain. He opened one of his bottom desk drawers, took out a bottle of Jack Daniel's, and poured two healthy drinks into paper cups he produced from the same stash. Silently, he handed me one. I recognized this as one of his gestures of reconciliation, and as I drank I realized how much I needed it. Apparently he realized it too, because he refilled my cup without being asked.

"To answer your question," he said softly, "no, it doesn't make me happy. And based on what you've told me, I can't protect Barbara Perez."

He took a long drink and tilted his chair back as far as it would go. "Let's start with the adoption," he said. "The Morenos aren't about to press charges against Betancourt, because that would constitute an admission of guilt in an illegal transaction. And they could easily lose the baby in the process."

I took another swallow. It burned going down. "I can guar-

antee none of the other parents would press charges either, even
if you could track them down," he said. "And they wouldn't testify for the Morenos. Even if the state were to subpoena them
and force them into court, they would hire high-priced legal talent who would keep it all out of the courts for years."

Maybe it was the liquor, but I felt my face flush with anger.
"Charlie, you're talking like a goddamned lawyer."

He lit another cigarette and looked away. "You know better,
Lupe," he said. "I'm making sense, and it bothers you."

"I thought you'd get less irritating with age, Charlie, but I
was wrong."

He ignored what I had said. "And you have nothing substan-
tial linking Betancourt to the adoption scheme," he said, blowing a smoke ring. I felt dizzy. Drinking liquor in the afternoon
on an empty stomach was a new experience for me. "You have
photos of wealthy couples going into his home, but they could
be guests. You have Alberto Cruz and Barbara Perez on his dock
late at night delivering what you claim is a baby."

He pulled Miranda's photos closer and put on his reading
glasses. "But these pictures aren't even that clear. Alberto Cruz
owned that boat. Betancourt could say he was talking to Cruz
about buying it, about hiring him to repair a boat, or anything
else he wanted to make up. Alberto Cruz gets killed two days
after seeing Betancourt in his office? That proves nothing. No
one has come forward to say they witnessed the killing outside
Dirty Dave's, and no one will. From what you tell me, this Barbara wouldn't be a very good witness. We might offer her immunity for her testimony, but we'd need more corroboration. Lupe
honey, all you have is a series of unsubstantiated allegations di-
rected toward a very prominent lawyer in town. There's no case
here."

He was starting to wear me down. "What would make the
case for you?" I asked. "What do you need to go after Elio Betancourt?"

The room was full of cigarette smoke, and I was feeling hot

inside from the Jack Daniel's. It was a struggle to keep thinking straight.

Charlie seemed perfectly normal. "I need the same thing you need: one of the birth mothers. That's what the state would probably need to prosecute, and I can't even promise that. The mother broke the law by selling her baby, remember. Actually, I'm not even sure if this would be a state crime. It could be federal."

"Charlie, stop for a second. You're giving me a headache." I got up and sat on the edge of his desk. It was so like Charlie to hedge and cover his bases, but I knew what he was saying: Find the birth mother, and Barbara has her protection.

I walked over to the door and locked it. Charlie certainly didn't object. I had work to do, but I wasn't above talking a half hour to see where old chemistry might lead me.

It wouldn't be right to go to a convent reeking of bourbon and sex, so I stopped off at home after leaving Charlie's office to shower, change, and brush my teeth before visiting Lourdes. At certain times I get a feeling I need to talk to her, and she's always there waiting for me.

I was optimistic that Charlie felt charges could be pressed against Betancourt if I found Michelle's birth mother, but when the liquor wore off I remembered I was back where I started. I was upset, and I called Lourdes on her cellular phone. Although my sister is devout, there are some things she can't give up, and her cell phone is one of them. I used our prearranged signal—three hang-ups—to indicate that she should answer the fourth ring. We had decided a long time ago that that was a surefire way to reach her when she would normally be unavailable.

She was happy to hear from me, but she was at a retreat, so I would have to visit her at the Order of the Holy Rosary in Co-conut Grove rather than at the house she shared with the other sisters. She wasn't supposed to speak during her retreat, but I must have sounded pretty desperate, because she agreed to meet me in the pine woods behind the convent.

She rose from the grass when I arrived after parking my car inconspicuously near the woods. "So, *chica*, what's up?" she asked, hugging me. Her shoulders felt tight and firm. She was still working out.

"We need to talk," I said quietly.

I wasn't used to seeing her wearing her habit, and navy blue wasn't her best color. The Sisters of the Holy Rosary were considered a modern, activist order—they had sent money to the Sandinistas in Nicaragua, for example. Lourdes disapproved of that. She joined on the condition that she wouldn't have to participate in activities she disagreed with.

Usually nuns didn't have the clout to stipulate the terms of their service, but Papi's donation helped her cause. The Catholic hierarchy is nothing if not practical. Lourdes's social activism was limited to teaching underprivileged children in Little Havana, and she stayed out of politics altogether.

We walked arm in arm to the stone wall facing the bay, shaded by Florida pines and caressed by a fresh breeze that cut through the humid air. We sat on the wall like children, our feet dangling over the water, our faces cooled by mist from the lapping waves.

I could make out the outline of Lourdes's cellular phone attached to the triple rope of heavy wooden rosary beads wrapped around her waist. Once a CAP—Cuban-American Princess—always a CAP. My sister spent an efficient thirty seconds, at the most, unlacing her sturdy black shoes and peeling off her thick, knee-high black socks.

"Damn, these things are uncomfortable," she said, tossing the shoes away from her. They landed on the grass with a hollow thud.

"So, little sister, tell me," Lourdes said, staring at the blue horizon. "What can be so bad that you're drinking in the middle of the day?"

"What are you talking about?"

"I may be a nun, but I know what liquor smells like," she said. "And I smell it on your breath. It doesn't matter how many times you brushed your teeth."

I felt as though I were ten years old again, begging her to run interference with Mami and Papi after I did something wrong. The all-knowing Lourdes. I wanted her to hold me and make it all go away, just like she used to.

"Lourdes, I screwed up on a case," I said, feeling my emotions come out in a great rush. "I made such a mess, you can't even imagine."

Lourdes pulled uncomfortably on her habit, twirling a blade of grass in her hands. "I don't want you to tell me about the case," she said. "I just want to know if you can do anything to salvage the situation. Look at it objectively. Is there anything you can do, realistically, to fix your problem?"

"Lourdes, I think I really burned my bridges. I . . ."

She took my face in her hands and looked into my eyes. I felt my heart lurch and suddenly felt very tired and spent. She stared for a moment longer, then released me.

"I wasn't kidding about the drinking," she said. "I like a drink or two myself, but you have to stay away from the stuff when you have to make critical decisions."

Our closeness the moment before had made me uncomfortable, and I suddenly realized why. For an instant, I felt as though I was looking into my sister's familiar eyes but there was something else behind them, something greater than her or me, and it was scrutinizing me. I pulled away from her a little and started searching through my purse for a tissue.

"Did you really screw up, or are you exaggerating?" Lourdes asked, picking a new blade of grass. "I love you with all my heart, Lupe, but you know how you are sometimes."

"I wish I was exaggerating, but I really and truly fucked up."

"Fine, we're back to that," she said patiently. "What can you do to unfuck the situation?"

"I'm not sure."

"Well, that's the question you have to answer—not to me, but to yourself."

We stayed on the wall watching the sunset until Lourdes had to go back inside. "If I sit out here any longer," she said, checking her watch, "then I won't get credit for the retreat. When we're here we're only supposed to talk to God and the saints—not other people, especially half-drunk private investigators."

I kissed her goodbye and left her putting on her socks and shoes. I hoped the Catholic church would come to its senses soon and start admitting women as priests. My sister looked much better in black than in blue.

I spent the following afternoon in my car, looking out on Alberto Cruz's old stomping grounds. The sun beat down with particularly intense wrath, and I was still there, hoping Barbara Perez would show up at the *Mamita*. I'd failed to find out where she lived, and I had no messages from her.

Every mosquito in Dade County had taken a bite of some part of my body, and I was sure their cousins from Broward County would be visiting soon to share the feast. I was sweaty, frustrated, and feeling half crazy, but I was prepared to wait days if I had to. Six hours later the sun was gone and the neighborhood began to come to life, underworld style. It probably wasn't a smart idea to stay there much longer, but I did anyway, the Beretta tucked under the seat.

It was close to midnight when I saw Barbara approach the boat. She wore the same outfit as yesterday—I guess the money she made from Betancourt went for her six kids and not for maternity wear.

I waited until she was inside the boat to approach her. "Barbara, it's me, Lupe," I called out from the dock. "I have to talk to you."

"Lupe, what the hell are you doing here?" she called back.

"I have no other way of contacting you, in case you forgot. I'm tired, and I'm hungry. I have people trying to find you, and failing, and I'm in no mood to play games. The only thing that kept me going was that I figured if I couldn't find you, then Betancourt couldn't either."

"You could put a hundred of your best people on me and they wouldn't find me, so save your energy for getting us out of this mess."

Barbara stuck her head out from below, scanning the dock around me with binoculars to make sure I was alone. "And I don't care if you're tired and hungry, Lupe. You got me into this."

All right, so I wasn't going to win the sympathy vote. The vague camaraderie we developed in our last meeting was gone, replaced by an antagonistic edge in her voice. To be fair, I would have acted the same if I were pregnant and scared.

Barbara climbed quickly up to the *Mamita*'s deck, looking all around us suspiciously. "You know how I feel. You guarantee my safety and we can talk about anything."

"Let's go below and talk," I said, pleading a little. "I've been sitting in my car all day waiting for you. Look at what the mosquitoes did to me." I showed her the welts on my arms.

She examined my flesh with the blasé air of an experienced mother. Bug bites apparently didn't mean much to her. Scowling, she started inside. "All right, come on," she said.

I jumped on board the boat. I was so stiff from sitting in the Jeep that my back creaked like a rusty hinge. My body felt folded up like an accordion.

I followed Barbara into the main cabin, where she lit a wall lamp and stood glowering at me in the flickering shadows. I was so grateful to be out of the car that I didn't really care what kind of attitude she wanted to give me. She pulled down two plastic tumblers from a shelf, poured healthy splashes of rum into each, and topped them off with tepid Coke from an already opened can, leaving me to fervently hope that the baby would not be harmed or inherit an alcoholic gene from her. Stirring the drinks, she lit a formidable cigar and took a long drag. The drinks weren't very promising, but I hoped mine at least wasn't garnished with ashes.

"What news do you have for me?" she asked, handing me a cup.

"Nothing definite. I can't guarantee anything. I went to see a friend, a lawyer for the government, and told him about the trouble you're in."

Her eyes opened wide. "You told someone from the government? Are you an idiot? Now we have more problems than ever."

"This is someone I trust," I said, sipping the drink. The Coke was completely flat. "Remember, I'm in trouble too. This was a friend I came to for advice."

Barbara laughed bitterly. "I didn't think you were a fool," she said. "But now I know you are. There's no such thing as a friend in the government."

"He's a friend first and a state attorney second," I said.

"Oh, I see," she said, regarding me with an uncharacteristic girlish smile. "So you and this man are more than friends?"

"We used to be—" I began, then stopped myself. "That doesn't matter. What's important is that he promised me total secrecy."

"You trusted a man to keep his promises?" Barbara asked incredulously, waving clouds of cigar smoke around the cabin. "So you made two mistakes. What did this man from the government have to say to you?"

"That you're in serious trouble with the United States government for trafficking in babies, but more immediately you're in trouble because you're the only person alive who can link Betancourt to the crime. It's just like I told you."

Barbara took a long pull on her drink and winced from the strong liquor. I was nursing mine, remembering what Lourdes had said.

"He said the government will probably give you immunity if you testify against Betancourt, but to make the case really airtight we have to produce one of the birth mothers. For my purposes, we need the mother I came to Alberto to find."

"That's the only way I'll come out of this alive?" she asked. "Taking the mother to the government?"

"Barbara, I found a way to protect you. You should be happy."

She drank again and stared at me with haunted eyes. "Well then, Lupe, we'd better start saying our prayers. There's no chance of that."

"What? Don't you know where they are? You've been doing this with Alberto for years." I was fishing, but she didn't contradict me. It was a small victory; I sensed that her fatalistic attitude was based on something very solid she knew.

"Lupe, I didn't know anything about the business. Alberto took care of that. My part was just to go on the trips with him, to be a wet nurse and help him sail the boat. In Cuba, you know, there's no bottled milk, so I had to be there to feed the babies on the trip back."

It took me a moment to register what she had said. When I did I tried very hard not to let my jaw drop, and failed. Barbara didn't even notice, she was so lost in her despair.

The babies came from Cuba. Barbara and Alberto sailed there regularly to fetch them.

"Holy shit," I whispered. Barbara said nothing, staring at the butt end of her stinky cigar.

I didn't know what to ask. For some reason my mind fixated on the logistics of the trips. "What about taking bottled milk?" I said. "Wouldn't that have been easier? What about feeding the babies formula?"

Barbara nodded. "I thought of that. Alberto said they used bottled formula in the beginning, but then the third baby he brought out died on the way. Alberto said Betancourt was convinced the baby formula killed it."

"Formula doesn't kill babies," I said.

"I know. I think Alberto just liked having me to help, so he convinced Betancourt they needed me. He knew I could help with the boat, but he was a man. He never would admit he needed a woman to help with his man's work, so he told the lawyer they needed me for the babies. And we had Cuban patrols and the Coast Guard, sometimes really close. Sound carries over water, so it was my job to keep the babies quiet."

I must have looked at her the wrong way, because Barbara turned defensive. "These were little newborn babies," she said. "They missed their mothers. So I rocked them, anything to keep them quiet. It's dangerous out there. One cry at the wrong time, and we'd be finished."

I could feel fear emanate from her as she remembered the patrols on the open seas. "How do you know so much about boats?" I asked. "Did you grow up around the water?"

Her eyes creased with a moment's softness. "I grew up in Cojimar, a little fishing town near Havana. It's a nice place—or it was, until Castro ruined it." She looked away from me. "My first husband was a fisherman. I married him at fifteen, had my first baby at sixteen."

I began to speak but she interrupted. "Someday I'll tell you how I got out of Cuba, but not now. It's private."

I decided not to press her, instead thinking of what Betancourt had accomplished. Betancourt specialized in Cuban babies for wealthy Cuban parents, but I had assumed since the beginning that they came from exiles in South Florida. Sure, I'd tossed some ideas in my head—that the mothers were taken to an island on the Keys to give birth, maybe even the Bahamas, then the babies were delivered by boat. But it made sense, and no wonder there was a seemingly endless supply. If you want Cuban babies, where better to go than Cuba, providing you can get in and out.

Now I understood what Barbara meant. We didn't have a chance in hell of producing one of the mothers, to say nothing of our odds of finding Michelle's. It seemed impossible that Alberto had made the treacherous passage from Florida to Cuba so many times without getting caught. I had no idea how to do it once.

Barbara leaned back in the captain's chair and looked out the porthole. "Let me tell you," she said, "those trips were hell sometimes. Those kids knew I wasn't their mama. A few times the kids didn't want to nurse and were fussy the whole way. Not all tit milk is the same, you know."

"You . . . were always pregnant?" I stammered.

"Alberto liked it when I was pregnant. He knew it meant milk for the children." She looked down with wonder at the enormous breasts straining against her shirt. "In ten years I don't think I've ever been without milk."

"Why did you do it?" I asked, giving up on my drink and resting it on the floor. "You have a family. Why take such a risk?"

Barbara shrugged. "Because Alberto asked me to. He was my man once, a long time ago, and he was good to me. Not all of them were, you know. A woman like me . . . so many children, so much of a past. Cuban men don't like that, you know. It's hard to find a good man. Alberto needed my help."

I was tempted to feel sorry for her, but she spoke about danger as though it was nothing. She knew how to survive, and didn't need pity from me.

"We didn't always do this, you know," she said wistfully. "We started out fishing. It wasn't much of a living, but we could eat, buy rum and cigars, live on the boat on the river. It wasn't the *Mamita* then but another boat, a tugboat. Alberto would do odd jobs around the marina for rich people too."

"And that's how he met Betancourt."

Barbara bit her lip and stared at the floor. "Alberto was working on some rich man's boat when he got hurt. Betancourt was the lawyer for the insurance company that handled the claim. They started talking, and Alberto started doing jobs for Betancourt. Me and Alberto split up years ago, but after a couple of years he called me about the babies. I wasn't doing anything much, just having babies and taking care of them. He didn't pay me a lot, but I don't need much, just enough to feed my children."

She was growing sad with her memories of Alberto, and I was having trouble following her. I was still in shock. How on earth had Betancourt set this up? It was brilliant, really—he probably paid the pregnant Cuban women a pittance. And he knew none of the mothers would come back to him years later and try to claim their biological children, which happened all the time in America. The only people who ran a great risk were Alberto and Barbara.

"Why can't you make the trip to Cuba without Alberto?"

"The trip isn't the problem," she answered. "I can do it. I know I can. I was always better on a boat than Alberto, anyway. It's dangerous, but if you're careful it can be done. You just need the right supplies, decent weather, and Santa Barbara at your side."

I ignored her reference to the Santeria goddess. "So you really think you can do it?" I asked, half dreading the answer.

She didn't say anything for a moment, looking around the boat. "Maybe it's time to tell you how I got out of Cuba thirty years ago."

I simply looked at her. Maybe it was.

"Remember how I told you I married a fisherman? Well, Eduardo, he was my *novio* all my life. I don't know where he is now, but that's not important. We were sweethearts all our lives, you understand? We even *thought* the same."

I had a sip of my drink. It wasn't half bad.

"After we got married, we could only think about how to get out of Cuba. We had no future there. We were watched all the time by the *chivato* government spies, because Eduardo owned a boat and might try to escape. In the beginning he would go out fishing with his brother, but then his brother got sick."

Barbara paused to inhale deeply from her cigar. I wondered if secondhand smoke from a cigar was as deadly as from cigarettes. Then I realized it didn't matter. It was probably one of the least dangerous things I had to worry about.

"After I had my baby, a son, we knew we had to leave." Barbara spoke slowly, as thought to ensure I understood her. "Neither of us wanted to bring up a child there. So we made a plan. I started helping Eduardo with the fishing; we'd go out early in the morning and return late at night. The men all laughed, because men didn't take women on the seas with them, but after a while no one said anything. The *chivatos* didn't care, because I always left the baby with my mother in Cojimar. They knew we weren't going anywhere without him."

A wide grin beamed across her face; this was obviously her favorite part of the story. She was so excited she forgot to blow smoke in my face.

"See, Eduardo and I knew that if we failed, we'd be thrown in jail for twenty years. We had to be careful. But then we started holding back some of the fish we caught, putting it in a cooler behind Eduardo's brother's house. After a month it was full to the top. It was a crime to hold back fish, you know. We were already taking a risk."

A creaking sailboat went by outside. Barbara stood up and peered out the porthole. "Then we got Eduardo's brother to help us," she said. "Once a week he had to go to the clinic to get medicine for his heart. So when the fish cooler was full, we had him tell the nurse he couldn't sleep. He was a good patient and never asked for anything, so she gave him some sleeping medicine without any problem."

The boat passed us and moved on. It would have taken a federal raid to move me from my seat by that point.

"Early in the morning, I gave the medicine to baby Jose," she said. "He was only nine months, and this was adult medicine, so I had to guess how much to give him. Eduardo covered him in an old blanket and put him in the bottom of the boat's fish locker. Then we covered him with fish from the chest behind Eduardo's brother's house."

"Weren't you worried Jose would suffocate?"

She laughed. "Of course I worried. But what kind of a mother would I be if I didn't try to give him a better life?"

I had no reply. "So we sailed to Key West," she said quickly. "We were stopped three times by Cuban patrol boats, and got searched twice. They even looked in the fish locker, but they didn't unload it. They wanted to know why we sailed so far north, and we told them we heard the fishing was good out there. They were stupid, and they let us be. As soon as we were in international waters I took Jose out and washed him off."

Thirty years later, the memory seemed as fresh as if it had happened today. "I can't tell you how long it took me to get the fish smell off the boy!" she roared.

I thought about why she bothered to tell me all this as she lit a fresh cigar, her eyes wide to see if I appreciated her story. It wasn't hard to figure out. She wanted me to know that she was a woman of courage, of action. She was still the woman who risked her own and her child's life thirty years before.

Then she changed the subject. I wished she hadn't. "But you have to understand about the babies. Once I get to Cuba, I don't know what to do. Like I told you, Alberto took care of all the business."

I hated to badger her, but I finally had part of the answer. I needed the rest. "As long as Betancourt knows about you, you're always going to be in deep trouble," I said coldly. "The man is ruthless. He killed once that we know about, so I don't think he'll hesitate to do it again."

Now her gaze turned critical. "You, too, then," she said thoughtfully. "He'll come after you, too. Right?"

"We have to stick together, it's the only way." I reached over to her and took her hands in mine.

Her rough hands squeezed mine in response. I figured we were partners now, so I told her about the cigarette butts outside my office and about the break-in at my apartment.

"You really think Alberto would spy on you that way? That's not the Alberto I knew," she said. I could see that her trust in me was still fragile, that she wouldn't accept everything I told her. I decided to let it pass.

"I knew I shouldn't have come back to the *Mamita* tonight," she added, her voice full of disappointment. "I had a feeling."

"What made you come back?" I was grateful she'd brought up the subject; I had wanted to, but I didn't know how she might react.

"I was looking for the money," she said. "The ten thousand you gave Alberto. I was sure he hid it in here somewhere. It's the only place he ever felt safe."

"Did you find it?"

She let out a full, throaty laugh. "*Querida,* if I had, I wouldn't be talking to you right now. You can be sure of that."

We had a lot to work on. "Maybe it's for the best you didn't find it," I said weakly. "These troubles aren't going to go away."

Barbara's eyes clouded over, her weather-beaten face creased into a frown. She wasn't a complainer, that was certain. She didn't blame Alberto, or anyone else, for her troubles. In the face of everything she sat there calmly, smoking her cigar, drinking her rum—a Cuban Madonna.

Early the next morning Barbara was waiting for me on the stoop outside my office. She called just after dawn, waking me, and ordered me to meet her there. Her face was impassive and rigid as she watched me approach.

She looked so out of place I would have been scared of her if I didn't know her. From the cigar ashes scattered around the steps, I could tell she had been waiting awhile. I opened the door, turned off the alarm, and ushered her in.

Barbara scanned the room and seemed to dismiss the office waiting area as beneath her scrutiny. "Two men in suits were asking for me yesterday at the marina," she said, sitting on the edge of Leonardo's desk. "I don't even know men who wear suits. They must have come from Betancourt."

I put on some coffee and opened the blinds. "Who told you this?"

"My son Jose told me when I got home last night. The guys who work around the marina told him. They thought the men were there to make trouble for me."

"What did your friends at the marina tell them?"

"Nothing," Barbara answered proudly. "We all stick together. Like a family."

"Those men will be back. This is just the beginning." I spoke over the tap as I rinsed two coffee cups. "Yesterday they might have just wanted to intimidate you, but who knows? They'll start watching your children, your home. If they want to find you, they will eventually."

"I know that. I'm not stupid, Lupe."

I poured coffee, and she accepted a cup. I figured a pregnant woman who smoked and drank rum probably hadn't sworn off caffeine, and I was right.

Michelle was running out of time, and now so was Barbara. It was just a matter of time before someone came after *me*. I suddenly realized I'd lost the luxury of speculating whether or not to go to Cuba.

When I looked at Barbara, I saw she shared my thoughts. "I want to go, Lupe," she said simply. "I have to finish this."

I knew what my answer would be. I was as trapped as she was. "I watched the Weather Channel this morning while I was getting dressed," I offered. "There are no storms around."

Barbara sneered. "Weather channel? Don't be ridiculous. I don't watch any weather channel! I smell the sea and know all the storms! I don't need any fancy people with fancy educations telling me about the weather. I have this!" She pointed at her nose.

I was taken aback and just stared at her. Her dark eyes shining, Barbara suddenly threw her head back and roared with laughter. "I had you going for a second, didn't I?"

We were planning to enter communist Cuba illegally, and she was seeing how gullible I was. Great.

"There's no point waiting," I said, and her smile disappeared. "Betancourt could send someone for us anytime. We should make preparations and leave tomorrow."

"I need money to get the boat ready," she said, extending her hand.

Barbara was as plain and unadorned in her speech as in her manner. I had come to appreciate and respect that. Maybe the Miami social circles I moved in were so shallow that I was moved by any kind of directness.

At the same time, there was something mercurial and volatile about her, and it scared me. I opened the office safe and pulled out several hundred dollars. "Here," I said. "That should be enough for the boat expenses."

"I also need money for Alberto's relatives, and for provisions to give them," she said. The bills I already gave her looked dwarfed and tiny in her huge hand.

I reached for the money and started to speak. She interrupted. "I'll explain what I mean. I'll explain everything before we go."

Another couple hundred was enough to satisfy her, and she raised her loose white cotton shirt and tucked the cash into her expansive brassiere. I caught a glimpse of her belly. Unless she was carrying twins, she was definitely farther into her pregnancy than I had thought.

"By the way, do you get seasick?" she asked, rearranging her clothes. "The trip can be rough."

"I never have before," I lied, trying to keep the nausea out of my voice. "But don't worry, I'll hold up my end. But now I need to know everything about the trips you took with Alberto. And I mean that, Barbara—if we're going to get out of this alive, I'm going to have to know as much as you do."

"I understand," Barbara said. She looked at me strangely. "You're more scared than I am, but that's okay. Remember, the sea will be your friend as long as you treat her with respect."

"My father always said that."

Barbara smiled and grasped my shoulder maternally. Her grip was alarmingly strong. Standing over Leonardo's desk, she delicately picked up his papers and placed them neatly on his chair. Lifting up her blouse, she took out a long roll of papers tucked in her skirt. I shuddered when I saw again how distended her belly was.

She spread the papers on my desk, and I saw that they were sea charts. "I came prepared in case you agreed to go," she said.

Bending over the charts, she identified the long island of Cuba and pointed at a small spot east of Havana marked in pencil. "We landed here," she went on. "A little fishing village called Isabela de Sagua, in the province of Las Villas."

I took a closer look. The town was on the northern part of the island, just to the south of Sagua la Grande, which I had heard of from Papi, and almost halfway between the provinces of Havana and Oriente. It looked like an ideal spot to land, protected from the open sea by a string of small cays lining the coast. The promontory the town rested on reminded me of Cape Cod, though on a much smaller scale.

"Why there?"

"Because Alberto has relatives there, and because Betancourt suggested it for his own reasons. The two came together. Alberto knew those waters from when he was small. He came from a family of fishermen, and he used to fish with them there."

She handed me a small black notebook. "Alberto always took notes so he was the only one who knew what happened on the trips. He had a feeling he might need it one day. But there's a problem. I think he took down the notes in code."

It looked so innocent, like a little kid's diary, but to Elio Betancourt it was lethal, and Alberto knew it. If Marisol Velez wasn't so honest, Betancourt's ass would have been partially covered.

"What do you mean, you think he wrote in code?"

Barbara stared at me confrontationally. "You're smart, you figure it out." Her quick anger diminishing already, she stared at the charts. "I can't read, all right?"

"But how are we—"

"I can't read that book, and I can't read the names of the places on this chart. But I can read the chart better than anyone," she said, jabbing a meaty finger into the Atlantic Ocean. "The coastline, the currents, the sandbars. I was raised by sailors, and I know the sea."

I opened Alberto's notebook and tried to read the entries. The writing was in a sort of hieroglyphics. I decided not to waste time on it. I locked the notebook in the office safe.

"So I was right?" she asked, watching me. "He wrote in code?"

"I have no idea what it says," I admitted.

"Alberto was a smart man," Barbara said admiringly. "You see? You can read, but you can't read about what he did."

"He was a genius. He was so great that he outsmarted us out of information that could save our lives."

The front door clattered open behind us and we turned as one, both scared out of our wits. It was Leonardo, and he arrived at work to see a huge pregnant woman staring at him with her fists raised. He looked at me uncertainly and started moving back out the door.

"It's all right, Leonardo," I said. "Barbara, this is my cousin. He works with me here."

Barbara lowered her fists and extended her hand. Leonardo winced when she shook it. "Am I interrupting anything?" he asked.

"Not really," I said. I didn't want him in on this. We were moving into a territory where knowing what we planned and what we had done without reporting it was borderline illegal. "But maybe we should move into my office."

Leonardo couldn't take his eyes off Barbara; he was transfixed. "No, no, no," he said quickly. "You can use my desk. I'll go into the other room and close the door. I missed a workout yesterday, anyway."

I thanked him as he quickly disappeared into the workout room. "That's an attractive boy," Barbara said, nudging me.

"I'll set you up with him if we live through this," I said. "But, for now, keep talking. How did you know when to leave for Isabela de Sagua?"

"You're serious about setting me up with your cousin?" she asked in reply. She saw I wasn't biting, and sighed. "All right. Betancourt would call Alberto two days before we had to leave. It was always the same: Alberto would go to Betancourt's office late at night to pick up an envelope with money for expenses and to give to his contacts in Cuba. Then Alberto would get the *Mamita* ready—fill her tanks, get food and ice, everything."

"So you were the only ones involved?"

"Well, my boy Jose would check out the engines. He's a mechanic, a good one. His father, Eduardo, used to fix his own engines on the fishing boat."

"Then did you ever consider taking Jose along on one of the trips to Cuba?" I asked. "It would seem like a good precaution, in case anything went wrong with the boat."

Barbara shook her head with such violence that wisps of hair escaped from her braid. "You know how I got Jose and me out of Cuba," she said. "Santa Barbara was with me at that time, but you don't ask the gods for two miracles. The trip is dangerous, Lupe, don't fool yourself about that. I tempted fate too many times, and my luck will run out soon—that's my business. But to take my son back to Cuba after what I risked to bring him to America . . ."

I saw her point. "Did Alberto agree with you?"

"No, we had big fights about that. So big that one time he went without me, and he learned his lesson then!" She spoke almost as though Alberto were in the room with us. "He saw he couldn't do it without me, so he shut up about Jose. Besides, Jose doesn't know where we go. He thinks I go fishing. I don't want him or my other children to know anything about the babies—that's my secret."

Somehow I felt touched that Barbara—the adventurer, with all her bluster—worried what her kids thought about her. At the same time, I had to consider: This woman kept secrets.

"All right, go on. How did the trips start?"

"When the *Mamita* was ready, Alberto would tell me what time to meet him at the dock. We would usually leave at noon so we could be at the marina in Key West by late afternoon. We waited there until after midnight, resting; then we set sail for Cuba before first light. We motored like hell, and the *Mamita* burns gas like a bitch because of the special engines Alberto installed, so we had to top off the tanks in Key West before we left. Gas is rationed in Cuba, you know."

"How did you get through the Cuban and American patrols?" I asked. The thought of being captured by Cuban soldiers filled me with dread.

"We were careful."

She had nothing else to say, so I got up for more coffee to keep myself from screaming. "Who met you at Isabela de Sagua?" I asked when I brought the cups back to the desk.

"Two of Alberto's relatives, two men, always the same ones." She blew on her coffee. "Alberto brought them provisions along with Betancourt's cash payment. The payments got higher over time. I think Alberto had to bribe them not to turn him in. Family is family, but things are bad in Cuba. You can't trust anyone."

"So Betancourt hired Alberto to pick up babies in the very province that Alberto grew up in?" I asked.

Barbara nodded. "Alberto said it was the luckiest thing that ever happened to him in his entire life."

Alberto was wrong. "What happened after you met the relatives?"

"We anchored in a little bay just before the town, pretty well hidden. Then the two men would take the provisions we brought them. Alberto would go off in a dinghy with them while I stayed on board. A couple of hours later he would come back with a baby. We waited until dark and then left."

"You don't know where he went to get those babies?" I asked nervously. "You never went with him?"

"Never. I always stayed in the boat," Barbara said, a hint of dismay entering her voice.

"So it was always pretty smooth. You never spent so much as twenty-four hours in Cuba."

"Never," she said. "We would get there before first light, and leave after sunset. It was always the same."

"How many trips do you think you made?"

"Oh, I don't know. The sea is worse in winter, so we didn't go very much then. I went to Cuba with Alberto for . . ." She looked at me as though expecting me to finish her sentence for her. "Three or four years now. It wasn't regular—sometimes in the summer we'd go two or three times a month, and I missed some trips when I had babies myself. So I went . . . maybe twenty times."

As if on cue, Leonardo groaned from the next room. Even behind the closed door, it sounded as if baby number twenty-one was well on the way.

Barbara demurely asked where our office bathroom was, then excused herself quietly. She was a bundle of contradictions. I didn't really think I had any reliable answers from her about the baby-selling scheme, since Alberto purposefully kept her in the dark. What amazed me was that they had made the trip twenty times and that Betancourt had arranged as many adoptions. There were wealthy Cubans all through Miami buying babies from Cuba. And I still didn't know precisely where those children came from.

There was another question that troubled me, and when Barbara returned from the rest room it was my first priority.

"Barbara, when I first saw you, I thought you were about six months pregnant," I said delicately. "How far along are you really?"

"Six, seven months. Maybe more, I'm not sure. It's hard to tell when you're nursing and pregnant at the same time."

Leonardo grunted loudly again. You could have tape-recorded that sound and used it to teach Lamaze classes. I hoped Barbara's baby didn't hear and get the wrong idea.

"Don't worry," Barbara said. "I've made this trip up to eight months pregnant. If anything happens, I know what to do."

Planned Parenthood would be terrified. Barbara Perez was a baby machine. The La Leche League crowd should have hired her as its poster girl. And I didn't even want to know what she meant by saying she "knew what to do."

"Do you have any babies?" she asked. "A husband?"

"Neither," I said quickly.

I didn't consider for an instant telling Barbara my views on marriage—it would be a waste of time, and this was no time to make her think I might be unhinged. She may have lived an unusual life, but I could tell she had conventional ideas about women and their children. Barbara had the Cuban view: that motherhood was and should be every woman's greatest goal in life. Sometimes I wonder if it was this pressure that drove Lourdes into the religious life.

My poor parents: they certainly got shortchanged in the way their daughters dealt with marriage and motherhood. One was a nun, one was divorced from a scoundrel, and the third was a confirmed single girl.

I wasn't against marriage in general, just for me in particular. After Fatima's fiasco, then working hundreds of domestic cases over the years, I saw that my parents' happy marriage was a rarity. To give up my unwedded bliss I would have to be convinced that a man would improve my life beyond measure. Charlie was fairly persuasive, then Tommy, but so far I had resisted. I saw no need. Leonardo said that sometimes I thought more like a man than a woman. That was pretty perceptive, but of course I wouldn't give him satisfaction by admitting it.

Barbara shook her head as though she pitied me, and I understood something about her. She relied on no one but herself, and saw her huge family as a joy and a sign of her independence and ability to make her own way in the world. I admired her, if reluctantly. She took part in and profited by unlawful, even immoral acts, but when the time came to pay the price she accepted it without complaining or feeling sorry for herself. I knew then that I could rely on her completely.

"What about the actual trip through the waters?" I asked. "It has to be dangerous."

"Well, there's the Coast Guard, and then the Cuban patrols," she said casually. "But the Cubans aren't out there as much as they want you to think—the gas shortage keeps them home a lot of the time."

Still, I shuddered at the thought. The Cuban military was known to treat Cuban-Americans ruthlessly. I also knew the Coast Guard did a lot of patrols to keep Cuban exile groups from launching attacks on the island from Florida—not to mention looking out for Cuban and Haitian refugee rafters—so they would be out in force. The DEA would also be around, seeking to intercept drug shipments from the Bahamas. And then there would be the legitimate boaters, cruise ships, freighters.

Barbara watched me intently. I could tell she saw my wheels spinning. "Lupe, don't think so much," she said. "The more you worry, the more likely your nightmares will come true."

I didn't know if she was right, but I had to put it out of my mind. "Then how did Alberto notify the men at Isabela de Sagua that he was coming for a pickup?"

"He sent them a message on that Cuban radio station, Radio Ritmo. He would call and ask them to play 'Aquellos Ojos Verdes' at exactly six o'clock the night before we set out. His relatives in Cuba monitored the station, so they knew when to be waiting for us at the cove. Alberto used to say the simplest plans were the best."

I thought that Alberto had watched one too many D-Day invasion movies, but I didn't say it. The more I heard about him, the more entrepreneurial and creative he sounded. I hoped he was also cautious.

"We have to do the same thing, then," I said. "We'll buy supplies, request the song, and set out at the same time he used to."

I tried to sound as confident as I could. Our plan was shot if the family contacts in Cuba had heard about Alberto's death. Actually, there were too many weak points in our plan to start numbering them. It was the only plan we had, and we had to go with it.

I couldn't even ask Lourdes to pray for us, because I had no intention of letting anyone in my family know what I planned to do. If Fidel Castro didn't kill me, my father would. In fact, I would rather face Fidel than my father when he was angry.

"And then once we've arrived?" I asked hopefully.

"We play it by ear."

Great.

twenty-one

"Tommy?"

"Mmmm."

"I want you to do me a favor."

He nestled deeper into his pillow. "Sure, sweetie. Anything."

"I want you to prepare my will for me."

He turned over. In the dark I saw that he opened his eyes. "Sure," he said hesitantly. "Come by my office next week."

"No, I mean right now."

He turned on his side and propped himself on an elbow. "This very second? You have to be kidding."

Then a resigned flash of understanding passed across his face and he got out of bed and walked over to his apartment's sliding door. Tommy was confident of his sexual prowess, but he wasn't conceited enough to think that was the entire reason I'd asked to come over on short notice. He had to know I would eventually get around to telling him why I demanded we meet at his place.

There was only one apartment per floor in his building, affording views of Biscayne Bay to the east and Miami to the west. Tommy usually kept the doors to both decks open, allowing a sweet cross-breeze to pass through the room. Still naked, I joined him outside on the wraparound balcony. The view from the fortieth floor was stunning.

He had completely changed the configuration of the apartment when he bought it, turning the living room into his bedroom. The condo board readily approved his plans, even though a tenant had never proposed such a change, because at one time or another most of them had been his clients. Tommy figured he would do most of his entertaining in the bedroom and spend limited amounts of time in the living room.

"I just have a feeling about something," I said, looking down on the city below. "You know, Cuban intuition. I want to put my affairs in order right away."

Tommy leaned against the rail and laughed. "Cuban intuition. Cuban superstition, you mean. Have you been with the Santeros again?" He scrutinized me in the darkness as he spoke. I knew my request had upset him.

I had done a case for the Santeros—African-American priests who practiced the Santeria religion in Miami—a few years back, and gotten involved in a few of their ceremonies. I finally balked at witnessing the ritual killing of animals in Hialeah.

"It's not that," I said. "I just thought everyone should have a will."

"All right, I'll play along. Do you have many assets? If it's going to be complicated, I should recommend a will and trust specialist. He'd know all the tax laws and ramifications of what you want to do." He paused, then asked, "Lupe, why do you want to do this now?"

"Don't ask questions, Tommy. Please. Will you help me, or do I have to call a lawyer out of the yellow pages?"

He gripped the rail hard with both hands. We typically had a carefree, no-strings relationship, and rarely exchanged harsh words with each other. "I'll do it for you," he said. "I don't like it, but if you want it I'll do it."

Tommy walked back inside and drained his glass of champagne next to the bed before pulling on his blue-striped boxer shorts. After I put on his flannel robe, he turned on the lights and stood over his marble dining room table, which was covered in a blizzard of papers. Shaking his head and muttering to himself, he searched out a legal pad and motioned to an empty chair.

In a tired voice he began asking me questions, writing down

my answers as I spoke. It was all pretty straightforward. In addition to my jewelry, I left half my cash to Fatima's girls. The other half I divided equally between cancer research in honor of my mother and Hermanos al Rescate—Brothers to the Rescue—a group of volunteer exile pilots who searched the waters off Cuba for rafters. I left all the gym equipment Solano Investigations had paid for to Leonardo. I knew he would put it to good use.

"This all seems pretty clear," Tommy said, examining the document before typing it into his computer. "Come by the office tomorrow and I'll have it ready for you to sign. My secretary is a notary, so she can witness it."

I was relieved to finally put my financial world in order. If anything happened to me on tomorrow's expedition to Cuba, I wouldn't want my father to endure the additional pain of a contested probate. I wished I had life insurance, but it was too late to apply. I wondered: If I bought gas for the *Mamita* with my American Express card, would that be considered insurance? Would the company have to pay off my heirs in the case of death or dismemberment, like it says on the back of airline tickets? I doubted it.

It made me wonder what Barbara was doing. Was she with her children, savoring every moment, knowing it might be her last night with her family? Or was she on the *Mamita,* smoking cigars and drinking rum, thinking quietly about the life she had led and the dangerous turn it had taken?

Tommy typed up the will and printed it in fifteen minutes. He took the document and, with an air of ceremony, put it inside his leather briefcase. I knew it took a lot for him not to ask me questions. It was almost a declaration of love.

There was no way Tommy would charge me money for his service, so I expressed my gratitude in a way I knew he would appreciate even more. I quickly discovered there's nothing like fear of death to inspire passion.

· · ·

At home we ate late that night, speaking little. Papi went to bed, and Fatima put the twins to bed. Lourdes came into my room, looking annoyed.

"Little sister, what's going on?" she asked, her arms folded. Sometimes it was a liability to have a sister who could practically read my mind.

"What do you mean?" I asked innocently.

Lourdes chuckled at my feeble acting. "You know you can't hide things from me," she said. "There's something important bothering you. I can't force you to talk, but you know I'm available for consultation." She lay down on the bed next to me, the way she did when we were children.

I stared at the ceiling. "Well, I *am* a little worried about a case," I said. "But everything should be wrapped up pretty soon."

No sale. Lourdes sat up and stared at me. "Don't bullshit me, Guadalupe. Just because I'm a nun doesn't mean I can't smell bullshit, especially coming from you."

There was no point fighting it. "You're right. I'm not being completely honest with you. The truth is, this case is driving me crazy."

Lourdes hopped off the bed and opened the closet door. She took out the extra pillows Aida stored there, fluffed them against the headboard, settled herself in, and stared at me expectantly. "I'm comfortable now. Start."

When Lourdes was onto something, she wouldn't let go. She was a little pit bull. I wished I hadn't begun it, but now I knew she would stay in my room until I leveled with her.

"Lourdes, if I tell you this, you have to swear you won't tell anyone. Promise me."

"I promise."

"I'm sorry, but that's not enough."

She looked up in surprise. She was a nun, after all, and not used to having her word questioned. I reached out to the picture of Mami I kept on the bedside table.

"Give me your rosary beads," I said. I put them on Mami's picture. "Now swear," I commanded.

To say Lourdes was shocked would be a disservice to her reaction. Her eyes bulged so much they almost shot out of her head. This was nothing compared to how she was going to look when I told her what I intended to do.

"I swear," she said. "I promise, all right?"

"Fine. I'm going to Cuba."

Lourdes crossed herself, her hand trembling. "I don't think I heard you right. Or maybe I heard you right and I'm hoping I heard you wrong. You can't have said what I thought you just said."

She was babbling. It was a good thing I made her swear on the rosary and Mami's photo.

"It's for this case that's got me so screwed up," I interrupted. "I have to go to Cuba for it."

"But how are you going to get a visa?" she asked breathlessly. "I've heard it's almost impossible for Cuban-Americans to get clearance."

"Lourdes, I don't need a visa. I'm going in by boat."

"What . . . like a cruise ship?" she asked hopefully.

"Not exactly. By sailboat." As I watched Lourdes coming to grips with this, I understood that I had hoped she would make me tell her my plan. If anything happened to me, someone should know where to look.

Lourdes left the room without a word, and in a moment I heard the door open to the upstairs den. She returned with a bottle of champagne and two fluted glasses. Opening the bottle with an experienced, fluid motion, she filled the glasses and handed me one.

"*Salud.* I think we're both going to need this." She drained her glass and waited for me to do the same. "Okay. Now I'm ready."

I told her the story from beginning to end. I knew by the twitches at the side of her otherwise clenched lips that she was horrified. She squirmed and emptied another glass when I got to the part about Alberto Cruz's murder.

When I had finished, Lourdes, for once, had nothing to say. She rose from the bed and paced the room a few times. I waited.

"Lupe," she said loudly, then spoke softer. "I can see why you feel you have to go to Cuba, but *really*. This is carrying your sense of responsibility too far. Why don't you let Papi contact Stanley Zimmerman to get you out of this mess?"

I could hear her talking herself into this implausible idea. "Think about it," she said. "You could go away to a spa for a while—maybe the Golden Door in California, or the Canyon Ranch. Mami liked that one. By the time you get back, all this will be taken care of. Papi can give that Barbara woman enough money for her and her kids to move away. Everything will be back to normal."

"Lourdes," I said, "Stanley Zimmerman can't do anything with Elio Betancourt. Betancourt is up against the wall. He's not going to just back down and wait to be charged."

"But—" she began.

"And what about the little girl?" I asked. "If she doesn't get that transfusion immediately she's going to die."

"Lupe, surely the Morenos can't expect you to risk your life going to Cuba on this wild-goose chase. You've done all you could for them, more than enough."

"If I don't go," I said simply, "I'll never be able to live with myself."

"Lupe, it's against the law to go into Cuba. If the Americans catch you, they might accuse you of planning a raid and throw the book at you. They're always arresting those Alpha Sixty-six guys."

"I know."

"And the Cuban government! If they catch you, they'll throw you in jail—if they don't torture you to death. And if Castro finds out our family has money, they might hold you for ransom."

I hadn't thought of that, and Lourdes pressed on, sensing she had found a weakness.

"It's not unheard of, you know," she said, sitting down next to me. "Remember Mami's friend, the one she used to play bridge with?"

"They held her sister and brother-in-law for ransom until the family paid," I said. "I remember."

"That's right," she said triumphantly. "The Cuban government is desperate for cash. They wouldn't be above keeping you until Papi deposited a few million in an account in Switzerland. Do you really want to put the family through that?"

Lourdes could play an incredible game of hardball. "I have to run that risk," I said. "Barbara is in danger, I'm in danger."

"That could all be—"

So I did it. I told her about Alberto breaking into my apartment, then spying on me in the office. Then I told her about the men in suits who were looking for Barbara. Going in for the kill, I told her about my visit to Michelle Moreno. I knew Lourdes liked logic, so I tried to put forth all of this in a concise way. She just listened.

She was skeptical, I could see, but it was a relief to spill everything to her. I had agonized so much about going to Cuba that talking about it like this made me feel as though my emotional dam had finally given way. I also recognized that although my decision was the only reasonable one, I wasn't in the most stable frame of mind.

"It's just a matter of time before Betancourt comes after me," I said. "The only card I can play is producing the birth mother. It's not just a matter of saving Michelle's life, or Barbara's. It's mine, too. Betancourt can take his time before doing anything to me, and I can't have that hanging over me. And what if he gets to Barbara? Then there's no witness to tie the whole thing together, and no way to find the mother. Then it's over for all of us!"

I stopped, realizing I was raving. Lourdes's eyes shone at

me. "Is this really the best plan, little sister?" she asked quietly. "Or do you just think it's your only choice?"

Lourdes was no fool. But I knew what would appeal to her. "And the Morenos," I said. "We know what they're going through. Imagine how we would have felt if someone could have saved Mami but didn't have the courage."

Lourdes looked as though she had just seen a revelation. "I know you'll be careful," she whispered. "But if something happens to you, I'll never forgive you. Never."

"Lourdes, I—"

"Shut up. Just tell me how you're going to do it."

twenty-two

The police hadn't yet searched the *Mamita,* which meant they weren't really pursuing the investigation. Early that morning I asked a cop, a friend of mine with Metro, for the case status, and he told me nothing was happening. Apparently Alberto Cruz's murder had yet to move to the front burner. My friend pointed out that there were no relatives bugging the cops about finding the killer, so there was little motivation to investigate. This was a good break. The last thing we needed was some zealous detective impounding the boat for evidence the very day we were leaving.

Barbara had moved the *Mamita* out of the river marina where Alberto kept her to a private dock in Coconut Grove the night before, just in case. The fees were exorbitant, but if the cops changed their minds at the last minute, we wanted to make the boat harder to find. We now sat together in the stifling cabin. At least we were out of the morning sun, which beat down mercilessly out of a cloudless sky.

"Is there anything else we have to do before starting out?" I asked Barbara, feeling as though a part of my life had ended and another begun.

"No. And I spent all your money, in case you're wondering," she said. "We're going to need more when we get to Key West. Gas is expensive there, and we need to fill the tank."

"Fine, I'll bring more cash. Anything else?"

"No, we're ready." Barbara looked out the hatch and fanned herself with a yellowed newspaper. "I told my family I'm going on a five-day charter, in case those men come around my house asking for me. That way they'll leave my children alone."

"Good idea," I said. "My sister is going to tell my family I've gone to Naples to visit a boyfriend's family."

Something occurred to me. "Barbara . . ." I said, hesitating, "in case something happens to us, have you provided for your kids?"

She was expressionless. "My son Jose gets plenty of work on boats," she said. "He can take care of his brothers and sisters."

"It's just that . . . well, I could make some arrangements before I left. Nothing extravagant, but enough to—"

"Hush," Barbara said, shaking her head. "Don't talk that way. That's how bad things start."

I saw she meant it. "All right," I said, standing. "If there's nothing else, I'll be going. I have a lot to do before noon."

"We'll be fine, Lupe. Worrying never solved anything."

To my total astonishment, Barbara waddled over and hugged me. She held me tight, and I smelled tobacco and perfume. I suppose she meant to reassure me, but she scared me silly, and I felt unbearably awkward. It's always been hard for me to show physical affection to another woman, not to mention one with a gigantic protruding belly.

I had already telephoned Tommy's secretary to let her know I would come over to sign the will at around nine-thirty. She faxed it to me at home for final approval before preparing it for me to sign. Tommy did an outstanding job. It was precisely what I wanted.

He was in court when I arrived, which was just as well. I signed the will and gave his secretary—a pert little blonde in her early twenties—a two-pound box of Godiva chocolates as a thank-you for processing the document so quickly.

I had a feeling that if Barbara knew I had ordered a will the night before our trip, she would have strangled me. I'm not superstitious—just because I draw a will doesn't mean I'll get hit by a bus, or killed by Cuban soldiers, the very next day. But Barbara was a classic superstitious Cuban—like Fatima.

My sister Fatima takes the usual superstitions—no walking under ladders, no seating thirteen people at a dinner table, no lighting three cigarettes from the same match—completely over the edge, even consulting fortune-tellers now and then for advice about the future. And she isn't discerning. She follows any recommendation, no matter how ridiculous, in order to ward off evil spirits. Once I came home to find Aida in a fury after spending the morning vacuuming the powdered armadillo testicles that Fatima had sprinkled throughout the house. But then I shouldn't leave out Lourdes, even if she takes a more traditional approach. She still puts little bottles of holy water all over the place.

You can get really caught up in that sort of thing in Miami, but I was never tempted: once I saw an ad in the *Herald* that said, "Psychics Wanted. Will Train." That took care of it for me.

I suddenly realized I was sitting in my car in front of Tommy's building, crying at the thought of my sisters. I had two and a half hours before Barbara and I were scheduled to leave, and I had to find some way to occupy myself.

I remembered Regina and called her on the car phone, after blowing my nose and fixing my eye makeup. Strangely—because she was almost always home when I called, and answered on the first ring—she didn't pick up.

I wasn't surprised she didn't have an answering machine. Cuban ladies of her generation seldom did. But maybe she was on her way home. Lately her story about having no luck finding Dr. Samuels's address, or remembering anything more about him, had worn thin. I could stop by her house in Sweetwater. It didn't take long to get there, so if she wasn't home it was no great loss.

Face it, Lupe, I said to myself, putting the Mercedes in gear, *you need something to do, or you're going to lose it.*

I parked in front of her house, as I had before, and was relieved to see it looked undisturbed. I'm not sure what I expected to find, but I was suddenly thankful that nothing seemed wrong. I let myself in the gate and rang the bell repeatedly, but there was no answer. After an eternity, an elderly woman I didn't recognize came to the door and peered through the window.

"What do you want?" she cried out, her voice muffled by the glass between us.

"I'm looking for Regina Larrea," I yelled. "She's not answering her telephone. Can you help me?"

"She's not here," the woman said, peering at me suspiciously. "She's on a trip."

"When will she be back? I have to speak to her."

"She said a few days. That's all I know." She cracked the door's window a fraction and put her mouth to the screen. "I'm her neighbor. I'm just here to pick up her mail and to dust while she's gone."

"Do you know where she went?" I thought I might as well press my luck. The old lady was getting positively chatty.

"She didn't say where. I think it was somewhere up north."

"When she gets back can you tell her I was here and ask her to give me a call? My name is Lupe Solano." I pushed one of my business cards through the mail slot in what I hoped was a friendly manner, then left, my vocal cords hurting.

Well, at least Regina was alive. I had entertained visions of her lying on the floor, near death. I think I'd watched too many scary TV commercials about elderly people falling down and not being able to get up again.

As I drove away I wondered where she could have gone. "Up north" could have meant anywhere, when your starting point was Miami. She could have been headed for Orlando or for Canada. And there was something secretive in the way she left without calling me, since she knew I was waiting for her information. Women like Regina didn't usually do something so spontaneous.

I couldn't dwell on it. I had problems of my own.

twenty-three

"Fast, right?" Barbara grinned fiendishly at me over her shoulder as she gunned the *Mamita*'s engines. "With horses like these, we can go as fast as any Cigarette."

"Very nice." I could barely speak through the hot wind whipping against my face. I had to hold hard to a wooden rail to keep from falling when she popped the throttle.

"Alberto never let me drive. He always wanted to do it himself." Barbara looked up at the sky and yelled out, "Alberto! Alberto Cruz! I doubt you're up there, but in case you are, look at me! I'm driving the boat, you bastard!"

She threw her head back and cackled maniacally. I hoped Barbara hadn't started in on the rum before we set out. All I needed on this trip was a drunken pregnant lunatic for a captain.

The *Mamita* cruised so fast that the coastline passed in a blur. By the time I got used to the speed, we were out of Miami completely, riding through the brilliant blue toward the Keys.

"Smart, eh?" Barbara yelled out, watching me instead of the water ahead. "Alberto had a good idea when he put these engines inside a sailboat. He figured no one would bother us: drug runners have Donzis or Cigarettes, not wooden sailboats. He told me it took a guy a whole week to figure out how to change the *Mamita* so it could go this fast."

"Very smart," I shouted back at her. "He thought he would be in the business for a long time, right? That's why he put so much money into the boat."

The *Mamita* slowed down a bit as Barbara cut the engines,

ignoring my question. "We're making good time. I won't wear out the engines until we need to."

She settled her girth on the thick cushions behind the wheel, steering with her foot, completely relaxed. I seriously considered popping a couple of Valiums, but I knew I couldn't hold them down.

"Can I steer for a while?" I asked. I needed something to distract me.

"Sure, get the feel of her," she said, getting up from the seat with a grunt. "The practice might come in handy later."

Having something useful to do calmed me down a little. Within minutes, Barbara was asleep. I envied her.

The sea had only a mild chop, minimizing the jarring of the boat against the waves. The channels were clearly marked, and since it was a weekday, there weren't too many other boaters in sight. I might have actually enjoyed the trip down to the Keys, if my voyage ended there.

The last time I visited Key West was three years before, on a missing persons case involving a husband who disappeared one morning from his office in South Miami. He wasn't really missing at all. The wife couldn't accept what the police told her—that after twenty years of marriage her husband had left her and their four children for a restaurant owner in Key West.

I had the unpleasant job of confirming that not only had he left her, but the restaurant owner was a man. Even though the news must have been very difficult and shocking for her, I thought she took an inordinate interest in photographs of the two men eating crème brûlée with a single spoon.

I wouldn't normally have taken such a case, but I really love Key West. Besides, I had an old boyfriend down there I always enjoyed seeing. Sam Lamont before he quit was one of the best—if not *the* best—polygraph examiners in Dade County. His abilities were legendary because his confession rate approached a hundred percent. Once subjects were strapped into his machine, something happened that made them break down and tell the truth. He knew precisely what questions to ask, and was respected or feared by virtually everyone in the criminal justice system.

One day five years before, in the middle of an exam, he walked out of his office, climbed into his car, and disappeared. Six months later he turned up in Key West. He bought himself an old Victorian gingerbread house on Caroline Street and started renovating it. He'd made a good income as a polygraph examiner and was a notorious saver, so he was able to retire and indulge himself.

When I was in Key West on the missing husband case, I looked him up, not really knowing what to expect. I had never known anyone who just quit the grind the way he had, and thought maybe he had collapsed under the pressure. I found him as happy as I'd ever seen anyone, and he looked terrific—so much so that I moved out of my hotel room and stayed with him while I worked the case.

We stayed in touch after that, so I knew he was still there, still making additions and renovations to his beloved house. When I parked at the marina in Coconut Grove just before noon, I'd called him from the Mercedes and told him I might be dropping by for an hour or two. I wanted to squeeze everything I could out of life before we crossed into international waters headed for Cuba.

We were very close to Key West, and when I turned to wake Barbara I saw her face inches from mine. "That's it, over there to the right!" she screamed.

"I see it, I see it!" I screamed back, trying to duplicate her volume. "Shit! I thought you were still asleep." The woman had scared me out of my mind.

"Watch the channel markers! You're too close! Careful, careful, you're going to get us killed!" She furiously waved her arms, knocking me hard into the steering wheel.

Her hysteria was contagious. I released the wheel, only too

happy to turn over command. "You steer, you take her in. I can't handle it."

I was shaking with fear and anger. I'd been around boats all my life, but Barbara made me feel like a neophyte from some landlocked country.

She slapped me on the back and laughed. This was another one of her tests, I realized. "No, you do it, Lupe. You're fine. Take her into the marina."

The wind had picked up, pushing us too far to the west. We didn't want to attract attention. I cut the motor. With the engine's roar reduced to a purr, I suddenly felt aware of my surroundings: the cool insistent breeze off the water, the gentle pulse of the waves, the squawking of gulls circling above.

It was all I could do to keep the *Mamita* on course as the Truman Annex marina entrance grew closer and closer. I could easily see the harbormaster's office, where we would have to stop for our docking assignment slip. Even the prospect of screwing up that maneuver gave me a chill of fear. Barbara had certainly done a number on me.

Alberto chose the Truman Annex for several reasons, according to Barbara. The main reason was that it was the southernmost marina in Key West, and Cuba lay due south. It was also a public facility as well as a private marina, so it accepted transient boats. Any boat docked there for only one or two nights wouldn't attract attention. They were used to it.

When I pulled in, the harbormaster was waiting for us. He had spotted us coming and pointed out a slip for me to drive into. I cut the engines completely, and as we came to a stop, Barbara waved at him and smiled with a calm, easy familiarity.

The harbormaster's name tag identified him as Henry Abbot. He was a great, blond, suntanned bear of a man who oozed friendliness and mellow charm.

"Welcome!" he said, climbing on board and looking around the spotless deck with satisfaction. "Nice to see you back, Barbara."

"Hi, Henry." Barbara lit a cigar and leaned back on her cushions. "How have you been?"

"Great. Just great," he said in his deep voice, which sounded like the sea and days spent outside in the sun. He turned to me and smiled. "Where's Alberto?"

"He stayed in Miami. This is a girls' trip." Barbara stood and put her arm around me, her cigar perilously close to my face. "This is my friend Marta."

"Nice to meet you, Marta." Henry extended his huge palm to me. His handshake was soft, and his leathery palm scuffed against my hand.

In another place, another time, I could have gone for this guy. He was like a fireman or a forest ranger, rough and gentle at the same time. And I always had a weakness for big men with big blue eyes. From the look he gave me, I could see he felt the same way.

Henry's beeper went off, and he glanced down at the display. "Well, I'll be seeing you," he said. "If there's anything you need, anything at all, just call me."

He peered at me with those blue eyes, and I had to look away before I got into something I didn't have time for. I don't apologize for myself—if I were facing a firing squad, I would visualize the soldiers naked. It's my nature.

Barbara busied herself checking our supplies. When I offered to help, she waved me off.

"You're making me nervous," she said. "Why don't you go look up that friend you told me about? We have hours before we go."

"You're sure you don't need me to stick around?"

She chomped into her cigar like a Marine drill sergeant and shook her head. Obviously she considered me a hassle, or else she just wanted some time alone before we left.

As I leapt off the *Mamita* onto the dock, Barbara called out, "Leave me some money. I have to buy some things."

I handed her a thousand dollars that I had set aside for just such a request. Hopefully I would recoup the money from the Morenos.

At the marina entrance I telephoned Sam, and he agreed to pick me up. Henry spotted me waiting under a tree and rode over in his golf cart. He pulled up alongside me and sat there grinning, his eyes hidden by avaiator's sunglasses.

"You're Cuban, right?" he asked.

I nodded. "I live in Miami."

"Is this your first time at the marina?"

I nodded again and wiped beads of sweat from my forehead. It was hard to tell how old Henry was; years of sun had lined his forehead and cheeks with deep grooves that accentuated his deep-set eyes and somehow made him look innocent and open, like a surfer boy settled down into the quiet life.

"Here, hop in," he said, patting the empty seat next to him. "I'll show you something you might be interested in."

I slid next to him on the cart. His tanned arms were covered with thick golden hair. He was more attractive up close, so I tried to fix my eyes downward—feet are usually a passion killer. With chagrin I saw this wasn't the case with Henry. He wasn't wearing socks, and his tanned, muscular calves showed above his worn Top-Siders.

Henry drove to the edge of the pier, where the winds blew across open water, and slowed the cart to a stop. "This is where the boats came in during the Mariel boatlift," he said. "Come on, I'll show you."

I realized the significance of where I was. It was the landing point for what came to be called the Mariel, the mass exodus of 125,000 Cubans within a two-week period in 1980. Fidel Castro had announced that all Cubans who wanted to leave their homeland could, if they left from the north-coast fishing port of Mariel. Jimmy Carter responded by declaring that any Cubans who left would be welcomed into the United States. Instantly, exiles living in America mobilized into a flotilla and traveled home to pick up their relatives. Key West was the refugees' point of entry into their new home.

"I wasn't here then, but the harbormaster before me was, and he told me stories," Henry said. We got out of the cart and walked to the edge of the pier. "The boatlift was fifteen years ago, and they still come. Ninety miles of water due north, currents, storms, sharks, Cuban patrol boats, and they still do it. Whole families—men, women, children, babies, even pets. You wouldn't believe what they sail in. They throw themselves into the sea in anything that floats."

Henry looked at me for sympathy, his mouth pulled into a frown of disbelief. I swallowed hard. *Oh, Henry, if you only knew* . . .

"I guess people do what they have to," I said. It was a dumb, innocuous comment, but Henry nodded respectfully.

"Well, come on. I'll drive you back to the gate."

When Henry and I arrived at the marina entrance I saw Sam pull up in his familiar green Jeep, wearing dark glasses and a Florida Marlins baseball cap. He waved, and I called out his name.

"I'm sorry—I hope I didn't make you late to meet your friend," Henry said, stopping ten feet from Sam's car. He nodded at Sam and waved.

"Not at all, Henry," I said, and kissed him on the cheek. "You were sweet to take me out there. I'll always remember what you showed me."

Henry blushed with pleasure and pulled away quickly when I stepped out of the cart. Sam was waiting for me, and hugged me tight.

Sam hadn't changed a bit. He was easily a foot and a half taller than me, and he gave off an ease and relaxation that made the pressure cooker of Miami seem like a foreign country a thousand miles away. I worried a little about the cap, though.

Sam was vain, and vain men who lose their hair become great experts in headwear.

We climbed into the Jeep and Sam drove out, sending a hail of gravel behind us. "Margaritas when we get home? Just like old times?" he asked as we merged with the sparse traffic.

I hesitated. I thought I should be clearheaded for what lay ahead. "Sure," I said. Why not? If I was rushing blindly to my death, I sure as hell didn't want to pass up a last round of small pleasures.

I leaned back on a wicker sofa in his cool, shaded garden, brightly colored cushions carefully arranged around me, my legs tucked under. I closed my eyes and took a long swallow of the drink Sam made me.

"*Salud*, Sam."

"*Salud* yourself." He raised his glass. "To the confusion of our enemies." Now there was a toast I could get behind.

"So, you didn't tell me much on the phone. Why are you here?"

It was a natural question, and I loathed answering it. When he worked in Miami everyone talked about how they hated talking to Sam sometimes, because when they told the most innocent lie they felt he could detect it. His mystique ran so deep that people intuitively vested him with the divining power of his polygraph machine.

"Nothing important—just a case I'm working on. It should all take me two or three days at the most."

He pursed his lips and nodded. As always, I had no idea if I'd failed the test. "Anything I can help you with?" he asked.

"Not really," I said quickly. "But thanks anyway."

We sat comfortably without speaking, something I rarely experience with anyone. I spotted the open wood shower stall in the corner, big enough for two people, with hanging orchids. I could remember how it smelled in the shower, the richness of the wet wood, the flowers, the fresh ocean air.

Sam saw me looking and smiled. "It still works, in case you're wondering. Care to try it out again?"

"For old times' sake?" I asked, taking his hand.

An hour later Sam and I lay on his bed watching the ceiling fan blades go round and round. A moment of Catholic guilt overcame me, and I thought about Tommy and Charlie and Sam, and what the nuns at my elementary school would have said. But the hell with it, I thought.

"Sam," I said, stretching. "Why did you leave Miami the way you did?" I had never asked him that question before, one I had always wanted answered.

"I couldn't take the lying anymore," he said in a faraway voice. "I couldn't stand to watch another person trying to beat the system. I'd done it for fifteen years, and one day I thought what it would be like to do it for fifteen more. I made a lot of money, you know—at the end I charged more than a thousand dollars a test, and I could do three or four in a day. It just dawned on me all at once that I didn't have to put up with the bullshit anymore."

"Do you miss Miami?" I asked, turning and resting my head on his chest. "This is so different."

He stroked my hair lightly. "I'm content here. I have enough savings to last the rest of my life, even with this money pit of a house."

"There were a lot of rumors about you, you know."

I felt him shrug beneath me. "I'm sure there were. Rumors are started by people with nothing better to do."

I closed my eyes and tried to take it all in: Sam's hand on my hair, the soft whir of the fan, the smell of the flowers in the garden outside. If I could have stayed in that moment forever, I would have.

"Remember how we met?" I asked.

"Sure I do." He chuckled softly, and I listened raptly to his breathing. "It was the first time in my life I was ever happy to get caught in a lockdown."

Six years before, Sam was at Metro West, a jail miles outside Miami, to administer a polygraph to a client accused of cocaine trafficking. I was there to conduct an interview with a Cuban guy accused of murdering his neighbor, then barbecuing him. When we were each ready to leave, the supervisor told us everyone in the facility had to be detained because of a lockdown. The word sounds like what it is: all the prisoners are sent to their cells and kept there until every single one is accounted for, usually because of some kind of disturbance. In this case, one of them had set his mattress on fire, activating all the alarms.

I was one of ten visitors locked into a small interview room for almost four hours. Sam and I ended up next to each other at a chipped, brown wood table. At first we both used the time to work on reports, but as the hours passed and we realized we were going to be there for a long while, we started talking. We gave each other our best war stories. I knew Sam by reputation, but had never heard he was so good-looking, with intense green eyes and a full, sensuous mouth. After our release from Metro West, we went out for the drink we richly deserved—never mind that it was only midafternoon.

"It's funny," I said now. "I can't go back to Metro West without remembering two things: meeting you, and the recipe for the barbecue sauce my client marinated his neighbor in. It was actually pretty good with chicken."

I laughed, but Sam didn't, so I rolled over. Our faces were inches apart. "Lupe, I made my living for fifteen years by knowing when people were lying to me," he said. "And you're holding out on me. I think you're in some kind of trouble. I don't know what, but you can tell me."

I was tempted, but it was better he didn't know. Sam was good-hearted and protective; he would have tried to stop me.

After he failed he would have sat in agony until he heard I was all right.

"You're a sweetie," I said brightly. "But I think you've been watching too much TV. Believe me, I'm here for routine stuff. Little old ladies and puppy dogs."

"I guess my imagination is more exciting than real life," he said, and smiled wistfully. He didn't believe me, but he was too smart to argue. He would have made a great husband.

twenty-four

I'd left a note on Leonardo's desk that I was going away for four, maybe five days, hinting I was with a new boyfriend, a married man, so I needed secrecy. It was disappointing to think he might have believed me.

Sam dropped me off as the sky over Key West turned dusky and dim, and standing at the gate, I thought I'd check the office voice mail. To my surprise, Leonardo picked up. It was late for him to still be at work.

"Lupe! God, am I glad you called." I'd never heard him sound that way before: serious, frightened, unsure of himself.

"Why? What's the matter?"

"Two homicide detectives were here about an hour ago looking for you. They wanted to ask you about Regina Larrea."

The marina was quiet and nearly deserted. Fear wound a tight knot through my guts. "Oh shit. What happened? Did they tell you?"

The late-afternoon sun broke through the sparse cloud cover and seemed to direct its dying beam directly into my eyes. Drops of sweat slowly moved their way down my back under my T-shirt. The pleasant high from the two margaritas I drank at Sam's was gone, replaced by a feeling as though my brain were submerged in glue.

"She was found by her niece strangled in her house in Sweetwater," Leonardo said, his voice husky. "According to what the niece told the cops, her aunt had just got back from a trip somewhere and invited her over for lemonade. The niece was running late so she called Regina. There was no answer, so the niece hurried over and used her key to let herself into the house. She found Regina dead on the kitchen floor."

"Why did the cops want to talk to me?"

"They did a neighborhood canvass to see if anyone saw or heard anything. No one had, but the next-door neighbor showed them your business card. She said you were there this morning, acting suspicious."

"Damn it," I said. I tried to imagine what had happened, and couldn't. Did Regina get close to Samuels, or Betancourt, without telling me? Was she killed for the same reason as Alberto—to keep her quiet—or was she involved in the baby-selling scheme on a deeper level? None of the pieces fit together.

"Lupe, you have to call these guys," Leonardo said. "Where are you, anyway?"

"You don't really need to know, Leonardo," I said. "At this point, the less you know, the better. Did the cops say anything else? Do they have any leads?"

"They didn't say much else. Mostly they wanted to get hold of you as soon as possible. Think about it, Lupe. First this little old Cuban lady goes off on some secret trip. A private investigator comes looking for her while she's still gone, then she's found dead. Don't you think the cops *should* be looking for you?"

"If the police come around again, tell them you gave me the message and I said I would call them. Tell them I wouldn't say where I was."

The last thing I needed was Leonardo lying to the cops to protect me. He would just end up in trouble, because he was such a lousy liar.

"I don't know, Lupe," Leonardo said. "This is serious."

"Just do as I say, Leonardo. Trust me." I paused. "Were there any other messages?"

"The usual stuff," Leonardo said. "Social calls, a couple of clients waiting for reports. There was one call on the machine that was really weird, though. I think it was a wrong number."

"Read it to me," I said.

"Well, the person had this deep voice, and it sounded like they were covering their mouth." I heard Leonardo rustle some papers. "Here it is. They said: 'I'm your friend. The answer to your question is an offense against God and His children.'"

I heard wind chimes rattle in the distance. "What the hell is that supposed to mean?" I asked.

"Don't ask me," Leonardo said. "It was probably just some nut."

"I have to go, Leonardo. Hang in there."

I stood there with my hand on the receiver for a few minutes after Leonardo hung up. Regina was dead. It was almost surely not a simple break-in gone wrong, since there was nothing valuable to steal in her house and people in the neighborhood would have known it. Something must have happened, maybe before her trip. Or she could have taken the trip to get away from whoever killed her, returning in the mistaken belief that she was safe.

The neighbor said Regina went "up north." That could have meant North Carolina, which meant she was trying to find Dr. Samuels on her own. But who killed her? Samuels? Betancourt? Whatever, she became involved in something related to this case, and someone felt she had to be killed. And I couldn't fool myself—I was responsible. First Alberto Cruz, now Regina Larrea. Alberto lived a dangerous life, and his end could have come at any time. But how could I rationalize putting an old woman in Sweetwater in mortal danger?

As for that second message, I didn't know what to think. They said they were a friend; they were talking about sin. Leonardo was probably right: some lunatic got hold of my office number.

Before I left I called my apartment and punched in the code to receive my personal messages. It worked right, for once. I put my free hand over my ear and listened to the first message.

"Lupe? Tommy. You'd better call me today. I'm worried, and—"

I pressed in the code for the next message.

"Lupe? This is Stanley Zimmerman." I closed my eyes and concentrated. What did my family attorney want with me? "I'm calling because your name came up today in a weekly meeting of the Jackson Memorial Public Health Trust. A woman named Larrea phoned in a complaint about a doctor called Samuels. He hasn't been on the staff for years, but she said she would come in person to pursue charges when she got back to town from wherever she was. Anyway, Lupe, she mentioned your name as a source. Are you involved in something you need help on? Give me a call when you can. I'll be out of the office until—"

The tape ran out. It didn't surprise me that Stanley was on Jackson's health trust—he was on so many governing boards in Miami that I was amazed he had time to run a law practice. What interested me was the nature of Regina's complaint. I thought we probably would never find out, but it was even clearer that Regina found out something she wasn't meant to know. Something that killed her. And I was even more certain that her death was my fault.

Slowly, I made my way to the *Mamita*, the orange sun low and close to the horizon. There was no sign of Henry, and only a few stragglers tended to their boats around the harbor, mostly locking up and storing their gear. When I reached the boat, Barbara wasn't on deck.

I was worried for an instant that something had happened to her, that somehow we were followed to Key West, but I found her napping in the cabin. I watched her. For all that she had gone through, she slept the untroubled slumber of a clear conscience. She didn't toss or turn or make any sounds. I was captivated by her even, peaceful breathing.

Without warning, she sat up, clear-eyed and awake. "Did you call the radio station and request the song?" she asked.

"*Sí.* I called from the harbor entrance, just in case it was

traced," I said. "They said they'll play it at six. Did you get all we
need for the crossing?"

Barbara grunted. I took that for a yes, and walked slowly to
the forward cabin and took off my shoes. "If you don't need me
for anything," I said, "I'm going to take a nap."

I shouldn't have even tried. My dreams were nightmares.
I kept seeing Regina dancing the merengue with Alberto. I
woke up several times drenched in sweat, and an hour later I
gave up.

It was almost six o'clock by then, so I turned on the radio.
The news was just ending, and the evening's music program
starting up.

"*Aquellos Ojos Verdes*" came on, its melody familiar to me
from years ago. We were on our way.

Two hours out of Key West, Barbara tensed and pointed out
some dim lights far ahead in the grainy dark.

"Over there, to the right. Looks like a freighter or a Cuban
patrol boat. They usually don't come this far out."

My heart lurched and I tasted bile in my mouth. What was I
doing? I was like a sleepwalker the past few days, driving myself
out there to the deep waters, never really understanding what it
all meant. I thought I had contemplated mortality watching
Mami's slow decline, but nothing prepared me for this.

"Hail Mary, full of grace, our Lord is with thee . . . Lord,
please be with us, too." Whoever said "once a Catholic, always a
Catholic" knew what he was talking about. My mind filled with
prayers to obscure saints I hadn't thought of since elementary
school.

Barbara pulled the binoculars hanging from her neck up to
her eyes and peered into the distance. "Well, whatever it is, it's
moving away," she said with satisfaction.

She turned to me with a stern expression, her eyes bright.
"Listen, Lupe, you have to get hold of yourself. You can't panic

like that every time we get a scare. You knew this was dangerous, and you can't be looking to heaven and calling out to God,
the Virgin, and the saints to save you. It makes me nervous as
hell."

"I'm sorry, I really am," I said. I wasn't, but faced with a
choice between worrying about some boat off in the distance
and dealing with an angry Barbara a yard away from me, I opted
to appease her. "It won't happen again."

I felt the boat's engines vibrate beneath my feet like a
purring cat. Barbara took one hand off the wheel and squeezed
my shoulder, showing me her sudden tenderness, which was as
shocking as her fits of rage.

"Don't feel bad," she said affectionately. "I was so scared the
first time I took this trip and a Cuban patrol boat passed us so
close we could smell their cigars, I threw up, and I was down-
wind, so it splattered all over Alberto!"

She laughed quietly between her teeth, her gaze focused on
the dark sea ahead. I appreciated that she was trying to help me
relax, but so far it wasn't working. My belly felt like it had turned
over, and I could barely breathe. I knew I couldn't sustain this
level of anxiety for the next twenty-four hours, so I started doing
the yoga breathing exercises I learned in high school. They had
never really helped me before, but they did now. Maybe I had
never felt true anxiety until then. After a while I could breathe,
and I was able to focus on things around me.

Mercifully, the waves carried only a light chop, and out on
the water there was a cool salty breeze. The moon was only a
small silver crescent, and pinpricks of light played on the deep
blue water.

"There's someone," Barbara said, pointing astern.

I panicked, grabbing the rail, ready to jump off the boat. I
don't know what I was thinking.

"Get back here," Barbara commanded in a voice she must
have developed from having so many kids. I froze, waiting for a
slap on the wrist. "Look," she said, pointing again.

It was a school of dolphins, moving easily through the water alongside the boat, playfully following us.

"See, if you relax you might even enjoy yourself," Barbara said. "The sky, the dolphins, the night air. You don't have to worry about driving the boat, and if we get caught we get caught. I've done this twenty times, and I know we'll get there. Pretend you're on a cruise."

I didn't even want to consider what kind of cruise Barbara might run. Besides, we were making good time with the *Mamita's* powerful engines. Now was the time to tell her the full scope of what I was trying to accomplish, and to see if she was still holding out on me.

"Barbara, I never told you why I went to see Alberto in the first place," I said.

She glanced at me quizzically. "He said you were looking for the mother of a baby girl we brought out four years ago."

"He didn't know the whole story. There's more."

She was silent for a moment, pondering. "What do you mean, more? He told you who the mother was, right? So you know who you're looking for?"

"Not exactly," I said.

"I don't understand you. We're going to bring out that mother, the one Alberto told you about, right? What's the problem?"

She didn't know. I hadn't wanted to press her earlier, to see if Alberto had given her the mother's name, because I hadn't felt the lines between us were completely open. But now, out on the sea, there was absolutely no reason for her to hide anything. It was as bad as I thought.

"I don't know the mother's name—I never did. Alberto got killed before he could tell me who she was," I said. "I could see he knew when I first met with him, when I showed him the little girl's picture, but he was stalling for time and money. To tell you the truth, I had hoped he confided in you before Betancourt got to him."

Barbara looked up to the sky, as though she could see Alberto there. "Son of a bitch," she said. "He didn't tell me anything. We're going into Cuba to find this girl, and you don't know who she is. You don't even know if she's still alive, do you?"

"I thought Alberto needed time to check on her whereabouts." I evaded her question. She didn't know she was the one who told me the babies came from Cuba. "But I guess we won't know if we can find her until we get there."

Barbara was silent, holding the wheel and peering into the distance. The *Mamita* cruised through the favorable current as though it were floating.

"Look, you might not think I'm smart," she said, still looking forward. "I don't usually know people like you. When we saw Henry at the marina I even thought he would know something was wrong, because a classy girl like you wouldn't be traveling with someone like me."

She wasn't angry now; rather, I had hurt her feelings. "I wasn't trying to trick you into taking me to Cuba," I said. "But a little girl's life is at stake. We're doing a lot more than just protecting ourselves to put Betancourt in jail."

"We have a couple of hours before we reach Isabela de Sagua," Barbara said. "So talk."

Well, at least she didn't throw me overboard. I had rationalized not telling her about Michelle's mother, and that I had no idea whether she could be found in Isabela de Sagua, by insisting to myself that Barbara hadn't asked for details. But now I was changing the rules as we went along, and I could see Barbara felt trapped. So I told her everything, stressing Michelle's illness, hoping I would evoke her maternal instincts.

"So that's why you want to go to Cuba so badly," she finally said when she knew everything. "You think you're the only person who can save this girl's life. *¡Mi Madre!* I'm on the high seas with a do-gooder with stars in her eyes who wants to save the world!"

She sat back on the pilot's seat and rubbed her belly,

chortling with a deep, throaty laughter. "And I thought you were in it to save your ass and maybe get some money!" She rocked back and forth, barking like a congested seal.

I knew then that I was right not to tell her before we left, even though it was selfish of me to withhold such information. Once I had made the determination not to level with her, I had serious pangs of conscience, but I did what I had to do to save Michelle's life. She never would have taken such an increased risk—because I wasn't leaving the island without Michelle's mother, unless I found her dead—if she knew I was on an altruistic mission. She could be as tender as she could be violent, but I understood that she had been backed into a corner too many times in her life—by her children, by Alberto, by Betancourt—to be motivated by anything but greed and self-preservation. She must have thought I was frivolous, a spoiled rich girl with the luxury of wanting to make the world perfect.

But then she surprised me. When she was done laughing, ending with a tobacco cough that rattled me where I stood, she turned to me with great seriousness. "All right then," she said. "Tell me what you know about this mother."

I took this as a commitment to see the journey through to its end. "It was four years ago. The little girl was different—she had a prominent birthmark on the side of her neck."

Barbara nodded quickly. "Sure, I remember that one, all right. I didn't want to bring her out. Birthmarks are bad luck, you know. Alberto and I had a bitch of a fight because I wouldn't take her on board."

It took me a moment to register what she was saying. "You really remember that trip?" I asked.

"That was the only time I really stood up to Alberto," she said. "I was sure something would happen with that baby. Birthmarks and boats are a bad combination. We were lucky nothing happened on that trip. But I see now—the bad luck just took a little while to set in."

Her dark forehead glistening in the light from the instrument panel, Barbara took a drink from a water bottle.

"After that, I made Alberto ask beforehand if the babies had marks," she said. "I wasn't coming on a trip with a baby who had a problem like that. It's too dangerous as it is."

"What else do you remember? Did you see the mother?"

Barbara gave me a wary look, which I didn't understand. "I always stayed on board the boat," she said. "But Alberto told me he'd seen the mother. When I started the fight about the baby's birthmark, I remember he said it wasn't the baby's fault, because the mother had one too—on the same side of the neck and everything. Like that made it all better! I certainly didn't want to breast-feed the little thing."

"Enough about the birthmark," I said, then softened my tone when she glared at me. "What else did Alberto tell you about the mother? He must have mentioned something else."

"He usually never even met the mothers. He met this one because she almost died. I remember when he got back to the boat, he was pale as a sheet. I was scared shitless because he was gone a long time, but he just shut me up. He waited until we were on the way back to tell me what he saw. Ay, *coño!* That birthmark will haunt me until the day I die!"

Barbara was so excited she hit me in the eye with a fine spray of spittle. I wiped it away. "What do you mean, she was dying?"

"She could be dead now, from what Alberto told me."

It took a lot of self-control not to jump on her then and pummel out the information. What we were doing might be pointless. Michelle would die, Betancourt could walk, and Barbara and I were dead on arrival. I felt my lower lip quiver.

"Lupe, come on," Barbara said. "I didn't say she was dead. I'm just telling you, Alberto said she was near death."

"Barbara, you're killing me," I whined.

"Look, I'll tell you what I remember," she said. "The people in Isabela de Sagua told Betancourt the baby was born and ready to go, but they lied. They needed money and supplies, so they called before the baby was born."

"I thought these people were relatively trustworthy," I said hopelessly.

"I never said that." Barbara shook her head. "Well, Alberto had a fit and he threatened to leave. He said they were liars, that they were trying to rip him off. So they took him to see the mother, to prove she was about to have the baby. When they got there, she had actually just finished giving birth. He never saw one of the birth mothers before this, and he said he'd never forget it. He said the stench of blood almost gagged him."

"But the mother was still alive?"

"Another girl was there, cleaning out the afterbirth. And someone was stitching her up. He wasn't sure she was going to make it, though, there was so much blood. But you know how men are—cowards when it comes to blood. He told me all about the mother's birthmark, that brown thing on her neck. He said he couldn't keep his eyes off it."

I knew that sometimes Michelle's kind of birthmark was hereditary, so it hadn't been a surprise to hear her mother also had it. That was good news: it would make my job easier. But still . . . "So you're telling me she was definitely alive?"

I could see Barbara's profile outlined against the moonlit sky. Her face was like wood, seamless and smooth. She steered the *Mamita*, taking her time before answering me.

"You know, Lupe," she said, "I would have gone into this before if you had trusted me with the truth. This is the first you tell me about bringing out the sick girl's mother. One that's probably dead. You can see that's damned stupid, can't you?"

"I . . ." She was right. "I don't blame you for being angry, Barbara. I was wrong. We can turn back now, if you really want to."

Barbara shrugged, considering this, but we stayed on the same course. We were well on the halfway mark by now, I knew. Part of me wished she would turn us around, to take our chances with Betancourt. Another part wanted to rush on, risking our lives on a nearly impossible chase. Ultimately, either way we were screwed.

The sea quietly glided past us, and we continued for five minutes in complete silence. Suddenly Barbara handed me the wheel and heaved herself below. She emerged in a moment with a bottle of rum. I hoped this wasn't the same bottle I'd seen on the *Mamita* the day before, because there were only two fingers of liquid left at the bottom. Barbara took a hefty swig and handed it to me.

"I guess this means we keep going," I said.

"I guess so," she replied. She took the wheel again. "One more thing. The last Alberto saw of the birth mother was when a priest was giving her extreme unction."

She didn't tell me anything else, and I had heard enough. In the end, it was just a business: hand over the money, take the baby, and get out. I had to hope that Michelle's mother was alive somewhere near Isabela de Sagua, or that Alberto's contacts would remember her. I found that hope a little hard to come by.

More clouds covered the sky now, and only the strongest lights from the heavens poked through with feeble pinpoints of illumination. Barbara lit a cigar, and all I could see of her was the fiery torch stuck in her mouth. This was how it must be before going into battle, I thought, feeling my adrenaline surge as I checked my watch: we were less than an hour from the coast.

"Isabela de Sagua is a shithole if you ask me," Barbara volunteered. Her voice sounded alien to me now that I couldn't see her face. "It was a nothing little fishing village until people started getting desperate to leave the country. It's only fifty miles to Cay Sal."

"In the Bahamas," I said.

Barbara nodded in agreement. "It's such a small town that everyone knows everyone else," she said. "Alberto said that worked for us—if anyone tried to turn us in, everyone would know who did it. People there depend on the things we brought them from Miami. They'd kill anyone who spoiled it."

I wondered how I was going to deal with these people, and if I could get them to help me find Michelle's mother simply because it was the right thing to do.

"Now is when we have to start looking for the Cuban navy boats," Barbara announced, tossing her cigar overboard.

"I thought you said they didn't patrol much because of the gas shortage," I said.

"It's true, but remember what I told you about the Bahamas. Castro makes the boats patrol a lot here. He doesn't like to be embarrassed by anyone leaving without his permission."

Barbara picked up the night-vision binoculars I'd packed and peered into the distance. I felt as if a low current were running through my body, a sickly tension that seemed like it would never leave. We cruised in silence for another few minutes, until Barbara reached down to the throttle and cut our engine speed.

"You know, I was really trying not to think about the patrol boats," I said. "I wish you hadn't brought it up. I mean, you're right—I'll worry about it when something happens."

"Worry about it," she said, cutting the engines even more. "It's happening."

twenty-five

Barbara cut the engines until we were propelled through the water only by our own momentum. Instinctively, we both crouched. I took the binoculars from her and looked into the night.

It was closer than I thought it would be, and bigger, a steel ship moving toward us at an angle. There was a gun mounted on its deck, pointed straight at us.

"Just stay calm," Barbara said. "These engines aren't only fast, they're quiet. They won't see us unless they're looking for us. We're still too far away."

"But they're moving this way."

Barbara hunched her bulk behind the wheel, keeping us on an even course, veering away from the patrol boat but still moving south. The moon appeared through the clouds for an instant, and I saw her eyes bulging and her mouth contorted with fear.

That was enough for me. If Barbara was scared, I was terrified.

I dropped to the deck and leaned against the *Mamita*'s side rail. Through the binoculars' green tint I watched the boat as it neared. It was lit from inside and, though we were too far away for me to be sure, it seemed as though small figures moved around on the bridge. A searchlight scanned the seas in a slow, menacing arc. "Is it getting closer?" Barbara whispered.

"It's still moving this way," I said, also whispering, though the boat was still several hundred feet away.

Barbara cut the instrument panel as well as the engine, so

we were cruising in total darkness. It felt as though we were floating on the sea atop a raft or the back of some big fish instead of the sturdy *Mamita*. Without the engines pushing us, the boat lurched over each swell in the ocean, rocking us forward and back. If I hadn't been so petrified I surely would have thrown up over the side.

They got nearer, and I realized we had an advantage: their searchlight was bright and covered a lot of sea, but it must have hampered their longer-range vision. In the same way, you can stand in the dark outside a house that's lit inside—you can see in but they can't see out. Unless we moved directly into their search beam we might just float by them.

I kept up an internal prayer while I watched, a talent that can be acquired only through years of Catholic school. Convinced I had begged Mary sufficiently, I moved on to the disciples. After them, I bothered Saint Jude, the patron saint of lost causes. I was fairly sure I could recall some other, pretty obscure saints—who might do us extra good because they didn't get called on very often—if things got any worse.

"They've seen us!" Barbara said, pulling the wheel violently, steering us away from the patrol boat. "I'm going to start the engines."

"Don't!"

"It's that damned birthmark. The baby and the mother—I should have known we'd have twice the bad luck. I'm going to turn us around and try to outrun them."

"Wait," I said. Through the binoculars I saw the boat pull parallel to us. I could see its wide wake in the water and painted markings on its side. It was Cuban, and it kept moving on through the water, passing us without slowing down at all.

"They didn't see us," I said. "They're moving on."

Barbara picked up her binoculars and looked behind us. I was right: the patrol boat had passed close to us, but not close enough for visual contact. I watched its searching beam probe the seas we had come from, moving north.

I stood up and brushed myself off. Though the breeze was still cool I was soaked in sweat, and my heart beat in my ears.

After a few minutes Barbara started the engines again, cruising for a while, then kicking in the throttle and turning on the instrument panel. Soon we were moving at our previous clip. Neither of us said anything about what had happened, as though mentioning it would bring them back on our course.

The sky began to grow a little lighter on the horizon. Barbara, rigid behind the wheel, scanned the ocean ahead continuously. She hadn't opened the charts even once, I realized.

"I think I see the lighthouse," she said after a time. "Over there, port side. See that light? Count to ten—it'll come around again."

To hear Barbara, you'd think the coastline of Cuba had suddenly appeared before her. I couldn't see a thing. I concentrated and squinted through Alberto's binoculars until little dots appeared in front of my eyes.

"Barbara," I said, "before we get there, I wanted to ask you. Did Alberto ever tell you if anyone special was in charge here? I mean, there must have been some kind of boss who kept things running and kept the Cuban government away."

"You have a hard time believing me, Lupe," she said, still steering with one hand and holding the binoculars in the other. "But Alberto covered the business end of things. Now look, there's the lighthouse again."

She was right. I could make out the bare outline of something indistinct straight ahead. Incredibly, I saw the lighthouse beacon turn toward us and disappear again. As we moved closer I saw dim lights and a murky darkness that I realized was land.

Though I was born in the United States, Cuba has dominated my entire life since my birth. Papi's family was sixth-generation Cuban, and Mami's ancestors came over from Spain in the early eighteenth century. I have grown up knowing a homeland that is always just beyond my reach, and have lived my life exiled from my history by politics and a ridiculously short distance of ocean. I'm not unique in this—Dade County lives, breathes, and dreams Cuba. We are exiles in the sense that we know and believe we will return home one day.

I realized my cheeks were wet.

"We made good time," Barbara said. If she noticed my reaction, she said nothing. "We'll be in the cove before dawn, and they'll be waiting for us there. Don't worry. If we can see Cuba, our contacts can see us."

As we moved in to the coast, the sea was so easy and clear that it felt as though we were returning from a casual overnight sailing trip. Barbara slowly cut the powerful engines until we were cruising at a slow speed. We entered a channel bordered on the west by sandbars and by a marshy coastline without vegetation, the country inland a vibrant green.

I was in awe of this land and felt the blood of my ancestors moving through me, beckoning me home. I took a moment to experience it all—the air, the water, every detail—knowing I would have to catalogue everything into my memory for when I returned to Miami. I had to forget the awe, the yearning, because I was about to meet people who might kill me to protect themselves from being found out. These people weren't going to understand that my lifelong dream was coming true.

We carefully motored farther up the canal until we reached the cove. I could see why Alberto selected it as a rendezvous spot. The water was shallow there, allowing for easy anchoring. There was only one entrance, with good visibility for miles.

I dropped anchor. Barbara cut the motor completely, and we sat down on the deck to wait. Dawn was coming soon.

twenty-six

I realized with a shock that I was in more real danger than ever before in my life. But I still couldn't get over the fact that Guadalupe Solano had finally made it to Cuba. Who cared if I was stuck in a sailboat, eaten by mosquitoes, with a hugely pregnant woman I didn't really know? I was home, for the first time.

Looking around, I felt that my eyes would never get enough of the place. I saw royal palms in the distance—the symbol of Cuba—as tall and regal as I always imagined. I think every Cuban exile family has something—a painting, a photograph— of that symbol in their home, always reminding them of their heritage and origins.

From the bow of the *Mamita* I could see mountains in the distance. I flared with anger at myself for not knowing more about Cuban geography, for not knowing the landmarks. In my dreams of going home to Cuba it was always through Havana, stepping from a 747, clutching my Louis Vuitton carry-on bag. I never pictured arriving in a sailboat at some godforsaken fishing village on the rocky northern coast.

I took out the binoculars and looked around some more, every colorful detail imprinted upon my memory forever. I looked at the butterflies circling up the coast, and at the lush plant life—captivated for the first time ever by the wild variety of nature. Osvaldo would have been proud. But I couldn't sustain this level of wonder for too long; reality started to intrude on my thoughts more and more.

Two hours passed. The morning sun seemed more tropical, reflecting against the water and making my skin feel too hot. Absolutely nothing had happened: no one appeared, the Cuban navy didn't arrive to arrest us. I had started to pick at my cuticles—definitely a bad sign—and I watched Barbara smoke her way through an entire Montecristo Number One. No small feat.

The silence rang in my ears through the stagnant air, broken only by the buzzing of insects. Mosquitoes had begun to dive-bomb us in exotic, military-style formations. I told myself that if nothing happened in the next hour, we had to come up with another plan. Miami never sounded so good.

"There's someone in the bushes there, to the left of that palm tree," Barbara whispered, her lips barely moving. "Two men, maybe three of them. They've been there for a few minutes now, watching us."

My heart beat so fiercely in my chest I was sure the men could hear it. I tried to glance casually at the trees and the high grass, but I couldn't see a thing. Part of me wanted something to happen; the other part wished nothing ever would. If I closed my eyes long and tight enough, when I opened them I would be in my chintz bedroom palace in Cocoplum.

"There's three of them, and they're coming closer." Barbara held out a hand for me to stay still. "I recognize two of them, Alberto's cousins, but there's an older one I don't know."

The hell with it. I turned and looked straight at the three men approaching the shore near the *Mamita*. They looked harmless enough, if you didn't mind the rifles they were carrying. They climbed into a small wooden dinghy hidden in the marshes and rowed toward us.

"Barbara, welcome back," the man in the front of the boat called out. His face and those of his companions were obscured by wide straw hats typical of Cuban peasants, and all three wore shabby canvas work pants and short-sleeved button-up shirts. They all looked poor.

When the boat got closer the man in front stared at me and called out, "I don't see Alberto. Where is he?"

"He didn't come, Pedro, he had another job he had to do

this time." Barbara smiled and pointed to me. "Marta here came instead."

"*Hola.* Nice to meet you," he said. I smiled with as much confidence as I could manage, keeping my hands where the men could see them.

I looked over at Barbara and saw her nostrils flare with anxiety. She tried not to, but she kept staring at the older man. He was obviously not part of the usual picture, and I knew that we had already lost control of the situation. I wouldn't have been too worried, but Barbara was graver than I'd ever seen her. I wondered if we should have brought some muscle along for the trip. It hadn't seemed necessary, since the Cubans were desperate and motivated by greed—which I figured would ensure our safety. Now I wasn't so sure.

Something definitely wasn't right. The men gave me the once-over, and apparently accepted my presence. As they carefully climbed aboard the *Mamita*, Barbara stealthily placed her machete under the waistband of her long skirt.

"I'm so sorry," she said as they came on board. "I forgot my manners. Marta, these are Alberto's cousins, Pedro and Tomas. I'm afraid I've never met their friend before."

The old man's face clouded when Barbara drew attention to him. He stood behind Pedro and Tomas, preoccupied with the boat's instrument panel. There was something at once different and familiar about him. The cousins resembled each other, though Pedro was obviously a few years older than Tomas, with more lines of age and sun in his Spanish features, but the older man seemed unrelated to them. His hair was white, long, and sparse, and a thin snowy beard partially obscured his angular features.

"My name is Alvaro," he said, bowing to Barbara and me in a courtly manner. He had a slight accent, difficult to place.

Pedro stood with his arms folded, squinting into the morning sun. "Well, since Alberto couldn't come, we might as well start our business. What did you bring us from Miami?" A demanding tone crept into his voice. "I hope you were generous. Things here lately have been very, very bad."

We watched warily—it seemed the prudent thing to do—as the three men went into the cabin and began to search it. They opened the cabinets and found a manila envelope full of cash Barbara had left there.

The cabin started to smell of the men's sweat. They opened all the cargo holds with a sense of ownership, within fifteen minutes taking everything Barbara purchased for them, as well as our own clothes and most of the few possessions we brought. I really didn't care what they took, as long as they didn't make off with the gasoline we needed to return to Miami. I half expected to see them roll out big gas drums, but thankfully they didn't.

Pedro handed the goods down to Tomas and dispatched him and Alvaro to the shore, where they unloaded everything into a metal cart.

"You did well," Pedro said approvingly to Barbara. "This should last us awhile."

Pedro was right. I was astounded by what she bought with the cash I gave her. She should have won Shopper of the Year: She brought the Cubans all sorts of toiletries—shampoo by the gallon, soap, toothpaste, deodorant, hand lotion. She bought all kinds of small electrical appliances, batteries, fans, flashlights. There was at least a pantryful of canned goods, with rice and flour, and beer on ice. An impressive stash, and the Cubans recognized it.

Tomas returned for another load while Alvaro stood on the shore, watching us and smoking a cigarette. Barbara and I stood with Pedro in the hot cabin, looking at each other like uncomfortable guests at a strange party, not knowing how to break the ice.

Tomas dropped the last of the goods into the cart and returned with the dinghy. Alvaro called out from the shore, "Barbara and Marta, you come with us to the house while we get organized."

His tone didn't encourage debate. Until then I thought Pedro was the de facto leader of this group, but it seemed that Alvaro was going to make the policy decisions. I didn't like that, because I couldn't read him at all and because he was the only member of the group Barbara hadn't met before.

She and I were reluctant to leave the safety of the *Mamita*, but we had little choice. We secured the cabin and took the dinghy to shore.

We walked with the men for about a mile through scrub brush along the coastline, with Tomas pushing the heavy cart on the rough path carved through the countryside. The place had an air of desolation about it, and I turned away when I felt Pedro's eyes on me. Alvaro took the lead, whistling softly to himself and saying nothing.

We passed through a clearing into a small grove of palms and were suddenly at the outskirts of a tiny village. Smells of the sea permeated the air. Drying, half-torn fishing nets were strewn everywhere, with dilapidated boats up on racks in need of repair. A few shacks were arranged in a circle, each begging for a coat of paint.

There were no people around anywhere, and the whole place had an abandoned air about it. We were still on the outskirts of the town, but it was strange not to see anyone. With every step we took I felt more and more sure that I was losing control of the situation—and a growing certainty that I had miscalculated. The men kept their rifles pointed toward the ground, but somehow I understood they were ready to use them.

Barbara and I walked side by side, and I suddenly noticed that the men were on either side of us. I felt like a prisoner rather than an honored guest. When we reached a gate in front of a newer, marginally better-kept house, Alvaro turned on us without warning.

"We stop here," he said. His face was in shadows again, covered by the straw hat.

He opened the gate, which led to a path covered in little

white stones that crunched as we stepped on them. Dust clouds whirled around our feet as we made our way up to the front door.

Alvaro motioned toward the door. "Please come in."

We were still alone in Isabela de Sagua, if that was where they had taken us. The dilapidated, abandoned air of this place made me fear that Alberto's cousins and their friend had taken us somewhere else.

We had no choice. Alvaro led us into a relatively large, sparsely furnished living room. He motioned toward a door to the left of us.

Before following his orders like lambs going to slaughter—and that's what it felt like—I had a close look around. I wanted to remember as much as I could about the place, in case I needed the knowledge later on. I had Papi to thank for teaching me from an early age to read blueprints and pay attention to architectural layouts—once a contractor's daughter, always a contractor's daughter.

The front door led directly into the square-tiled living/dining room. I tried not to let the revolutionary posters on the wall distract me, though it was hard to ignore the heroes of the "glorious Cuban revolution"—Fidel, Che, and Camilo—watching my every move. The ceiling was high, easily fifteen feet. I counted five doors off this main room, two to each side and one directly opposite the front door. I could see inside the latter door a little, where there was a dirty kitchen. The other doors were closed. I feared the only way into the place was through the front door.

The house was in poor shape, all peeling paint and sagging walls. There was mildew on the wood. The sole couch and pair of armchairs arranged around a glass coffee table looked cheap and dirty and lent the place the air of somewhere unlived in and uncared for. Fatima would say it had bad vibes. I thought it looked like a place where nothing good could happen.

Alvaro apparently decided we'd waited too long to follow his command. He cleared his throat with a nicotine rumble—very charming—and held the door open for us. This was obviously more than an invitation.

"If you would like to freshen up, everything you need is in there," he said politely.

I knew what was about to happen. We entered the room slowly, Barbara first, then me. When we were inside, the door shut behind us. We heard the key turn in the lock, then the front door closing. Then there was nothing.

Barbara stared at the door. "Well, I guess this is where we start playing it by ear," she said.

"My guess is, this isn't how they treated Alberto when he came down here," I said.

The room was perfect for its current function: it was a place for confining people. There was no furniture, save for two twin beds bolted to the floor along opposite walls. The only source of light was a sorry-looking fixture in the middle of the high ceiling. A small open window faced the alley that ran alongside the house, but the opening was far too high to be of any use to us. A tiny closet containing a dirty toilet and sink lay to the right of the door; it also had a small, high window. I hoped this wouldn't be our home away from home for very long.

Barbara and I sat heavily on our respective beds. It felt like the first day at a particularly wretched summer camp.

"How did we let this happen?" I asked. "It was so fast, I just didn't think. I should have done something when they started going through our things."

Barbara put her fingers to her lips to shush me, grinning. Slowly, with the air of someone unwrapping a prize gift, she pulled at the waistband of her skirt to reveal the machete she had hidden there. As great actors do at the end of a superb performance, she took a bow when I silently applauded.

She apparently didn't know that I saw her put the blade in her skirt on the *Mamita,* and I didn't want to deny her the enjoyment of giving a show. I had a bad feeling that this would be the most fun we would have for quite a while.

As she fumbled with her skirt, I was appalled to see that her stomach had grown over the last few days—which should have been medically impossible. Even worse, it seemed to have dropped considerably. I recalled Fatima's graphic pregnancy lectures, that when the baby drops like that it's in the birth canal, ready to be born.

Barbara saw me looking and stared back expectantly, as though waiting to see if I could match her ingenuity. I trusted Barbara—hell, I crossed the Florida Straits with her—but there was something about her, some volatility that disturbed me. I thought her a loose cannon, but I needed to trust her implicitly. Anyway, I knew how intuitive she was. If I held back anything again, she would see it in a flash and probably never forgive me. She was disappointed when she found out about Michelle's mother, and she surely wasn't one for second chances.

So it was my turn. I stood up and unbuttoned my walking shorts. Barbara gasped with pleasure when she saw the Beretta strapped to the inside of my thigh. Several years ago, Esteban handmade this special holster for me. It was uncomfortable, sort of like a chastity belt that always slipped, but it was efficient. Barbara's eyes fixed on the gun and she cooed with appreciation.

My momentary happiness faded quickly. Guns and blades were fine if you wanted to kill people and probably get killed yourself. Barbara seemed comfortable with her machete, but I'd never shot anyone in my life, and I didn't want to start. Hacking and shooting my way to Michelle's mother wasn't going to work.

My other problem was that none of the men who met us in the cove said anything about a baby. In fact, they didn't say much of anything at all. It was wishful thinking, but maybe this was how things worked with Alberto. Perhaps the goods we brought over from Miami had to be examined and distributed before the exchange was made, and we were locked in the room to make sure we stayed out of trouble. I certainly had no idea what we would do if an actual live infant was handed over to us.

I tried to stay calm by telling myself that nothing truly

threatening had happened yet. No one made any move to physically harm us, and as yet we had no reason to think they would. I would have been happier having the run of the village so I could locate Michelle's mother, but I was in no position to make demands.

Barbara, apparently satisfied that I would blast us to safety if anyone tried anything, lay down on her small bed and started to drift off. I was no expert, but she looked like she was going to have that baby soon. I again remembered living through Fatima's pregnancy with her, and from the shape of her stomach it *definitely* looked as if Barbara's baby had dropped into position.

I was determined not to dwell on it. A woman who crossed the treacherous Florida Straits eight months pregnant and kept a machete hidden in her skirt probably could look out for herself.

It quickly became obvious that nothing was happening soon, and the day passed with excruciating slowness. I wasn't used to lying around with nothing to do, so I played memory games with myself. First I tried to remember geometry proofs and theorems from high school, but it was hopeless. Then I found more fertile ground: counting the number of men I had slept with since my first at eighteen. When the number started creeping up with alarming speed, I divided my list into two categories—the Latinos and the Americans. I also made a third category, Europeans, in the spirit of accuracy.

When I finished I tried to reconstruct the map of Africa in my mind, but I got bogged down in all those countries in the interior. I had just started in on the states of the American Northwest when the door opened. It was dinnertime.

Tomas was our waiter for the evening, bearing two plates of white rice topped with black beans. The plates and spoons were made of cheap, beaten tin. Along with dinner we were given two glasses of water in dirty plastic tumblers. A four-star restaurant it was not.

"Hey, Tomas, is everything going well? Will we have the

merchandise soon?" I asked as he carefully set the glasses on the floor. He was younger than I thought: hatless now, he had a baby face prematurely aged by sun. He kept his eyes averted and didn't answer, backing out the door and locking it again.

Barbara tore into her food. I realized she was feeding another little person inside her, and though it almost killed me to do it, I offered her my portion. She gratefully took half. Thirty minutes later Tomas entered again and took the dinnerware. Again, he refused to speak to me.

Something was very, very wrong. "What was your usual turnaround time here?" I whispered to Barbara.

She sat in bed, her hands in her lap. "A couple of hours. We always left the same day."

"Talk quietly," I said. "They might be listening in on us to see what we're up to." It was a B-movie precaution, but listening devices were relatively cheap, and I had found them in more unlikely places.

My warning seemed to have brought out an anxiety in Barbara that she had hidden until then. "It looks like we're going to be here for the night," she said, glancing at the high window. The sun had shifted. "Lupe, tell me. What do you think?"

She looked tired. I hadn't thought about the physical strain she must be under, carrying her bulk around. "I don't know," I said. "It looks like they're trying to frighten or intimidate us, but I have no idea why. Maybe something will happen tonight."

Barbara lay back on her cot, and her breathing quickly grew heavy and regular. I did the same, but sleep was impossible. I reconstructed my memory of everything that had happened since we came to land, and something kept bothering me.

I drifted into a half sleep, almost a kind of waking dream, and tossed for what seemed like hours. I got up twice to use the bathroom, seeing it was dark outside, and when I returned from the second trip something stuck in my mind. It was Alvaro, something about the bearded old man. He didn't belong with

the others, and he had some kind of authority over them. I pictured his face in my mind like a photograph, and then it hit me.
I almost cried out, it was so obvious.

"Barbara, wake up!" I shook her and whispered in her ear.
"We have to talk."

She went for the machete when she came awake, but recognized me and stared up uncomprehendingly. It might have been
silly, but I pushed her into the bathroom, sat her down on the
toilet, and ran water in the sink. If anyone heard us talking, they
might have to kill us for what I now knew.

"What's wrong with you?" Barbara asked, rubbing her eyes.
"You want me to watch you wash your hands?"

I leaned close to her ear. "The old man, Alvaro," I whispered. "It's Samuels, the doctor Betancourt listed on the phony
birth certificates as delivering the babies. I recognize him from a
photograph I saw of him from his retirement party."

"Are you sure?" she asked, looking at me as though I might
have lost my mind from confinement.

"Yes, yes. I got a good look at him on the *Mamita*. He's a few
years older, and he grew out his hair and his beard—that's why I
didn't recognize him immediately." I leaned back against the
wall. "Barbara, we're in deep shit."

"Where did you see this picture?"

I told her about Regina, her connection to Samuels and her
little house in Sweetwater. As gently as I could, I also told her
about Regina's trip north and subsequent murder. I couldn't
hold out on her anymore. She was entitled to the truth, the
whole truth. After all we had been through, it was the very least
I could do.

I dreaded it, assuming Barbara would think I betrayed her
again, but she was beyond anger. She was tired and worried, and
looked older somehow than hours before. The Barbara I knew
would have chewed me out or beat me up for not telling her
about Regina. I could have taken that better than her actual re-

action—she stared at me with an alarming passivity as I spoke. I didn't need this. I needed Barbara the survivor.

"She was killed?" Barbara said quietly. "That means Betancourt is working with this doctor down here, and they had that old lady killed the same as Alberto—because they knew too much. We're dead, too."

Her voice broke and her lips trembled with the beginnings of a convulsive sob. I took her head in my hands and pressed my face against hers. "Don't lose it, Barbara," I said. "We have to think this through. First we have to figure out how to get the hell out of here. We have to forget about the birth mother with the birthmark—hell, *all* the birth mothers—and get to the *Mamita* so we can go home to Miami."

My tone seemed to calm Barbara, and she sat on the toilet while I leaned against the wall next to her.

I had an idea. "Barbara, I weigh a hundred pounds. Can you carry me if I stand on your shoulders?"

"A hundred pounds. That's all?" She stood up and flexed her thick arms. "Two hundred, three. I can do it all."

"Which window do you think is bigger?" I asked softly in her ear. "The bedroom or the bathroom?"

She pointed up at the bathroom window. She was right. It was slightly wider and taller than the one in the other room, but not by much. Still, with what I had in mind, inches counted.

"Stand here. I'm going to climb up on your shoulders and stand up to see what I can out the window."

As quietly as I could, I stood first on the sink, then carefully hoisted myself up on Barbara's shoulders. She teetered a little, and I almost fell because the smooth wall afforded me nothing to hold on to. Carefully, I balanced and stood up.

"*¡Mierda!*" I cursed. "I can just see the tops of the trees."

"When I count to three, stand on your toes. I'll do the same." Barbara grabbed her stomach and exhaled below me. "One, two, three!"

I strained until I could reach the corners of the window, then raised myself up on my elbows until my head was outside. Warm night air hit my face, and it took me a second to get my bearings. It was almost pitch-dark out there. In revolutionary Cuba, they apparently didn't believe in spending money on decadent luxuries such as streetlights.

"What do you see? What's out there?" Barbara whispered.

"There's a tree right out there, by an alley. If I could get out this window I could jump to the tree and climb down to the ground. I can see some docks down the street. There's no one around, and no lights anywhere. I think this place is deserted."

I couldn't hold myself up much longer. I felt my elbows rubbed raw on the plaster, and when I shifted I saw blood on the sill.

"I'm coming down." I landed as gently as possible on Barbara's shoulders. Even so, I came down hard, and she barely stayed on her feet.

We sat down in our reserved spots, Barbara on the toilet and me on the floor. I brushed away fragments of plaster from the window that were sprinkled across my T-shirt.

"Can you fit through that window? You're small." Barbara wiped sweat from her forehead.

"It's too narrow. I couldn't get my shoulders through."

Barbara rose from the toilet and disappeared into the next room. I contemplated the dirty floor until she returned with the machete.

"What if you use this?" she asked. "That plaster is all over you, so we know it's soft. You could chip away at it until you have a space wide enough to wiggle through."

"But what about you? I'm not going to leave you behind, and there's no way you're going to fit through that window, unless we tear down the wall with a sledgehammer."

Barbara patted her belly, thinking. "I don't expect you to

leave me here. You have to come back in through the house and get me out. What time is it?"

I couldn't believe so much time had passed. "Two in the morning," I said, checking my watch. "We know Tomas is out there, because we didn't hear him leave after he fed us. Pedro might be out there too."

"They're probably asleep," Barbara said. "If they were awake, they would want to know why we've been running that tap all this time."

She was right. I was so used to the water running that it hadn't occurred to me how strange it would seem from the front of the house.

"Come on, then," Barbara said, taking a deep breath and assuming her position under the window.

I tried to work as quickly and efficiently as I could, but the machete was so heavy and unwieldy I could barely hold on to it. I was also acutely aware that Barbara was having a hard time bearing my weight, because she had started to pant underneath me.

"I need a break," she finally said, almost dropping me. We both collapsed on the floor. "How are you doing up there?"

"It hurts like hell, but it's getting there. How long can you hold out?"

Barbara stretched her back, propelling her belly into me. Her face and hair were covered with white plaster fragments. "Just don't take too long," she said. "Or you'll have to rescue two of us."

At a few minutes to four I finally carved out a hole big enough for me to crawl through. I handed down the machete, giving Barbara a farewell squeeze on the shoulder, and heaved myself up as far as I could. My forearms screamed with pain as I pulled myself up and out the opening, trying to spring out with my legs to catch the tree.

Unfortunately I pushed too hard and overshot the thick branch I had chosen—it was a lot closer than I thought, almost directly under me. I sailed headfirst out to the alley, but instead of hitting the dirt road I landed on something soft.

The young woman I landed on grunted in pain, but quickly recovered. She dusted herself off.

"Lupe?" she asked in a girlish voice. "Lourdes warned us you were on your way."

I lay stunned on the ground after rolling off Lourdes's welcoming committee. Looking back at the window I'd just leapt from, I was amazed I hadn't killed myself. I'd miscalculated just about everything: the window was a full two stories off the ground, and the branch I hoped to catch couldn't possibly bear my weight. I closed my eyes and slowly opened them again. Everything seemed to still work.

"Can you move?" the young woman asked, standing over me. Even in the poor light I could see she was pretty, in a plain sort of way, with medium-length curly hair and wide eyes. I nodded feebly and tried to stand. It hurt more than I thought it would.

She grabbed my arm and pulled me across the alley to a group of palm trees a few yards from the house. When we were safely hidden from sight, she poked and prodded me to make sure nothing was broken.

"As soon as you feel well enough to walk, I'll lead you away from here," she said. "They'll be looking for you soon."

"My companion, Barbara, is inside," I said, looking at the darkened house. "I can't leave without her."

At that precise moment the machete sailed out of the bathroom window, landing on the spot in the alley where my new friend and I had recovered after my fall. If we hadn't moved out of sight, the thing would have killed us. I moved quickly, retrieving it and returning to our hiding place. I lay down for a few moments, cradling the machete and waiting for my sudden burst of dizziness to pass.

"Who are you, exactly?" I asked, sitting up again.

"My name is Maria Rosario," she said, bowing her head to me. "I am a novice sister from the Order of the Holy Rosary, which Lourdes also belongs to. Yesterday we received a message from her about your trip to Isabela de Sagua."

Maybe the fall had scrambled my brains. I shook my head and squinted at her. "You talked to Lourdes?"

"Our convent is the next town over in Sagua la Grande," she said. "Lourdes talked to Mother Superior, who knew I was from Isabela. She asked me to bicycle over to see what I could observe, and report back to her. If there was any way I could help you, without risk, I should do so."

"You've helped a lot," I said. "If you hadn't broken my fall I would have killed myself."

"I watched the men bring you to that house from your boat," she said. "I was about to leave for home when I heard the noises from that window up there. I couldn't believe you were crazy enough to try to get out that way."

"You're telling me. I can understand why those men didn't bother to put bars over the windows. Only an idiot would try to jump out."

Maria Rosario smiled shyly, not contradicting me. "I'm glad I could help you."

"You've been out here since yesterday afternoon," I said. "How many men are in there now?"

"Two. I know them—Tomas and Pedro. They're very dangerous. People say they even killed and tortured prisoners when they worked for the government. I don't know where the old man went, or who he was. He left in the early evening and hasn't returned."

"Well, you've put yourself in enough danger," I said. I unzipped my shorts and took out the Beretta, making sure it was correctly loaded with the safety off, and prepared myself mentally to use it. Maria Rosario watched my preparations in silence.

She crossed herself and started praying, her lips moving without a sound.

I tucked the machete in the back of my shorts, hoping I wouldn't stab myself. I guess Barbara tossed it out for me to use, but it was too heavy for me to swing at anyone—if I could get past my squeamishness and actually try it. What worried me was that Barbara had left herself unarmed.

"I have to go in there for my friend," I said. "We'll get to the boat anchored in the cove and head for Miami. Do you want to come with us?"

She saw that I was serious, and shook her head sadly. "No, my work is here. There are very few religious people left in Cuba. The revolution took care of that. It would be a sin to abandon my people."

"Let me know if you change your mind," I said. The house was there waiting for me, and I realized I was absolutely terrified out of my mind. So I stalled. "How did Lourdes send the message I was coming?" I asked.

"Oh, we communicate regularly with Miami by ham radio," she said, staring at my gun. "We have a sophisticated code, so the government hasn't been able to catch us."

"Was there anything else in the message?"

"Your sister said you were coming here for a young woman from our town, which isn't unusual. People sometimes come by speedboat from Miami for their family members. We use the radio to tell the relatives when to be ready for the pickup. We've helped thousands of people over the years, because we don't want people throwing themselves into the sea on rafts."

"That's all Lourdes said, that I was coming to take someone out? Nothing else?"

Maria Rosario started crossing herself again. This conversation was making her nervous. "No, our messages have to be short. If we stay on the air too long, the government agents—the *chivatos*—locate the equipment and arrest the operator. We've lost two already."

"I see," I said. Maria Rosario looked at me strangely. "What's wrong?" I asked her.

"I thought you were going in there for your friend."

She was right. Barbara must have been getting desperate. I took a deep breath, checked to make sure the machete hadn't slipped deeper into my shorts, and tightened my grip on the Beretta.

"I'll wait out here for you," Maria Rosario said, stepping behind a tree.

"What, you're not going to help?" I asked. Her eyes widened. "Just kidding. But if anything happens to me, make sure you get word to Lourdes in Miami. Tell her I forgive her for breaking her promise to me."

With that, I sneaked up on the house. Never again would I make fun of Sylvester Stallone when he armed himself to the teeth in those superviolent movies. One of those macho megaguns would have been a great reassurance.

I reached the veranda and crouched by the window near the door. Glancing back the way I'd come, I saw Maria Rosario kneeling in the shadows, her hands clasped in prayer. When she saw me watching her, she smiled worriedly and offered a thumbs-up.

I peered in the window and saw Pedro and Tomas sleeping soundly in the twin armchairs. I was so frightened I started to hyperventilate. My private investigator's training never taught me how to stage a commando raid on a house full of armed men.

The best way to get through this was to pretend it was years ago. As a teenager in Cocoplum, I used to sneak back into the house after breaking curfew. So I took off my shoes and quietly dropped them in the scrub grass under the window.

I prayed the front door would be unlocked, but was confident it would be—after all, I had a nun watching out for me not a hundred feet away. Slowly, I turned the handle and felt the doorknob turn with just a bit of resistance.

When I opened the front door its hinges creaked, and for a

moment I was prepared to die. But nothing happened, and when I pushed it open a little more and stuck my head inside, I saw an empty bottle of rum between the sleeping men. I pointed the gun at them, but they didn't stir.

Barbara waited for me in the back room with the lights out, and I passed her the machete and led her out. "What took you so long?" she whispered.

"Be quiet! You'll wake them!" I said as we reached the front room. The dim moonlight barely lit the place, but my eyes were so used to the darkness that I could clearly see Pedro when he stirred, rubbing his eyes and reaching for the handgun he'd left next to an overflowing ashtray.

He should have stayed asleep. Without hesitating, Barbara descended on him and slit his neck open with the machete before he could alert Tomas. He died quickly, the blood shooting out in pulsing spurts as he grabbed at his wound in vain.

Barbara looked up at me, her eyes glassy and distant. Then she turned to Tomas, reaching him in two quick steps and cutting his throat in his sleep. He made a terrible gurgling sound as he died, his expression one of outraged surprise.

"Let's get out," Barbara said, grabbing my arm to lead me out of the house. I was incapable of leaving on my own.

When she saw us emerge from the house, Maria Rosario emerged from hiding, tightly embracing me. For once, physical affection from another woman didn't bother me in the least. I wondered if the young novice would have been so welcoming if she'd witnessed the carnage inside.

Barbara had blood on her blouse, but had wiped the machete clean somewhere before leaving the house. I felt strangely frightened of her.

"Barbara, this is Sister Maria Rosario," I said weakly. "She's from here. My sister asked her Mother Superior for help. She saved my life when I jumped out the window. Sister, this is Barbara," I was babbling and almost incoherent, but at least I remembered my manners.

When Barbara moved toward Maria Rosario, I feared for an instant that her sudden bloodlust might be out of control. The young nun saw the stains on Barbara's clothes and moved away from her.

"I'm so happy you got out of there," Maria Rosario said, stepping closer to me. "I was afraid those men would kill you."

"Don't worry," Barbara said, and she seemed more herself. "They won't bother anyone."

"You had better hurry," Maria Rosario said to me. "The old man might be coming back."

I kissed her on the cheek. "Thank you," I said. "You can still come with us, you know. This is your last chance."

She smiled sweetly and shook her head. I realized that an invitation to take a boat trip with a homicidal pregnant woman wasn't such an attractive offer.

"No, thank you," Maria Rosario said. She turned and began to walk away, calling out over her shoulder, "Go now."

Even in the dark we could find our way back to the *Mamita,* along the coastal path we took the day before. Barbara and I didn't speak the entire way, but I thought I knew her well enough to tell what she would have said about the bloodshed in the house: we did the village a favor by eliminating Pedro and Tomas. I wished my own conscience could have been settled so easily.

twenty-nine

I thought running the mile back to the *Mamita* would be difficult for Barbara, but our only problem was the hard time I had
keeping up with her. I kept looking back, but no one was behind
us. Samuels must not have discoverd Pedro and Tomas yet, and
the *Mamita* looked undisturbed anchored in the cove.

We stood in the shallow water and mud on either side of the
dinghy, the moon low in the sky. "Are you up to leaving now?" I
asked Barbara. "We can take a rest for an hour or so before we
set out."

The truth was, I couldn't wait to put Cuba behind me, but I
was worried about Barbara's condition. She was pushing her
pregnant body too hard, and her face was haggard and sweaty.

"No, no, we'll go now," she answered. She looked down at
her bloody skirt and then up at me shamefully. "Lupe, I just
want you to know, I've never done anything like that before.
Those two men—I was scared, scared for my baby."

"I understand," I said as we pulled the dinghy into the water
and boarded. I didn't understand, not really, but then I never
was a mother. Perhaps Pedro and Tomas had the bad luck to get
between a mama bear and her unborn cub—I didn't know.
Killing is something I've never understood.

We rowed slowly toward the *Mamita,* and my tension evapo-
rated into a kind of languor. Disappointment set in: I was leaving
without finding Michelle's birth mother. I knew nothing more
about the adoption scheme than before, except that Samuels was
in Cuba, and I had no idea how to even find any of the mothers.
When we returned to Miami, nothing would have changed—

Betancourt might be waiting for us, little Michelle would still be sick.

"I know what you're thinking," Barbara said as she pulled the oar through the shallow water. "Forget it. We've pushed our luck enough, and there's no way I'm going to stay and find that woman. I've killed two men. I want to go home, pack up, and get the hell out of Cuba."

I didn't answer her, and a minute later I tied up alongside the boat and waited for Barbara to board first, helping her up. Her movements were slow and labored.

When I climbed up to join her, I found her leaning against the steering wheel, her eyes closed. "Go below and lie down," I said. "I'll get the *Mamita* ready to sail. I can even drive the boat if I have to."

She didn't object, which made me realize how exhausted she must have been. Alone on the deck, I started the engines and checked all the pressure gauges and charts. The boat hadn't been tampered with in the slightest. All I had to do was lift anchor and we would be on our way home.

I went below to see if she would at least be able to help me navigate the waters. The main cabin was empty, so I opened the door to the forward cabin. It took me a few seconds to adjust to the gloom inside the barely lit space. Barbara sat on the bunk, speechless and terrified.

I approached her. It had to be the baby. "What's wrong, Barbara? Are you sick?"

Her eyes widened as I moved toward her. She shook her head and mouthed the word "no." I couldn't understand what she meant. Then everything became clear.

"What your friend is trying to tell you, Miss Solano, is not to come in any closer. But it's too late for that, isn't it?"

I felt the unmistakable poke of a gun barrel pressing into the small of my back. In the mirror facing me I saw the smiling face of Dr. Allen Samuels close behind me. In an instant I mentally stripped away his beard and long, unwashed hair. I saw the grinning doctor surrounded by nurses at his bittersweet going-away party.

"I was just thanking Barbara for getting rid of Pedro and Tomas for me," he said to my reflection. His voice was deep and rich, a good doctor's voice. "They were getting too greedy for their own good, which leads to carelessness. And they were *chivatos*, so the payoffs cut into my own profits."

"He set us up," Barbara said, a hint of wonder in her voice.

"I drugged their rum," Samuels said, obviously pleased with himself. "I didn't think you would go to such lengths to escape, since you could have just walked out the front door. I saw Barbara here put that machete in her skirt when we first picked you up, so I assumed she knew how to use it."

"Why didn't you just kill them yourself?" I asked.

Samuels looked as though I'd asked him to carry a tray of urine samples. "They were dangerous men, Miss Solano, even drugged. You don't live to a ripe old age by taking chances like that."

I'd had guns pointed at me before, which helped. I didn't panic. He hadn't shot me the second I walked in, which meant he didn't really want to kill me. He might eventually, but it was against his nature. My Beretta was tucked inside my holster, and it would take me a few seconds to get to it. For now, I had to keep the conversation going. Who would have thought that years of parties and dinners would come in handy in a situation like this?

"Dr. Samuels, I know a little about you," I said. "You were in obstetrics for years at Jackson Memorial. How on earth did you end up in Isabela de Sagua?"

Rule number one when dealing with a man you want something from: Keep him talking about himself. It worked. Samuels motioned for me to turn around, keeping several feet between us and the gun trained straight ahead. He could still shoot both of us before we could do anything to stop him.

"My record at Jackson was spotless," he said, the edge of

malice gone from his voice. "But about four or five years ago I was caught in a minor impropriety and the administration over-reacted. They were counting on a penny tax increase for funding and were scared to death of any scandal developing. So they offered me early retirement instead of a public inquiry."

The fore cabin was hot and nearly airless, and we were all beginning to perspire. A thin line of sweat trickled from Samuels's neck down into his peasant's shirt. I moved around the cabin table and lowered myself at the far end of Barbara's bunk while Samuels spoke. He didn't object.

"I'm glad I'm not in America now, actually, with all the political pressures on doctors." The gun was still on us, but his mind was wandering. How long had it been since he aired his old grievances? I wondered. "The Jackson board even made me re-sign from the AMA. And after all the years I busted my ass, de-livering babies in the middle of the night, working weekends. *They* created this situation, actually, by making it impossible for me to make a living legally."

Samuels had started waving his gun to punctuate his speech. He looked and acted like a man stuck on a desert island for years, with no one to talk to. I took a chance and nudged Bar-bara, staring pointedly at my right thigh. I saw recognition in her eyes.

"What about Elio Betancourt?" I asked politely, like a stu-dent in class. "How would a reputable doctor like you end up as-sociated with someone like him?"

"I know what you mean," he said, leaning against the table. He held the gun lower. "What a terrible man."

"The worst," I said agreeably.

"You see, I delivered his daughter. His wife was a patient of mine for fifteen years—since I was in private practice. She had a hard time getting pregnant, and I recommended specialists for her. Elio and I had a lot of conversations during that time. It was hard on them both."

Samuels smiled and chuckled, shaking his head. "At one

point they even considered adopting. Elio joked with me, saying how great it would be if someone just started selling babies, bypassing all the legal formalities. He said he could even make it happen, if he wanted to. When I left Jackson a few years later, I remembered all this and gave him a call."

"So you made a deal with the devil," I said, trying to sound understanding. "You were backed into a corner."

"I'm not sure what I expected," Samuels said. He seemed to remember the gun in his hand, and raised it a fraction. "I knew Elio had a lot of criminal connections—he was always making little jokes."

"And he knew wealthy Cuban couples would be perfect customers for Cuban babies." Now I was fishing, but I also hoped Samuels was a normal person underneath it all and not a sociopath: if we talked long enough it would humanize me, making it harder for him to shoot me.

"The plan wasn't that elaborate at first," he said. "I thought we could deliver babies in Dade County and buy them from their mothers. But Elio had gone to Havana a year before for a legal convention and had an affair with a prostitute from Sagua la Grande. She told him about all the poor young girls from her town who ended up in Havana prostituting themselves with foreign tourists and getting pregnant."

I glanced at Barbara. She was watching Samuels intently.

His attention was focused on me, and he droned on as though he were giving a medical case study. "It's terrible, you know. A lot of them die from botched abortions." His brow wrinkled in disgust. "And if they decide to have the babies, the families are shamed, and they don't have the resources to feed themselves, much less another addition."

Barbara's hand inched toward my leg. "So these girls are trapped," I offered, as though pondering what he said. I glanced at Barbara and she nodded, almost imperceptibly.

I cried out. "Barbara, what is it? Are you all right? Is it the baby?" She looked confused for an instant but recovered, grabbing her belly and grimacing in pain.

Samuels's instincts as a doctor took over, and his face filled with concern. The gun forgotten for an instant, he moved close to Barbara and reached out for her.

She kicked Samuels in the groin with enough force to double him over in outraged shock and pain, his eyes wide and full of tears as he dropped the gun. I reached into my shorts, pulled out the Beretta, and held it to his head. I was amazed how steady my hand was. To this day I think I could have fired the gun without hesitation.

"If you shoot me, you'll never get to the girl," Samuels said, kneeling with his hands covering his crotch. "You know who I'm talking about, the whore with the birthmark. The one you need to save the little girl's life."

"How do you know about that?" I asked. I tried hard to concentrate, to keep the cold edge within myself that emerged when I first pressed the gun to his head.

"Alberto Cruz told Betancourt you were looking for the mother of the little girl with the birthmark," Samuels said. He looked small and old, his ashen face cast down to the floor. "Betancourt keeps records. It wasn't hard to look into the situation."

Barbara moved forward on the bunk, leaning over Samuels. "Who killed Alberto?"

Samuels said nothing.

A quiver passed over Barbara's wide mouth. "Who killed him?" she repeated.

Samuels looked up at her despairingly, obviously unsure how to save himself from Barbara's increasing anger. He knew what she was capable of, and he began to stammer when she rose violently from the bunk, taking his dropped gun from the floor, and strode off into the main cabin. She returned seconds later brandishing a long fishing knife. Samuels and I both stared aghast at the long serrated edge.

"Wait, wait," Samuels said, but Barbara moved with chilling efficiency. She pulled him toward the table, grabbing his hand and holding it to the varnished wood surface. With a quick slice she cut across his knuckles.

All three of us watched in fascination as a thin red line emerged at the base of his almost severed fingers. Blood dripped quickly from the wound, spilling over the table and running onto the floor. Samuels watched, mesmerized, as though it were happening to someone else.

I took a step away from them and tightened my grip on the Beretta.

"Who killed Alberto?" she asked again.

This time there was no hesitation. "Betancourt. Elio did it himself. He said too many people were involved already."

Samuels seemed far away, his eyes focused in the distance. "What about Regina Larrea?" I asked.

He turned to me, suddenly showing pain. "Betancourt. Elio killed her, too. She went to North Carolina to find me. She got curious when you came asking about me, and she wanted to find the real reason I left Jackson. I don't know what she found, but she called Elio from Raleigh because his name came up in connection with mine. She was innocent, really. But Elio is frightened."

Samuels swayed on his knees, his blood dripping to the floor in the stifling hot cabin. He made no attempt to stanch the bleeding.

Barbara sat down on the bunk again with a heavy sigh, the bloody knife on her lap. She stared at Samuels with an odd combination of hatred and sadness.

"Dr. Samuels, where is the girl?" I asked. "The mother with the birthmark—do you know where I can find her?"

He answered instantly. "In Sagua la Grande. They're all from around there. But she wouldn't go back with you to Miami. You're wasting your time."

"How do you know that? What makes you so certain?" I

asked. He fell back to lean against the bulkhead, saying nothing, and Barbara gripped the knife in her hand. Samuels didn't even try to pull away when she slashed him again, this time across his wrist. His bleeding became worse.

I knew what Barbara was doing, symbolically: avenging Alberto. Where she came from, a man without the use of his hands was no longer a man. Samuels leaned back, his spirit completely gone, as though the weight of all he had done pressed on him for the last time. I wished Barbara would stop, but I was too frightened to try to intervene.

Samuels grimaced and looked at me with something approaching admiration. "You're the really tough one, tougher than you look. A girl from a nice Cocoplum family! Who'd have known?"

"What are you talking about?" I asked. I felt a tide of panic within me. It seemed that violence covered me like a shroud.

"Betancourt tried to scare you off the case," he said. "But you didn't fall for it, did you?"

Blood was everywhere. Samuels stared at his wounds but still made no move to stanch them. He was a doctor, he knew what was happening to him, but he did nothing.

"How did he try to scare me off?" I asked. Though I had a sickening sense that I was watching him die, I needed answers.

"With the cigarettes, you idiot!" Samuels said, chuckling.

"I . . . I don't get it." It felt as though my brain were shutting itself off. The heat, the stench, the sleeplessness, all combined horribly, making my mind feel sluggish and dead.

"Alberto Cruz told Elio you were sniffing that smoky apartment of his when you first came to see him," Samuels said in a distant singsong voice. "You were too polite to say anything, but Alberto could tell you were thinking about it. Not that I disagree. That man's apartment was like a smokehouse."

I listened in shock. True, I was preoccupied for a moment with Gauloises cigarettes in Albert's apartment, but I thought I hid it well. Apparently, I had fooled only myself.

"Alberto watched you walk back to your car. You were smelling your hair and your clothes the whole way." Samuels took a deep, labored breath.

"That's why you and Betancourt sent him to break into my apartment," I said. "So I would smell the smoke and know Alberto had been there? And the butts outside my office—they were just a sign to frighten me?"

"Sure," Samuels said. "Even Elio isn't a complete barbarian. He figured you would give in once you were frightened."

I shook my head, amazed with myself. I didn't think I had the energy to get so angry. "Well, you screwed up," I said. "All you did was convince me I had to break the case."

Samuels didn't answer. Behind me, Barbara had lain down on one of the berths, listening silently, her face covered with a sheen of sweat. It must have been a hundred degrees in the cabin, and there was no ventilation. Three adults—one pregnant, one very wounded, and one sort of all right—all breathed each other's carbon dioxide. Samuels looked terrible, but I had to depend on him for the truth.

"If you knew why we were coming to Cuba," I asked, "why didn't you try to stop us?"

"I agreed with Elio," Samuels said in a slurred voice. "The game was up soon with you asking so much, but we had to be rid of you first. When we knew you were coming here, it was perfect. There would be no official record of your entry, and the Cuban government would never cooperate with an American murder investigation. When I saw you came armed, I saw a chance to be rid of the *chivatos* as well."

Barbara had cut into a major artery, it was obvious, and Samuels had turned completely pallid. I saw with chilling clarity, in his vacant eyes and slouched posture, that the man now wanted to die.

"How did you know it was us coming?" I asked. "And where in Sagua la Grande is the birth mother? What's her name?"

"Lupe, he's not going to tell us anything," Barbara said, staring at his inert form without concern.

"I'll get a shirt to use as a tourniquet," I said. "We can stop the bleeding and take him to the police in Miami."

Samuels let out a low moan: "No." He sank all the way to the floor, staring up at the ceiling. With a long final exhalation, he died.

"He's staining the wood," Barbara said, putting down the knife. "I'll get some trash bags to put him in. I don't want him smelling up the place."

She rummaged efficiently in the closet for large plastic bags while I stood in shock. Within a minute, she had stuffed his body into them, taping them shut. She was right. He was beginning to smell up the cabin.

"What do we do with him now?" she asked. "We can't leave him out in this heat."

I stared at the body. In his last moment, he'd said no to me. He didn't want to be taken to jail. I hoped God would forgive me for allowing his wish to be granted.

"The fish locker," I said. "There's probably ice left in there from the supplies you stored."

Ten minutes later, Dr. Allen Samuels, his life's journey taking him from Florida to North Carolina to living out the rest of his life in self-imposed exile in Cuba, was slowly cooling off for his trip to the Florida Straits. His life and crimes were no longer mine to judge.

thirty

I stood on the deck of the *Mamita,* my hand on the steering wheel. The engines grumbled quietly beneath my feet. All I had to do was activate the anchor hoist and we could be gone.

"Lupe, don't just stand there, let's go." Barbara emerged from below, changed into a clean floral-print maternity blouse and skirt—ones that Pedro and Tomas had overlooked when they ransacked the cabin on our arrival.

She was almost begging me to return with her. I don't think she was concerned only with crossing the straits alone—there was a delicacy in her voice, as though everything that had happened might have been too much for delicate little me.

Barbara sat down heavily in the captain's chair and looked up at me, then reached out and touched my face with surprising gentleness. "Lupe, let's leave," she said. "We've been through so much. Anyway, you're smart. You can think of some story, or hire a laywer to get us out of this mess when we're back in Miami."

"It's just that—"

"Lupe, think," she interrupted. "At least now we have a chance to get out alive. If we stay here we have no chance. Don't be stubborn. Those people, your clients, they don't expect you to risk your life any more. You've done everything you could."

I suddenly realized that Barbara had become my friend. I also knew there was no way I could make her understand what saving Michelle meant to me. Michelle Moreno had somehow become a symbol of the children I left on the oncology ward at Jackson. And I thought of my mother, who would have wanted me to continue—even though she surely wouldn't have let me.

"I can't go," I said, speaking without thinking. "I just can't leave without at least trying to find Michelle's mother. I'm so close."

Barbara closed her eyes, her dark cheeks flushed. "I just killed three people, Lupe. Maybe you think that's easy for me, that I'm some kind of savage, but it isn't easy. I need to get out of here."

"And counting Alberto and Regina, that's five people dead," I said. She stared at me. "All the more reason to make something good out of all this."

"What do you think the Cubans will do to us if they find Tomas and Pedro dead—not to mention Samuels in the locker?" she asked in a quiet, angry tone, as if talking to a child. "Now come on. Raise the anchor and let's go home."

"I've put too much into this, seen too much," I said. The sun had risen while we were in the boat, and I looked at its reflection on the still waters. "You can leave without me if you want."

"Lupe, don't do this," Barbara said. "Stop fooling. Please."

"You can make it back by yourself," I said hopefully. "It'll be difficult, but I know you can do it. You did most of the work coming over, anyway."

I felt like a real shit, suggesting she pilot the boat alone, and I didn't even want to think how I'd get home if she left. But this was stronger than I was. I had systematically screwed everything up, and the only way to redeem myself was by finding Michelle's mother. I didn't have time to explain to Barbara about the past, about what drove me.

I was genuinely surprised when Barbara, looking revived and energized, turned away from me and started walking the deck. With angry motions she unfastened the sail covers and started loosening ropes here and there. With a practiced hand she pushed her stomach to one side so she could crouch to reach a stubborn coil of rope tangled in a cleat on the deck.

She started to work her way back toward me, still focused on her tasks. For a fleeting instant I was afraid my friend had become my adversary, that she might even get rid of me with her machete. But then she turned toward me and slapped the boat's rail. "How do you even know she's alive? Don't tell me you believe Samuels, that she's really in Sagua la Grande?"

"It's the only lead I have," I said. "I have to believe he was telling the truth. Besides, I've been doing some thinking. I may have figured something out."

"I'll leave you here!" Barbara shouted, turning away from me again. "You think I'll do whatever you say, but I won't! I'll go home and take care of myself and the hell with you."

"I . . . I guess I'll help you get the boat going," I said.

She turned and stuck her finger in my face. "And suppose by some miracle you find her, what are you going to do then? Samuels said she wouldn't want to come with us."

"I thought you said you didn't believe Samuels."

Barbara stared at me as if I had slapped her. Then, with a weary heaviness about her, she took off her shoes, went below, and lay down on the bunk in the cabin, the bloody knife in her hands. I followed her down.

"There are some clothes in storage that you can put on, to help you fit in," she said, closing her eyes. "Just don't take too long. I don't want my baby born in Cuba."

I nearly fell out of the mango tree as I steadied my binoculars. After a two-mile hike through scrubland—twice hiding from passing wagons bearing fishing equipment and boisterous, smoking fishermen—I had asked a little girl and gotten directions to the convent of the Order of the Holy Rosary in Sagua la Grande on the near edge of the village. Thank God it was mango season—the sizable clumps of fruit kept me hidden from the few passersby. Also, I was finally able to eat something.

It had been years since I last climbed a tree, and I was

proud to get up there with little more than a few scrapes. Once I made sure my abrasions weren't too bad—and noticed they blended nicely with wounds incurred earlier in the day—I relaxed a little.

Looking north, I could see the convent clearly, without obstructions. While I didn't know as much as I would like about the local geography, I knew a little about Sagua la Grande from the bedtime stories Papi used to tell. It was one of the oldest cities in Cuba. Once it was illustrious—a bustling tobacco and coffee center with access to the sea. But since the revolution it had become a sleepy backwater town.

Papi used to tell us about the moro crabs and oysters from this part of the country, and about the cattle industry. Actually, he used to do cow imitations for us, but I got the picture. I also knew there were sugar mills in the area, since confiscated from their owners by the government.

I remembered another place Papi told us about—La Libertad, a wide, beautiful square in the center of town. He described the royal palms and the stone benches arrayed along lush flower beds. Ever the tourist, I stood up partway on my branch, hoping to catch a glimpse. A breeze caught the branch and I quickly settled in again. I whispered a quick prayer, hoping it would be answered efficiently—after all, I was so close to a convent.

From my perch I was able to see all four corners of the building. The binoculars were powerful, so I had no problem with visibility. So long as I didn't tumble to the ground and knock myself out, I was fine.

I was following a hunch. There were too many details that didn't fit what I knew so far. Something Maria Rosario inadvertently said during our brief conversation worried me. I'd never told Lourdes that Michelle's mother was from Sagua, because I had no way of knowing, and Maria Rosario clearly intimated that she was.

Maria Rosario knew a lot more than she could have learned from an abbreviated, clandestine radio transmission. It was hard for me to think a nun had lied to me, but there were too many coincidences. The more I considered it, the more I knew Maria Rosario was the key that would lead me to Michelle's mother.

I didn't even think about what she had said, in the rush back to the *Mamita*, until Samuels claimed the same to be true. And Samuels said that Betancourt had met a prostitute from Sagua la Grande while visiting Havana, sparking the entire baby-selling scheme. I felt the contours of an idea coming together, and my answers lay inside the innocent facade of the convent.

The convent was a beautiful Spanish-style, two-story old stone house, set far back in the walled courtyard. The long building itself made up the fourth wall of the compound, looking out on a life-size statue of the Virgin and a huge wood cross. In the tree I could smell perfume from the blooming roses planted in the garden.

About a dozen women of all ages, dressed in short-sleeved shirts and long skirts, moved in and out of the main building on their daily rounds. Scarves tied around their heads, kerchief style, were the only obvious signs of their calling. Now and then one of them would leave or enter through the imposing iron gate in front of the property.

Time passed, and I started to worry about Barbara on the *Mamita*. I was fairly confident she wouldn't leave without me—really, I had to be—but I worried that someone might have found Pedro and Tomas. The house we left them in seemed abandoned and out of the way, but I couldn't be sure.

I really didn't want to think what would happen if Barbara was captured. I had left her alone on that boat to follow up on a half-assed hunch. I felt responsible for her, and for her baby—hell, I felt responsible for a lot of people, and I could barely take care of myself.

After two hours of waiting and a lifetime of muscle cramps, I still hadn't spotted Maria Rosario. It was almost three in the afternoon, and I was exhausted. I don't do well without sleep, and hadn't had a decent rest in days. I began to wonder what the hell

I hoped to achieve by waiting in a mango tree all day, praying and worrying.

I almost yelled out in triumph when I saw her walking around the courtyard with another nun. They seemed to be talking about the garden, pointing at bare spots in the rough lawn. I hoped she would leave the enclave, but instead she ducked into an open door along the east side of the convent. At least I knew where she was, which was some consolation as I settled in for another long vigil.

Wedged in the branches with my back tight against the tree, I must have dozed off for a few minutes. I awoke, disoriented, to the mental clang of the heavy iron gate. It was Maria Rosario, alone, heading toward town. Fighting off the pins and needles in my legs, I shinnied down the tree and followed her until she was alone on the path. She was so intent on her errand she didn't notice me behind her until I tapped her shoulder. She turned and recoiled in horror.

"What are you doing here?" she asked, her eyes darting. "I thought you had gone!"

"We'll leave soon," I said, "But first I need to find the little girl's mother."

She examined the clothes I had borrowed from Barbara's locker—a man's shirt and pants, both way too big for me. She was young, and naive, and couldn't act well enough to convince me she wasn't hiding something.

"You shouldn't be here," she said, leading me under a tree by the side of the road. "It's too dangerous in Cuba for you and your friend. Where is she? Did she come with you?"

"She's on the boat, waiting for me."

We stood by the side of the main dirt road leading through the area, alone for the moment but basically in plain view of anyone who might pass. There was no vehicular traffic, because of poverty and the gas shortage, but I could see a group of people walking toward us. I'd been told that Cubans can spot foreigners, even in brilliant disguises such as mine. I took Maria

Rosario's arm and led her down a side path, toward the shadows of an obviously abandoned warehouse.

"I know you could get in trouble for being with me," I said when we were out of sight. "But do you know where I can find the woman I'm looking for?"

She looked down without saying anything. I knew then that she was under some kind of pressure not to answer. But I had spent my mango tree time well, and had put my ideas together.

"She's at the convent, isn't she?" I asked quickly, without giving her time to tell me a lie.

The young nun looked so thoroughly miserable, and youthfully conflicted, that I felt sorry for her. She took a deep breath. "Yes."

I tried to stay nonchalant, as though I had everything figured out. But I was on a roll. Not only was the birth mother alive, but she was only a few minutes away. Of course, those few minutes could have been light-years, I thought, remembering the walls and iron gates of the place.

On the main road the people I'd seen passed by. They didn't see us. "And when you said Mother Superior sent you to observe what happened to me, you only told me part of your duty. You were supposed to do more, weren't you?"

She nodded in response, and big silent tears rolled down her cheeks. I thought I sensed relief amid her torment.

"What exactly were you supposed to do?" I asked, pressing on even though I was pretty sure I knew the answer.

"I was supposed to help you if I could," she said, with genuine kindness. "And then I was supposed to make sure you left Isabela de Sagua as soon as possible."

"You did a good job," I said. "We almost left, and we will soon. I have another question for you. How many birth mothers do you have living at the convent?"

"There are eight of us. Wait!" Maria Rosario covered her mouth with her hand in astonishment. "How do you know?"

"Dr. Samuels told me," I said. "Well, sort of. I figured out most of it on my own."

I didn't want to tell her more than she needed to know, so I didn't mention that Samuels was dead. I didn't know if she would have told anyone about Pedro's and Tomas's deaths, but she probably hadn't—she didn't see the actual bodies and had told me how frightened she was of them.

Maria Rosario's innocent confession explained everything. When Samuels explained the scheme he developed with Betancourt, it made sense—to a point. I knew about the girls from the Cuban provinces who were driven to Havana in search of a living, and who found no way but to enter into prostitution. Maria Rosario's appearance raised new questions, especially after she slipped up and I realized she was lying about the supposed message from Lourdes.

The Catholic church's stance on abortion is well known. But the church is also practical. When Maria Rosario showed she knew too much, I understood: this tiny Cuban Catholic order was involved with Betancourt and Samuels. The church could help destitute young girls through their pregnancies in exchange for services after the babies were born. Maybe Betancourt paid the church for the babies, maybe he didn't. Some townspeople got goods and money, the church avoided abortions and got grateful young girls for novices, and Betancourt and Samuels got rich.

"I thought you believed me," Maria Rosario said, downcast. She was too calm, though, and I suspected that she knew more, that I had yet to figure everything out.

I actually found myself consoling her. "It wasn't your fault," I said. "And you probably saved my life under that window. I won't forget that."

She blushed and looked away. "I am sorry for everything."

"Then you'll tell me more," I said. "Lourdes had nothing to do with this, did she?"

"No," Maria Rosario said plainly. "At least, I don't think so. I've never heard of her before. I was simply told her name by Mother Superior when she asked me to follow you. In fact, we rarely have contact with other orders in America."

I guessed as much. Lourdes had sworn on Mami's image and rosary beads. She was protective, but it had nagged at me that she would break an oath so serious. I tried to piece it all together: The order wanted me out of Cuba quickly, because they were involved with Samuels and didn't want it discovered. Perhaps, knowing what he might be capable of, they also wanted to save me from Samuels, as long as I left without proof of their involvement in baby trafficking.

Maria Rosario remained fixated on her sense of guilt. "It was my fault you stayed. I failed," she said. She was going to make a good nun.

There was something else I had to tell her. "I received a message on my way here that I couldn't figure out at the time, and once we arrived I didn't have a lot of leisure time to think about it."

But in the mango trees I did. "Your friend" had to be Regina, home from her trip to North Carolina, and she must have left the message with Leonardo just before she was murdered. The "offense against God and His children" she talked about referred to those the church feels are particularly blessed by God—literally, children, in this case the unborn.

Combined with her never-filed complaint against Samuels, Regina's message told me what she had discovered: Samuels was dismissed from Jackson for performing third-trimester abortions. He was caught either for the illegal procedure or for falsifying records afterward. Regina must have been incensed to discover that a man she respected was responsible for crimes against her religious morality. I wished she'd never found a thing.

I told Maria Rosario about Samuels's background. She was

incredulous. "He told Mother Superior he helped us because he didn't believe in abortion."

If all the other girls were as naive as she, Betancourt and Samuels never had to worry about any trouble from the Cuban end of their operation. Samuels had claimed that Betancourt murdered Regina, which might have been true, but it was as much for the retired doctor's benefit as for the lawyer's.

I sat down on the ground, exhausted and unsure precisely what to do. Maria Rosario joined me. "What is the mother's name?" I asked.

She hesitated, then gave in. She had told me so much already, there was no point resisting. "Maribel Montero," she said.

"I need to speak to Maribel and explain why I need her to come to America," I said. "She can make her own decision then, but it's my job to tell her that she's needed in the States."

"Maribel is very young, younger than me," Maria Rosario said. "She's found a real home with us at the convent. You'll have to meet Mother Superior before you can speak with her."

That's what I was worried about. "Isn't Maribel free to come and go if she wishes?"

Maria Rosario glanced toward the road. "Mother Superior usually makes those decisions for us."

"I get your point," I said. "Let's go see Mother Superior."

We rose from our hiding place and started up the dirt road leading back to the convent. My legs were stiff, and I felt cold, tired, and hungry. I wanted to go to sleep with this nightmare over, in a hot bath with plenty of bubbles. I wanted a manicure. I wanted to go home.

This time I entered the convent through the front door, instead of hiding outside the wall in a mango tree like a maniac. Walking through the courtyard, I received a lot of curious stares. I wondered how many of the nuns had arrived here by way of the Havana streets.

Maria Rosario had told me about Mother Superior's past along the way, speaking in a near whisper.

"Mother Superior came from an aristocratic family that left Cuba for exile in Miami when Castro came to power," she said. "She was the only member of her family to stay, and she is here to carry on the good works she started under Batista. She has been left alone by the government because we are in such an isolated place, but it is still difficult. Her dealings with Dr. Samuels have given us money to keep going."

"Sure," I said as we approached the building. This speech sounded like a grand rationalization for something that resulted in nothing but misery and death. "It was all for a good cause. I'll keep it in mind."

Maria Rosario grasped my arm with surprising force as we reached a side door. "Don't talk so lightly," she said, bending close to me. "I tell you all this so you can understand. Mother Superior has sacrificed much in her life for God and for the girls under her care. You have no right to judge her."

With that, she moved ahead of me, avoiding my gaze, and motioned me toward a chair when we were inside. I was in a small reception room and had to wait while Maria Rosario told Mother Superior about me. They must have had a lot to talk

about, because they kept me waiting more than a half hour. I
drifted off, seduced into sleep by the tranquility of the place and
the birds singing softly in the trees outside.

I woke to find Maria Rosario standing over me. "Come on,"
she said softly. "Mother Superior will see you now."

She led me to a study, and something strange happened. I
felt like a fool. I began sweating, my knees shook, and I went
into my rapid-breathing mode—all because I was about to be in
the presence of a Mother Superior. I was regressing back to my
childhood. My sister was a nun. My mother was—by all accounts—a near-saint. I was named after an apparition. I really
had to get control over myself.

Mother Superior made her entrance. She looked to be in
her early sixties, with porcelain skin and strands of salt-and-
pepper hair peeking out from the sides of her cowl. She was tall
and thin, with a regal bearing. I took a deep breath as she approached.

"Lupe," she said, walking to me and kissing me on both
cheeks. "Lupe, child, I've been hoping we could meet. And here
you are."

I was blown away. I had expected an adversary, and instead
I found this charming woman who gave off an intense personal warmth. It was difficult to remember that she had a hand
in all the evil things that had happened to Barbara and me in
Cuba.

We sat in a pair of chairs near the window, and I had a look
around for the first time. No matter how bad the conditions on
the island, Mother Superior obviously didn't deny herself the
finer things in life. There was a massive mahogany desk, intri-
cately carved with scenes depicting the life of Christ. Our chairs
were leather, and behind the desk hung a floor-to-ceiling tapes-
try reminiscent of the Aubusson we kept at home in the dining
room.

"I know of your family," she said, staring into my eyes. "Your
mother and I met when we were both studying with the Ursu-

lines. She was a very good Catholic. I prayed for her when I heard she passed away."

"How—" I began.

"I am not so isolated that I cannot get news of people who have passed through my life." She smiled beatifically. "You look a great deal like her when she was young, but you must know that. Your mother was a very beautiful woman, physically and spiritually."

She knew how to get to me. I knew she was doing this for her own ends, but I was deeply touched—and was put on the defensive.

"Maria Rosario has told me of all the difficulties you have encountered in Cuba," she said in an even tone. Her eyes hadn't left mine. "I want to express my sympathies to you and your companion. I hope we didn't contribute to your travails in any way. We were only trying to help."

The spell was broken. She may have been a noble soul, she may have known my mother, but she was involved in something lethal and illegal. Apparently she'd decided that the tone of this meeting was to be cordial. The woman could win an Oscar any year, there was no doubt. She was a deceptively powerful woman, and she was my opponent. I did the only thing I could—I smiled sweetly.

"Coffee?" a voice called out, and I nearly jumped out of my chair.

Maria Rosario brought in a silver tray with two cups of aromatic Cuban coffee. I struggled to keep my hand from shaking as I held the delicate porcelain cup and saucer.

When we were alone again, Mother Superior gave me a thin-lipped smile. I felt like I'd been caught smoking in the girls' room.

"My dear, I understand you wish to speak to Maribel," she said. "Is that correct?"

"I have to talk to her about her daughter. It's gravely important."

"Then by all means do so." She rose and walked to the door. "Maria Rosario, would you ask Maribel to come in."

I couldn't believe it could possibly be so easy. And I was right.

The young woman who entered the sanctum was young and beautiful in every way; down to her absolutely spotless face and neck. There was no birthmark to be seen anywhere. I decided to play along.

"Maribel?" I asked. "My name is Lupe Solano. I'm a private investigator from Miami, and I've come to ask you to return with me to save your daughter's life."

The young woman looked searchingly at Mother Superior, who nodded. "Lupe is telling you the truth, child."

"Your daughter had been adopted by a couple in Miami who have taken very good care of her. But your child is sick."

Maria Rosario joined us, taking the girl's hand. I couldn't believe all three women were willing to put me through this farce. "Without a medical procedure only you can help with, your daughter will die."

"Maribel" did a bit of very poor acting, looking from me to Mother Superior as though grappling with the meaning of life. She knelt in front of Mother Superior, kissed her hand clumsily, rose and turned to me.

"I will go," she said.

She left the room, and I was led out to the entry chamber where I had languished while they cooked up this ridiculous scheme. Within minutes the young girl appeared again, with a small case containing what I presumed were all of her meager belongings.

Mother Superior saw us to the door. "Go with God, child," she said to me, kissing my cheek.

"Maribel," or whatever her name was, had already reached the front gate. She opened it with a resounding creak.

Afternoon had passed into that nowhere zone between day and night, the time of day you'd turn on your headlights without being sure it was necessary. But there were no headlights or cars on the dirt road leading away from the convent, and I was alone with the young nun. I waited until we reached an isolated bend in the road before jamming the Beretta in the small of the phony Maribel's back. It was surprisingly easy to threaten a nun.

I was really past caring whether I would go to hell or not—besides, I wasn't sure she really was a nun. It's not as though they have physical marks you can check. I realized just how desperate I felt when I instantly considered how long Barbara had already waited for me. I might have blown my window of opportunity; she might even have long since lifted anchor and headed home. I couldn't blame her if she had. I wanted nothing more than to return to the *Mamita,* cross the Florida Straits, go to Papi's house, and collapse in bed—all this in about ten to fifteen minutes.

The young girl stopped and looked over her shoulder slowly, as though she'd almost expected to be found out. When she did, I saw beads of sweat appear on her forehead. I didn't care how hot it was—real nuns didn't sweat. It's something Catholics know intuitively.

I took a step away and kept the gun pointed at her. "Where is she?" I asked.

She tried acting again, a bad move. She would need years of lessons from Mother Superior. "Who?" she asked.

"The real Maribel—or whatever the hell her name is. The girl with the birthmark that I came here for."

I got a little closer and pointed the gun at her face, knowing that would get my point across. All women share an instinctive fear of having their faces injured. I also thought it wouldn't hurt to let her see my frustration and desperation—it would be dark soon, and Barbara and I had to leave. If she wasn't halfway to Florida by then, I thought. Then I told myself to stop it. If that was true, then it was over for me.

The girl looked into my eyes and saw, I'm sure, total desperation. She didn't have to be the best judge of character in the world to know I wouldn't tolerate any more bullshit from her. I didn't know if she was behind Mother Superior's trickery, or if she was just along for the ride. It didn't matter. She was in my way, in either case.

I saw her consider her options: running away from me and risking getting shot in the back, putting up a fight, or simply giving in. I don't know what I would have done if she'd simply decided to attack me. I was too tired, too weak.

The girl threw her bag down to the ground petulantly, obviously angry that the plan had fallen apart so quickly. "She's been locked in a room at the convent the last three days," she said angrily. "Ever since she heard you were coming she wanted to go with you, but Mother Superior wouldn't allow it."

She couldn't keep her eyes from the gun barrel. "We're going in after her," I said. "Is there a way we can get to her without anyone seeing us?"

I took the safety off the gun, figuring she had seen enough movies to know what the gesture meant. It worked. The young girl threw her arms in the air, her eyes wide.

"There's a way, there's a way," she said. "Through the back halls—there's a door there. It's used mostly to take the garbage out to the dump behind the back wall, so no one spends any time there."

Pointing the gun at the ground—there was no reason to be unnecessarily rude—I asked, "And Maribel's room is close to that?"

She gave her bag a desultory kick. "Yes. Two doors down."

"Come here," I said, and her features froze. "Don't worry, I won't hurt you. My sister is a nun."

I pushed her toward some ficus trees behind tall weeds by the side of the road. Using my belt, I tied her hands together in front of her, then took off my socks and wrapped them around her mouth for a gag. Finally, and I really hated to do this because I knew it would be really uncomfortable for her, I took off my brassiere and tied her to one of the sturdier trees. I don't think Wacoal intended that their product be put to such a use, but it was Swiss-made so I knew it would be reliable. I hoped God would forgive me for tying up a nun, even a phony one.

Now that my belt was gone, the oversized pants I borrowed from Barbara were falling down. I'd already cuffed them about six inches, and now I had to tie the waist into a knot to keep them from falling around my ankles. I walked quickly down the road back toward the convent, thinking that if I lived to tell someone about all this I would omit describing the wardrobe I was forced to wear during my adventure.

It was almost dark now, the sun gone below the horizon, leaving only a dusky glow. I passed a single traveler on the road, an old man in a straw hat, and I shoved the gun in my pocket and kept my head down as we passed. I could feel him staring at me, but he continued on his way, humming softly to himself.

I reached my old friend the mango tree and again climbed it—as high as I could this time, to see better over the convent walls. Toward the top I heard squeaks of protest from the branches supporting me. I think if they'd given way I would have simply lain on the ground until someone came to arrest me.

But the tree held, and I was able to glimpse the far end of the convent's quadrangle. All seemed quiet, which was very

good. If Mother Superior had received word that the *Mamita*
was still in Cuban waters, she would have suspected that I didn't
fall for the fake Maribel's story.

Before coming down I had a last look around. The view was
better than before, when I was simply hiding lower in the tree.
Craning my neck, I could see the city of Sagua la Grande in the
distance, with lights interspersed across the dark land. When I
was ready to begin my descent, something caught my eye, and I
trained my binoculars on it. It was a clearing, ringed in low
lights. I wasn't sure, but I thought it was La Libertad, the square
Papi told me about. I decided to believe it was true. I needed a
good omen.

I was reluctant to leave the tree, when the moment came,
but the convent might not remain quiet. I had to hope the new
friend I'd tied to a tree told me the truth, and that my brassiere
would hold out a little longer. I took a deep breath for courage
before setting out.

The lights were on inside the convent, but none of the sisters was out in the courtyard. This time of day, I figured, they
would be either in evening prayers or seated together in their
dining hall. Hopping out of my mango tree, I crept along the
side wall, listening for any activity.

Behind the property was a long, vacant lot leading out to the
sparse wilderness. I walked carefully, trying not to step on too
many branches, and felt my way along the convent's back wall.
As I advanced I started to smell a stench, and took a look down.

I was up to my ankles in trash. Squinting into the darkness,
trying to make my eyes adjust, I saw that garbage was everywhere: food remnants, coffee grounds, dirty rags. Apparently
Mother Superior hadn't inspected the garbage dump in quite a
while, because the nuns were dumping their trash just outside
the convent. Looking up, I saw that the only windows looking
out the back were on the second floor, safely away from the
stink.

Crunching through the debris, I came to an open stretch of

dirt and soon reached a single back door. If it was locked, I suddenly realized, I had no secondary plan. But I couldn't have come so far to find a locked door.

It was locked. I pushed against it, finding it incredibly sturdy, made of thick wood on tarnished brass hinges. It would have taken a battering ram to get me inside.

I sat in the dirt and felt like crying. After everything I found myself sitting like a beggar in the trash, locked out from Michelle's mother, who was probably only yards away. What was I going to do, return to Miami and tell the Morenos I could have saved their daughter, but the security at the Order of the Holy Rosary was just too tight for me to breach?

Then I remembered something Esteban told me once: "When you're completely stuck, do something completely obvious."

In the trash, like a beggar, I thought. I mussed my dirty hair over my face, rubbing some grime onto my face for effect, gripped the Beretta beneath my peasant shirt, and knocked loudly at the door. I heard a single set of footsteps approach from inside.

The door opened, and a woman about my own age peered out warily, her body set in silhouette by a single lamp from the hall behind her. "Yes?" she asked.

"Could you spare a scrap of bread for a humble traveler passing from one town to the next?" I asked in a gravelly voice, mumbling as much as possible and kicking at the ground.

"I'm sorry, I don't understand you," the nun said, leaning closer.

I must have hesitated too long before answering, because she stepped back into the hallway and reached into the pocket of her skirt. After fumbling around for a moment she pulled out a long, dark, cylindrical object. In the darkness of the doorway I couldn't tell what it was, but I could safely assume it wasn't good for me.

She clutched the object possessively and took a half-step

back toward me. I didn't dare give myself away by speaking again, so I tried to look as harmless as I could. Ideally, she was about to invite me in for a three-course meal, but I guessed those kindnesses happened in the Bible rather than communist Cuba.

Keeping an eye on the dark object, meeting her eyes as she moved another foot closer without speaking, I realized this bride of Christ was a phenomenally brave woman. She was willing to confront a stinking, ragged stranger in the darkness alone. Then again, she might have had reason to feel safe. I was fairly certain that the object she held was a gun, or maybe a thin club. And when she drew near I saw she was a foot taller than me, and about a hundred pounds heavier.

Without a word she moved on me, swinging her arm and the object directly toward my head. Before I could react I heard a click—and I was blinded by a flashlight beam focused directly on my face. I reacted with pure reflex.

I pulled the gun from beneath my shirt and beaned her with it. She fell like a stringless marionette, and I bent over her to make sure she wasn't severely injured. I would have to spend the next year doing penance, but it had worked.

The nun was fine. I stuffed her in a small utility closet, knowing she would wake up with a bruise and a scary story to tell the other sisters. Behind her the long hall was completely silent, so I moved quickly, finding the second door. It was also locked.

From down the hall I heard voices, and I went into a crouch with the gun drawn. Then I stopped myself. This was ridiculous—what was I going to do, hold the entire convent at gunpoint? I'd sinned enough for a lifetime in the last day, and I didn't have a taste for more. So I leaned against the wall, waiting for them to come for me. I would surrender and plead my case to Mother Superior. If she wouldn't allow Maribel to come, then it was over.

The voices didn't come any closer, and I began to recognize

a steady, rhythmic quality in the sound. Then it came to me: evening prayers! Mother Superior was leading her charges through their nightly ritual. They had no idea I was there.

And to think I was ready to give up. I turned to the door and saw that there was a key in the hole. In a second I had it open, closed it behind me, and faced a frightened beautiful young girl crying alone in the dark room. She looked at me with a gleam of recognition and a spontaneous, heartrending smile.

She had a birthmark running from just behind her jawbone down her neck.

Maribel and I hugged and kissed, more in desperation than anything else. We had never met before, but we both knew our immediate present and futures were linked together.

"I'll tell you everything you want to know later," I whispered. "For now, you have to help me. What's the best way out of here?"

Maribel opened her mouth to answer, but before she could we heard footsteps approaching. I dived for the small space between the bed and the stone wall. For once I was glad to be tiny. A bigger person would never have fit.

I heard the door open, and felt Maribel's tension from the bed where she sat in silence. Then the door closed and locked from the outside. Someone was just checking up on her, and was apparently satisfied that everything was in order. That meant they hadn't found the *Mamita*, the girl tied to the tree, or the poor sister sleeping among the brooms and pails. What a trail I was leaving.

I emerged from my hiding place, motioning for Maribel to stay quiet until the footsteps outside were completely gone. "What's the best way out of here?" I asked again.

"Down the hall, in the shower room. There's a back door we can use," she said quickly. I must have looked surprised at how fast she answered. "I've had a lot of time to think, locked in here. I prayed you would come for me, and I know what to do."

She took a look around the bare room, the place of her captivity. I scarcely listened to her. First we had to get out of the room. "We're locked in," I said. "Did you think about that?"

"The lock is so old that you can turn the key from the inside," she said, smiling. "I did it once with my fingernail, and the key fell out. Maria Rosario found it and put it back in, so I wouldn't get in trouble."

She was still smiling. I didn't know how she found humor in all this, but more power to her, I thought. At least she was contributing.

Maribel sat down on the cement floor and settled herself in front of the door. "This place is centuries old," she said. "Nothing works."

I stifled a laugh—maybe I was a little giddy myself—when she spit on her hands and blessed herself before putting her little finger into the lock as far as it would go. She grimaced in pain as she tried to turn the key. Apparently it wasn't as easy as she described. After what seemed like far too long I heard a muffled click.

Maribel stood, her finger in her mouth. "Okay," she said from the side of her mouth. "We can go now."

She wiped her hand on her skirt, and I saw a bead of blood seeping from her little finger. I opened the door and stuck my head out into the hall, looking left and right. There was no one there, so I grabbed Maribel's shoulder and pulled her from that miserable room. She took the lead, walking quickly to the left past three closed doors before stepping inside a room.

I followed, and once inside I was almost overpowered by a strong odor of mildew. It was the shower room, and mildew grew freely at the bottom the plastic curtains, creating strange patterns—deranged Rorschach tests that would tax any psychiatrist's powers of analysis. We paused for a moment, both scared that someone might have followed us in. I saw the door Maribel had told me about, in the back of the room.

"The door was cut out years ago when men came to install plumbing for the convent," Maribel whispered as we edged across the tile. "Mother Superior said it would be disruptive for men to come and go through the front gates. They were supposed to seal the wall when they were done, but they never got around to it."

"Lucky for us," I said.

With one strong pull, I yanked the door handle toward me. Nothing. I felt tears well up in my eyes, and Maribel looked at me in shock. I remembered that doors in the tropics, especially if they haven't been used in years, tend to swell and become impossible to open.

Maribel pushed me out of the way and frantically pulled on the handle. Then I shoved her aside and did the same. When she was on her second try, the door gave a little. When we both pulled at the same time, it finally opened.

We ran nonstop for at least a mile in the heat through the rough underbrush. Maribel never once asked me what we would do next.

Barbara was waiting on the *Mamita*'s deck, the boat's engines quietly running and the anchor out of the water. She didn't seem at all surprised to see us.

She helped Maribel and me out of the dinghy, pulling me to the deck with complete ease. The rest seemed to have done her good. "I was fast asleep, and I dreamed I saw you running to the *Mamita*," she said, staring at Maribel. "I came up to the deck, and there you were."

With a quiet sob, Barbara took me in a crushing embrace. Over my shoulder, I saw her still looking at Maribel, and then I realized: the birthmark. "Don't say a word," I whispered. "She's coming with us."

We cruised almost silently, Barbara steering as I stood on the deck with binoculars, looking for patrol boats. The seas were quiet and still, the night air crisp and redolent of sea salt. Maribel was below, stretched out on a bunk, and I'd ordered her to stay there for a while. We had a final job to perform before we had the luxury of getting to know one another.

I started to drop chum over the side of the *Mamita*, watching for the sharks that I knew would come. Within minutes we had a small pack following us, gulping greedily at the food and snapping for more.

With Barbara's help, I pulled Dr. Samuels's body out of the fish locker and unceremoniously dumped it over the side. Barbara returned to the helm, gunning the engines to take us out of Cuban waters.

"What's the matter with you?" she asked when she saw me watching the sea behind us. "He's with the sharks now, with his own kind."

I watched the wake of the *Mamita* for a few moments until there was no trace left of Allen Samuels and the sharks had had enough. Barbara put the sailboat on autopilot and joined me, breathing gently and evenly. She reached over and held me, respectful of my feelings. As I turned to go below, she said, "Lupe, wait, there's something I want to show you. Look."

Barbara took a deep breath, accommodated her stomach so she could maneuver with more ease, and squatted as close as she could to the fish locker which ten minutes before had served as Dr. Samuels's final resting place on earth. She pushed aside some old, rotted burlap bags at the bottom, and presented me with what looked like a shoe box, wrapped in plastic.

"Go ahead, open it."

Carefully I peeled back the layers of dark green and opened the box. I gasped as I saw the neat piles of hundred-dollar bills.

"The Morenos' money?" I asked.

"Alberto hid it here. I found it before we left Key West, while you were with your boyfriend," Barbara informed me, a self-satisfied look on her face. "You see, Lupe, you're not the only one with secrets."

"We'll have to tell the Morenos," I said, as firmly as I could.

"Of course. It's their money," Barbara answered as she

wrapped the plastic around the shoe box and returned it to its hiding place. I couldn't help but think that those bills would carry the smell of rotting fish for a long, long time.

I crossed myself and said a silent prayer: for Regina, Alberto, for Tomas and Pedro, and for the soul of Dr. Allen Samuels. I don't know what sorts of punishments await those who commit evil in the world, and what rewards await the good, but I prayed anyway. And I watched my homeland, the birthplace of my ancestors, recede completely from view. I wondered if I would ever see it again.

t h i r t y - t h r e e

We had motored for two hours at full speed—Barbara leaning back on her cushions steering, me nervously watching the waters and seeing nothing save for a huge freighter far off in the distance—when I decided to approach Maribel. She hadn't emerged from below since I'd ordered her there while Barbara and I disposed of Samuels's body.

I found her lying on the bunk, her eyes closed, breathing deeply. For the first time since we escaped from the convent, I had a chance to really look at her. Apart from the birthmark on her neck, I saw little resemblance between her and her daughter—except, perhaps, in her high, smooth forehead and a widow's peak in her hairline that Michelle might one day develop.

"Hello," Maribel said, startling me. She opened her eyes. "I have had trouble sleeping lately, thinking about my daughter."

I took the bunk opposite hers. "How are you?"

"Because of you, I am good," she said. "I haven't had a chance to thank you. I know you risked your life coming to Cuba to help my daughter. That was very brave."

I didn't know if brave was the proper word. Insane, maybe. Foolhardy, probably. "What were you told about the reason for my trip?" I asked.

Maribel sat up and swung her legs over the side of the bunk. She had a quiet kind of beauty, an unadorned pristine quality that showed through her plain convent clothes and lack of makeup. She had large, wide-set brown eyes, short-cropped curly black hair, and an even complexion, save for the birthmark. She also had a presence, a serenity and maturity, beyond her years.

"Three days ago, in the evening, I heard Mother Superior talking on the telephone in her office," Maribel said, shyly looking away. "I could hear everything. The phone connections in Cuba are so bad that everyone has to shout. I shouldn't have listened, but I was sweeping the hall. That's my job for the month."

"What did you hear?"

"Mother Superior said: 'That girl must not come here.' I think she was speaking with Dr. Samuels."

"Why do you say that?"

Maribel paused. "I heard her talking to him before, when he was due to deliver a baby in the convent. She always sounded impatient with him. I don't think she liked him very much.

The engine hummed louder as Barbara gave it more power. The seas were so smooth I barely felt we were moving. "How did you know they were talking about you?"

"Oh, because they mentioned my mark." She unconsciously reached up to cover her neck. "I had no idea why someone from Miami would come to talk to me, until I realized it must have been something about my baby."

"You were right," I said gently. "What happened then?"

"Mother Superior called me to her office. She said she didn't think I was serious enough in my devotions, and told me I had to stay in my room and pray for guidance from the Holy Mother until she released me." Maribel bit her lip. "I knew my piety had nothing to do with it. It was that telephone call."

Maribel had a sharp mind. I could tell. The Morenos would be lucky if Michelle turned out like her. "Did you find out anything else?"

"My friend, Sister Maria Rosario, would tell me things when she brought my meals," Maribel said. "About how you came ashore, and how she helped you when you fell out the window of that house."

Maribel looked directly into my eyes for the first time.

"Maria Rosario didn't agree with Mother Superior," she said. "She didn't like having to deceive you. She's a very good, honest person."

I agreed. "Who was the girl they tried to pass off as you?"

"Her name is Mercedes; she's the younger sister of one of the girls at the convent." The cabin lurched as we hit a large swell in the ocean. "She's wanted to leave Cuba for a long time, so when you appeared it seemed a perfect opportunity."

"So she was a nun who wanted to leave?" I asked.

Maribel looked surprised. "No, of course not," she said. "Mother Superior wants all of the girls who come there from Havana to become nuns, but some of them just stay for a while, working until they can find a way to leave."

I was relieved. After all I had done, I didn't want my eternal résumé to say that I tied a nun to a tree with a lace brassiere. Every little bit counts when you're Catholic and go to meet your maker.

Maribel pulled her knees up to her chest, worried. "Tell me, please. What's the matter with my baby? Is she dying? I almost died when she was born, you know. It was a miracle I survived. Did that have anything to do with what's wrong with her today?"

"No, nothing like that," I answered.

"Thank the Virgin." Maribel blessed herself. "The Virgin saved me then, so I know she'll save my baby."

"She's a very sick little girl," I said. "I came for you because you're the only person who can save her. She needs bone marrow from you."

"What's that?" she asked, puzzled.

"It's a soft material inside your bones," I said. "I don't even know that much about it, but it has to come from you. Now that you're coming to Miami, we've saved her. I just feel it."

"Tell me about her," Maribel said, smiling. She suddenly showed her age, her features gleaming with pleasure and curiosity. "What is she like? What name did they give her?"

I looked through the few possessions that Pedro and Tomas

had left on the boat. Among them was a small envelope containing a picture of Maribel's daughter. "This is Michelle," I said, handing it to her.

She grabbed it and studied it for a long time, first with a grave expression, then with reserved pleasure. "She's beautiful," Maribel whispered, handing me the picture.

"Just like her mother."

Maribel blushed and looked away, rocking back and forth on the bunk like a little girl. "Tell me about the people who adopted her," she said. "I want to know everything about her and her life. These people must love her very much to go to all this trouble. They must be very rich, very smart."

I told Maribel all about the Morenos. Though she had been separated from her daughter virtually at birth, it was obvious the child had never left her thoughts. I wondered how she would handle leaving Michelle to her adoptive parents after the medical procedure was complete.

"Oh, it's so nice!" Maribel exclaimed. "They must have so many cars, and a house with dozens of rooms!"

"I . . . I've never been inside their house, but I've seen it from the outside. I'm sure it's very comfortable."

"And Michelle will have so many nice friends. She can go to American schools, and have parties on her birthdays." She paused for a moment, with a bittersweet smile. "God has been good. She will have all the things I never had. And these kind people will give her things I never could have."

Maribel's simple proclamation brought a warm stinging to my eyes. I had to change the subject before I curled up and let the stress and pain get to me. "How did you ever get in contact with the nuns?" I asked.

She also seemed eager to think about something else. "I was born in Isabela de Sagua," she said. The cabin lights shone on her dark curls. "It was always a fishing village, but when things turned bad in the country, people left in fishing boats for the Bahamas. That's why the village looks so deserted—almost every-one has left."

I remembered the dilapidated shells of small fishing craft, the torn nets, the small group of fishermen moving slowly along the dirt road.

"For the girls especially, there is nothing," Maribel contin-ued. Most of us leave for Havana, to try to get jobs. But there is not much there for a girl from the provinces, so we make a living the only way we can."

She turned her head down at the memory, and I moved across the cabin and sat down next to her. She took my hand but still stared at the floor.

"You know, we go with the tourists," she said plainly. "They pay the best, and they give presents. Isabela and the other vil-lages are small, and I always knew where to go if I got in trouble. As long as we come to the convent late at night, with our heads covered, no one knows we are there until after the baby is born and we can come out again. Mother Superior said it was best that our babies go to Miami, where they can have a future."

Tears began to fall from her cheeks, spotting her dark skirt. "There is nothing for the children in Cuba," she whispered. "We give our babies away so they have a chance for a good life."

"And some of you stay at the convent even after you have your babies?" I asked.

"We can leave if no one knows about the babies, if our fami-lies do not know our shame," she said. "At the convent there is always plenty to eat, and we were never bothered by the govern-ment. Some girls, like me, stay and become novices, devoting our lives to God to atone for our sins."

Betancourt and Samuels's plan created a good situation for everyone, ironically enough. No wonder they didn't want me nosing around and ruining their sweetheart deal. In my mind, the true villains were the lawyer and the doctor, who made the real profit. If I could ever decipher Alberto's book, I knew, I could find out exactly how much money they made over the years.

I left Maribel below and found Barbara at the wheel, lying almost flat on her pillows. "What's the matter?" I asked.

"Tired," she whispered. Her eyes were glassy and her hair was plastered to her forehead with sweat.

I had endured more than I could bear in the last two days, and nearly forgot about Barbara. I apologized to her, helping her and sending her below to Maribel. When she agreed without protest to bunk with a girl bearing a birthmark, I knew something was wrong. I begged her to call out for me if the baby started to come, but she ignored me and disappeared.

Standing at the wheel, I gave the engines a little more gas and steered through the last half hour across the Florida Straits. At one point I closed my eyes and listened to the wind, then opened them to the faint glow of red light that had appeared on the horizon.

When I saw the dull iron monument marking the southernmost point of the United States, I finally allowed myself to cry. I steered closer, until I could make out the faded American flag waving beside it, and then navigated through the tricky waters of the Truman Annex marina.

I cut the engines and motored back to our old slip—still empty, as though it knew all along we would make it back. I tied up the *Mamita* and sat on the deck, watching the sunrise alone.

Barbara and Maribel slept on. I didn't disturb them; we would all need some rest for what lay ahead. But I couldn't sleep, so I went below and found a fresh bottle of Alberto's rum. I mixed some with orange juice left in the cooler and took it out to the pier. It was early, with no one around yet, and I knew exactly where I was headed. I wanted to stand as far out on the jetty as I could, to be as close to Cuba as possible while still on land.

I sat down on the edge, my legs dangling over the water, sipping my drink and staring at the sea. My time in Cuba now felt like a dream, something that happened to someone else. Only my bruises confirmed that it was all real, that it hadn't been a dream or nightmare. I realized tears were running down my cheeks, that I was finally starting to let go of it all.

I was almost finished drinking my breakfast when I heard someone behind me. I didn't have to look up to see who it was when he stood beside me. The golden hairs on his legs were a dead giveaway.

"Marta?" Henry asked. "Is your name really Marta?"

I stared out at the water. "No. My name is Guadalupe Solano. Lupe to my friends."

"Somehow you didn't seem like a Marta to me." He sat down next to me, the sun shining on him, making him look like a blond Adonis. "Lupe sounds just right. So how did it go?"

"Fine. No problems. Routine." I shrugged and looked away, finishing my drink with a gulp.

Henry took the glass from me and sniffed it. "Lupe, honey, you don't seem like the type who needs alcohol to get going in the morning. You want to talk about anything? We don't know each other, but I'm a good listener."

I was tempted as hell to tell him everything. With another rum and orange juice in me, I would have told him the color of my underpants.

"There's nothing to tell, Henry," I said, smiling. "A little sailing. I wouldn't want to bore you."

Henry nodded and sat there for a while, watching the water with me, taking me at my word. He was a good man.

thirty-four

"Mr. Betancourt, this is Guadalupe Solano speaking. Thanks for taking my call." The son of a bitch. "I would like to meet with you at your earliest convenience."

He didn't sound at all surprised. "Certainly," he said in a deep, refined voice. "When and where did you have in mind?"

"Noon, here at my office. I'm sure you know where that is." I hung up without giving him a chance to disagree.

I downed the rest of my coffee. It had been a hard, busy twenty-four hours since I saw the shore of Florida from the deck of the *Mamita*, and I would have no time to get enough rest until after I finally met Betancourt face-to-face.

The Morenos had driven down to Key West to meet Maribel as soon as I called them. Jose Antonio and Lucia arrived at the Truman Annex in their blue Jaguar, running to the *Mamita* and showering Maribel with kisses and tears. They were doubly lucky, because Maribel had told me she wanted the transplant procedure to be done in such a way that she had no contact with her biological child. She planned to make no kind of custody claim and wanted to spare herself the pain of meeting Michelle. The Morenos had the good taste to hide their relief.

As they climbed into their car, the Morenos got a look at Barbara, who lumbered carefully off the boat to the dock. "I'll explain everything later," I said, waving them away.

Barbara had been so quiet on the way back from Cuba because her water broke while she was below deck; she didn't want to do anything that might bring on the birth. Always superstitious, she refused to have the baby in the cabin where Dr.

Samuels had bled to death two days before—not to mention that she knew I would be no help delivering the child.

I paid a couple weeks' docking fee for the *Mamita* to Henry, promising to give him a call sometime, and rented a car. I drove like lightning and soon had Barbara at Jackson Memorial's emergency entrance. I phoned her son Jose and told him where his mother was, making him swear to call me the minute the baby was born.

Before finally collapsing, I picked up Alberto's notebook and dropped it off with a cryptologist. For an extra four hundred dollars, he promised to have it ready early the next morning.

Following that I went home to my apartment, locked myself in my room, and slept for twelve hours. It wasn't enough. I had a bubble bath, disinfected the dozen wounds I'd picked up in Cuba, and nuked an enormous plate of chicken and rice from the freezer, courtesy of Aida. Lourdes stopped by while I was asleep, let herself in with her key, then went back home to Little Havana when she found me comatose, leaving a note on my coffee table. She qualified for sainthood for not waking me and demanding I tell her the whole story right away. When I'd slept, eaten, bathed, and eaten some more, I had a call to make.

"Tommy? Hi, I'm back." I tried to sound as sweet and innocent as I could. It wasn't hard. I needed Tommy to keep me out of trouble. And I missed him.

"Where the hell have you been?" Tommy roared. Not a good sign. He usually tried to hide his anger from me.

"Oh, Tommy, I'm fine. I need a favor from you." I had to salvage this. "I want you to represent me with a problem I have."

Tommy sighed. "You have *cojones*, don't you, Lupe? You disappear for days without an explanation—forcing me to make out a will for you before you leave—and then the first words out of your mouth are that you need a favor? You're fucking unbelievable!"

This wasn't how I had envisioned it going. I took a deep breath and decided to start over.

"Tommy, *querido*. Please, I need you." He chuckled. "I

mean it, Tommy. I'm sorry about disappearing, but it was for a case and it was important. Forgive me. When you hear what I have to say, you'll understand."

"Sure I will," he said.

"Please don't get angry with me," I pleaded. "I hate that. Please." I hated to beg, but I was desperate. And it would work.

"Maybe. If you're really nice to me," he said. He was warming up. "So what kind of trouble are you in now?"

"The cops are looking for me. They want to talk about the murder of a retired nurse who lived in Sweetwater."

"Uh-huh. Start at the beginning, and go slow."

This is what I loved about Tommy. He was completely non-judgmental as far as his clients were concerned—and I hoped I was one of them now. He was pure Joe Friday—just the facts, with no amazement or reproach. I told him as much as I could in a short time about the Moreno case. He listened without interrupting.

He was silent when I was done, and I knew what that meant: he was cooking up a strategy. "We'll stonewall," he said. "When the cops come after you, tell them to talk to your attorney—me. Don't worry about a thing. Just don't fuck up anymore."

"Oh, thanks, Tommy. I—"

"Did you hear me?" he asked.

"All right. No more trouble."

This had turned out better than I thought. Now I could operate freely without the cops interfering. When they found out Tommy McDonald was my lawyer, it would ruin their day for sure. They knew he was a bulldog who would do anything for his clients. Whatever the police might try would have to be firm, well thought out, and airtight. I was in the clear.

"Lupe, why don't I believe you?" he asked. "This is your lawyer speaking. Leave the case alone. It's over."

"Thank you so much, Tommy. I promise. It's over."

I hung up and uncrossed my fingers.

.　.　.

It was now eleven o'clock. The cryptologist's report had arrived at eight, as ordered, and I was ready for Betancourt. I walked out to the reception area and told Leonardo to expect Elio within the hour.

"Elio Betancourt?" Leonardo asked. He had dressed up for my return, in black sweatpants and a South Beach T-shirt that stretched across his biceps. "Coming here?"

I poured myself some more coffee. "At noon," I said. "And you don't have to be particularly nice to him."

Leonardo saw that I was stepping toward our office back porch and quickly got up from his desk. "Where are you going?" he asked.

"Outside. What's it to you?" I said, unlocking the curtained door. "I need to get some air and collect myself before Betancourt gets here."

"Okay, fine. It's just that . . ." Leonardo sheepishly reached out and opened the door for me. "I'd better go out there with you."

While I was away he had cleared out the mess on the back porch for Serenity's meditation and yoga classes, decorating it with posters of rock formations in Arizona at sunset. That didn't bother me much—the porch had been long overdue for a cleaning, anyway—but the spacey New Age music playing on a brand-new sound system did.

Leonardo put his hand on my shoulder. "Now, Lupe, I know what you're thinking, but this is an initial investment that's really going to pay off." He unrolled a crimson meditation pad. "I got good merchandise at a discount, and we already have five people signed up. I even got Serenity to agree to share the profits. I hope you're not mad."

I made him get up from the pad and pinched his cheek. That was always enough to make him blush. "Leonardo, after what I've been through this week, it's going to take more than this to get a rise out of me."

"Really?" Leonardo said. "Thanks, Lupe." He opened the

wide window. Fresh air rushed in, and the parrots were babbling to each other outside. "You know, I've also been meaning to mention . . ."

"Leonardo," I said, "don't push it."

"Sorry."

"By the way," I went on, "there's another visitor coming a few minutes after Betancourt. Have her wait outside until I ask her to come in."

At precisely noon my intercom buzzed. "Lupe, it's Elio Betancourt to see you," Leonardo said. His voice was part surly, part polite—just right for the atmosphere I wanted to create.

I rose from the materials I'd prepared and greeted him at the door. I suppose that I'd tried not to think what this moment would be like, finally meeting my until now unseen adversary. My first reaction, which I pushed away, was a burst of fear. I had been through too much to be scared of this man. My second reaction was to his intense personal charisma.

He was dressed impeccably, in a navy-blue suit over a perfectly ironed white silk shirt with subtle red striping. I recognized his tie as Hermès, a perfect choice. His nails were cut short and buffed, and I could see a tasteful narrow gold Patek Philippe watch adorning his wrist when he extended his hand.

I knew how to play the game as well, though, so I wasn't intimidated. I had dressed in my Armani suit and Walter Steiger suede pumps, with my Cartier tank watch.

"Please, have a seat," I said, motioning to one of the client's chairs. His short curly hair was scented with some kind of floral oil, and his skin seemed to glisten with wealth. When I sat at my desk opposite him, however, his veneer vanished. Under the lamp I'd turned on over the chair to simulate an interrogator's beam, I saw the patches of discolored skin, the rings under his eyes—Elio was an aging party boy, and from the looks of it the high life was taking a toll.

"You have a nice office," he said, settling his briefcase on the floor at his feet. He offered an affable grin.

"Mr. Betancourt, shall we get down to business?"

"If you like," he said, a bit disappointed. He held my gaze a little too long. "What can I do for you, Miss Solano?"

I decided to plunge in without checking the temperature of the water. "I think you're aware that I know all about your business venture with Dr. Allen Samuels in Cuba."

"What business is that, Miss Solano?" he asked with a blank look.

"Do I really have to go through all I know, Mr. Betancourt?"

"Call me Elio. And I did cancel all my appointments for this afternoon." He stretched and leaned back. "I have all the time in the world."

I pressed the intercom button. "Leonardo, could I ask you to bring in a tray with coffee, please? This meeting is going to last a while."

Betancourt frowned a little and tugged at his shirt cuff. "Do you have anything stronger?" he asked, grinning.

"I think we should keep our wits about us during this meeting," I said, staring at him. "We probably both will want to be careful what we say."

We waited in silence until Leonardo arrived with the coffee, glancing at Betancourt as though he were an annoyance. Betancourt looked nervous, shrinking in his seat at his proximity to Leonardo's bulk. I had to remember to use Leonardo as an enforcer in the future—who had to know he wept over sick kittens and had never been in a fight in his life?

After Leonardo left I served Betancourt with a grace Miss Manners would have been proud of. While he held the steaming cup in his hand, I gave him a copy of Alberto's journal entries as translated by the cryptologist.

"While you're enjoying your coffee, maybe you'd care to glance through these?" I asked, taking a sip of my own coffee.

A note from the cryptologist lay in my desk. Alberto's code

was fairly straightforward and easy to break. He had also been a meticulous record keeper: the journal contained an accounting of all cash that had passed through hands in Cuba, money to pay off the *chivatos* and money paid to Samuels for delivering the children. It also contained Betancourt's name and address.

"Where did you get this?" Betancourt asked. His voice was low, and I could tell he was barely controlling a surge of rage.

"From Alberto Cruz. You probably told him not to keep records, but he was a meticulous man," I said. "You can see he took twenty-one trips to Cuba during a four-and-a-half-year period. If all your clients paid you what you charged Jose Antonio and Lucia Moreno, then you made quite a bit of money. No wonder you wanted to hire someone to steal the book from Cruz's apartment."

He shook his head, but his hands were shaking as well. "Fifty thousand per baby times twenty-one trips," I went on, "equals more than a million dollars. I don't know what your expenses were, but you still cleared a lot of money. So how did you make your entry when you did your taxes? I don't recall seeing a heading for 'profits from baby selling' in the regular ten-forty forms."

I smiled sweetly at him, and he got up, placing his saucer carefully on the end table next to his chair. "This is ridiculous. You can't prove anything, and you know it. You're wasting my time."

"Maybe not with that alone," I said. "But along with a few other factors, I might be able to muddy the waters enough to warrant an investigation into your affairs. Speaking of affairs, this would be a good time for you to have a look at these. Before you leave, I mean."

I think he knew what was coming, because when he sat down again, he nervously fingered his gold wedding band. When he was cozy I handed him a manila envelope containing photographs of at least three different girlfriends, which my investigators took on surveillance. Most surveillances are stupefyingly boring, so when something actually happens most investigators go all out gathering evidence. In other words, some of these pictures left little to the imagination. It hadn't occurred to me before that they might become useful, but I had to keep hitting Betancourt, keep him reacting.

"You're disgusting," he sneered. He stood up again, so I did too. Betancourt towered over me, but that didn't matter. Since I'm not much over five feet, most people tower over me.

"I'd be careful how you use that word," I said. I pulled out a folder and pushed it across the desk. "This is a transcript from memory of a confession given by Dr. Allen Samuels in Isabela de Sagua, Cuba, two days ago. I have a witness to corroborate."

Betancourt put his hand on the folder, as though he refused to admit its existence. "This is ridiculous," he repeated.

"Dr. Samuels said you murdered Alberto Cruz and Regina Larrea." I opened the folder for him. He couldn't help but look.

"That's ridiculous. I didn't kill those people."

"Samuels said you did. He also told us everything about your operation in Cuba, right down to the personal history between the two of you. He's willing to go to the wall to convict you of murder if any of this becomes public."

"Allen is a liar and a lunatic," Betancourt said. "The old woman was no threat to anyone. I don't know how Samuels had her killed, but it wasn't necessary. He was upset about his reputation, which was ridiculous. That was long gone. He was a fool to think he would ever work as a doctor again."

He walked to the window and pressed his hand against the pane. For an instant, I thought he was going to jump out. Instead he turned to me, asking, "Where is Samuels? How did you get him to talk to you?"

"He's out of the loop now." That was the truth, but there was no need to say more. "Your business endeavor is over, and your ex-partner is willing to talk. I think, from your perspective, that's a real bitch of a situation."

He held out his hand to silence me, his head turned away. Then, as if nothing had happened, he returned to his chair and picked up his lukewarm coffee, sipping slowly. He looked at the items arrayed on my desk as though they were poison. His gaze darted from the typed lists from Alberto's book, to the pictures of him with his lovers, to the transcript of Samuels's last words.

"I'm a lawyer, which gives me a certain perspective," he said, opening his jacket. For a scary moment I thought he would pull a gun, but instead he produced a thick cigar. "Do you mind?" he asked.

"Why not? It's a special occasion." I gave him an ashtray from the bottom drawer of my desk.

"As I was saying, I know criminal defense as well as anyone in the country." He lit the cigar with a silver-plated lighter, exhaling a noxious cloud that filled the room. "And from what I see here, you don't have anything I should worry about."

I had to give him credit for at least trying. "Do we have to go through this?" I asked. "To begin—I'm sure the IRS would be interested in reviewing your tax returns for the last four years. I probably hate the IRS as much as you, but then I hear whoever reports a case of tax evasion gets a reward if the government successfully collects."

Another big cloud. Stony silence. "As far as your very visible wife is concerned, I'm sure you have less than an ideal marriage." His eyes narrowed. "But even in Miami, adulterers aren't looked upon kindly. I'm sure the *Herald* would be willing to break the story—especially with colorful pictures."

He waved the cigar at me. "Do you know what that would do to my daughter?" he asked.

"You should have thought of that when you were screwing around."

We sat there in silence. I was doing well. He absolutely hated me. "And then there's the U.S. Attorney's office. I'm sure he'd like nothing more than to hit the ground running by indicting one of the most prominent attorneys in town. Washington would be sure to notice, and I'm sure you've made a few enemies among federal prosecutors."

Betancourt laughed deeply, with something that resembled admiration. "You're really the scum of the earth, threatening me with blackmail. I should have you arrested."

"Oh, please, Elio." I took a sip of my cool coffee. I was pleased to notice that my hands were perfectly steady.

His smile vanished. In the bright light over his head, he seemed gaunt and drawn, his eyes sunk in their sockets. Here, backed into a corner, was the real Elio Betancourt: a calculating, self-serving shell of a human. "What do you want from me?" he asked.

"Two things. I want your word that you will never attempt to harm or interfere in any way with myself or Barbara Perez."

He nodded equanimously. "Agreed. And the other?"

"I want you to produce or reconstruct all your records on the babies you brought out of Cuba. No other set of parents should have to go through what you made the Morenos endure."

"I can't do that," he said, his expression vacant.

"Also, you will offer to change the status of the illegal adoptions you oversaw into legal births. At your cost, of course."

"You are insane," he said, looking up at the ceiling. His cigar burned unattended in the ashtray. "How the hell am I supposed to do that?"

"I don't know. That's your problem now."

"Forget it," he said, getting up again. He made a show of checking his watch. "I've indulged you long enough. We have no agreement."

"Fine," I said, pushing my intercom button. "Leonardo, will you send Maribel in, please?"

Maribel, dressed in jeans and a polo shirt I'd borrowed from Lourdes's closet, stepped uncertainly into the room. Betancourt stood with his briefcase, swaying uncertainly.

"That's him," Maribel said quietly. "That's the man."

Betancourt turned to me. "What trick is this? I've never seen her before in my life."

I got up and shut the office door, motioning toward the

chairs. Betancourt and Maribel remained standing. "You really don't remember?" I asked him.

Maribel folded her arms and recited: "You were a client of mine in Havana, in October 1990. You were there for a few days attending a conference on the law. I was working at Señora Anna's house in the Vedado. You were staying at the Hotel Nacional. You liked what I did so much that you returned three or four times before you went home to Miami."

Betancourt dropped the briefcase and fell into his chair. "Oh, God," he said. "Oh, my God."

"It's in here, too." I pointed to the Samuels documents. "Your friend Allen said that you were checking up on the baby-selling scheme during that trip to Havana."

"What—" Betancourt paused, his face flushed. "What are you trying to do to me?"

I sat on the edge of my desk, leaning close to him. "As I understand it, the only requirements to determine paternity are samples of the mother's blood, the father's blood, and the baby's blood. As an attorney, you must know that the courts accept medical findings as ninety-nine point ninety-five percent accurate."

"How did you know it was me?" he asked Maribel, staring at her face, her hands, her body, as though remembering.

She lowered her eyes. "You were the only one I was ever with. Señora Anna felt sorry for me after you left and I was pregnant, so she let me do housekeeping duties instead of staying with the men."

Betancourt stared at Maribel for a moment longer, then turned away from her. "Ask her to leave," he said. Maribel left quickly. "You win. I'll do anything you say."

"Of course, there's one more demand."

"Of course." Betancourt stood up again, his shoulders stooped. "I will have to provide for the girl."

"In monthly payments. I'll help you keep it discreet."

Betancourt looked at me as though I had offered him a

branch just before he tumbled off a cliff. Then he nodded and left. I saw him glance at Maribel on his way out.

Maribel came in and sat in the chair Betancourt had just vacated. It was probably still warm. "Do you have a handkerchief, Lupe?"

"Let me get you one." I gave her a scented linen hankie from my desk, and she furiously rubbed away the stage makeup I'd applied to cover her birthmark. When she was done we looked into each other's eyes and laughed like little girls.

"You're smart!" Maribel said, radiant with happiness. "I can't believe he would think I was another girl, even with my birthmark covered. Maria Rosario and I do look a little bit alike, but I never thought anyone would ever get us confused!"

I wished I had a cigar. I don't smoke, but it seemed appropriate. "We were lucky you and she spent so much time talking when Mother Superior had you locked up," I said. "Her story about Betancourt was perfect."

I told her about the support payments I'd demanded of Betancourt, and she covered her mouth. "But that's wrong," she said.

"This has all been wrong. But Michelle is going to be all right, and I got some money for you. Don't worry about it—he won't miss it, and it's the least he can do."

"I'm leaving soon," Maribel said, suddenly serious.

"Don't worry. I'll have the money sent to you."

She thought about it for a moment. "I will take his money."

"Good."

"They told me at the hospital that I have to donate the bone marrow one more time. Then I will be done. I still haven't seen my daughter, and I don't think I will ask to."

"I'm sorry," I said, and I was.

"Don't be sorry. I have a cousin in Union City, in New Jersey. I think I will go up there and find an order to live with. I'll make a life for myself here—until Castro falls. Then I will go home again."

"That's a good plan, sweetheart. I'll pray for you and Michelle." I went around the desk and embraced her.

When Maribel was gone, I thought what I would tell the police. After hearing Samuels and Betancourt give their respective accounts of who was to blame for Regina's death, I had to admit I believed the lawyer. Regina discovered Samuels's past and, being an old world Cuban Catholic, reacted badly and called Betancourt when his name came up. I would probably never know whom she talked to in North Carolina, or who did the killing that Samuels ordered, but the responsibility lay with Samuels. And he was beyond arrest and prison.

On the other hand, I believed Samuels in one respect: Betancourt killed Alberto Cruz. Alberto knew he was playing a rough game, and the man who paid him eventually killed him.

With that morbid thought, the phone rang. It was Barbara's son Jose, calling from Jackson Memorial. I could barely hear him with all the noise in the background. It sounded like a party had broken out.

An unmistakable voice screamed from the din, "Is that Lupe? Give me the phone!"

"Barbara, how are you?"

"Lupe—I had twins! A boy and a girl, can you believe it?" She cackled maniacally. "Hey, we had a good time, didn't we, Lupe?"

I tried to congratulate her and tell her the Morenos wanted her to keep the money Alberto had hidden in the fish locker, but Barbara began yelling at someone in her room, caught up in the party again. I hung up and called the florist, ordering their biggest flower arrangement—in pink and blue—to be sent to Barbara's room. Then I dialed a familiar number.

"Tommy? It's me. You want to go out tonight? Tear up the will and buy some champagne. You're going to have a great time, *querido*. I promise."